Talking to Water

—

A Dolphns Chronicles Book

John Tkac

ISBN-13: 9780979445415
ISBN-10: 0979445418
Library of Congress Control Number: 2013919932
John Tkac Enterprises LLC, Delray Beach, FL

Talking

to

Water

"Freedom for all, pirates forever!"

Phillip Radstone

Contents

Author's Note

When I started writing this story, historical accuracy caused me little concern. As I wrote, I performed a few cursory bits of research and gradually convinced myself that historical facts and chronology should be a part of *Talking to Water*. However, I always maintained my fiction writers' prerogative to stray from the facts for the sake of the story.

This story begins in 1714 in the village of Bantry on the southwest coast of Ireland. From the earliest times, England ruled Ireland in a brutal manner. The English confiscated much of the productive land in Ireland and became landlords. In the British Parliament, the Irish people were spoken of in subhuman terms, and English laws denied the Irish people their basic human rights.

During the rule of King Henry VIII, England pushed the Irish to abandon the Catholic faith and become Anglicans. The egregious effort to convert Catholic Ireland to the Protestant faith of England continued for four centuries, to no avail. This attack on Catholicism, probably more than anything else, served to foment the animosity between the Irish and the English. For centuries, Irish acts of violence and rebellion against the English persisted, but it was not until 1922 that Ireland gained its independence from Great Britain.

I depicted Lord Radstone as a benevolent English ruler. He is fictional, and it is debatable as to whether or not such a kind English nobleman ever existed in southern Ireland.

The first Europeans who landed in the Caribbean carried infectious diseases for which the native islanders had no immunity. Within a hundred years, the natives (mainly members of the Carib, Taino, and Ciboney tribes) were almost completely wiped out. At the time of this story, there were still a few native islanders roaming around the Caribbean.

From the time of Columbus, Spain controlled most of the islands of the Caribbean. Over the course of two centuries, Spain's power waned, and the English, French, and Dutch took control of many of the islands. In 1655, England took Jamaica away from Spain and established a formidable naval base at Port Royal (now Kingston). In 1692, an earthquake destroyed Port Royal, and although some rebuilding took place, the location never flourished again. My depictions of Port Royal are fanciful.

Pirates in the Caribbean were at their strongest and most numerous during the late sixteen hundreds and early seventeen hundreds. Most of them were out-of-work members of European navies. They settled in the Caribbean with dreams of owning and operating plantations as well as other businesses. Many of them failed at these endeavors and turned back to the sea, and piracy, to make a living. The governments of the day (England, France, Spain, Portugal, and The Netherlands) issued letters of marque to a few pirates. These documents gave the pirates legitimacy when attacking foreign ships. A pirate ship holding a letter of marque was considered a part of the navy of the issuing country. The pirates depicted in this book are fictional except for John Rackham. Calico Jack, as he was called, operated in and around the Bahamas during the time of this story.

The Atlantic slave trade is one of the most repugnant and bloodiest stains on the record of human history. Between the mid-fifteen hundreds and the mid-eighteen hundreds, over twelve million Africans were transported to South America, North America, and the Caribbean and sold into slavery. During these centuries, it is estimated that ten million Africans may have lost their lives because of the slave trade. Eight million died during capture and transportation to the west coast of Africa, and another two million perished at sea owing to the horrific conditions aboard the slave ships. Some historians think the number of deaths caused by the Atlantic slave trade could be as high as fifteen to twenty million.

Claire Riley, the heroine of the story, fights against the evils of the slave trade. Claire never existed, but she should have.

In 1807, the British government finally banned the Atlantic slave trade, and in 1837, the English Parliament made slavery illegal throughout the British Empire.

Lastly, history is rife with stories of dolphins helping humans. Dolphins have guided ships through treacherous waters, driven sharks away from swimmers, and saved people from drowning. Could it be that dolphins have true empathy toward humans? I think they do.

Glossary

This glossary contains words pertaining to life in the early eighteenth century and sailing terms from the period. You will find words such as baldric, doublet, bumbo, and powder monkey.

Aft – At, near, or toward the rear of a ship, also called the stern.

Baldric – A belt, sometimes richly ornamented, worn over one shoulder, across the breast, and under the opposite arm. Seamen hung multiple single-shot pistols from baldrics in order to have them at the ready when boarding ships or when in close combat.

Bos'un – A short form or abbreviation for boatswain. A superior and senior seaman in charge of the general operation of a ship. On warships, a noncommissioned or warrant officer who supervises seamen as to their everyday duties.

Bodice – A woman's sleeveless undergarment, worn above the waist and often laced at the front.

Boom line – A rope tied to the boom of a ship for the purpose of moving it so the sail catches the maximum amount of wind. The boom is a spar that swivels on a mast. The foot of a vessel's sail is attached to the boom.

Bow – The front end of a ship.

Bowsprit – A long spar protruding from a ship's bow.

Bow chasers – Forward-facing cannon on a warship, located in the bow.

Bumbo – A drink popular with pirates. A mixture of rum, water, sugar, and nutmeg.

Breeches – Trousers covering the leg to just below the knee, where they can be buckled to hold the hem or cuff in place.

Broadside – The firing of all the guns from one side of a warship.

Cutlass – A short sword with a slightly curved blade, used by sailors in the early eighteenth century.

Dirk – A short, double-edged, pointed dagger.

Doublet – A close-fitting garment, with or without sleeves, usually covering the body from the neck to the waist. A quilted vest containing small iron rings sewn between layers of heavy cloth to provide protection in combat. The equivalent of the modern-day flak jacket or bulletproof vest.

Fo'c'sle – A short form or abbreviation of forecastle, the area at the very front of a ship. Sometimes the forecastle is higher than the main deck, and it is traditionally the location of the crew's living quarters.

Fore – At, near, or toward the front of a ship.

Furl – To roll or fold up securely. To roll up the sails and tie them to the spars.

Fustian – A type of cotton and linen cloth of a coarse weave.

Gangplank – A moveable plank used to board or disembark a ship or boat.

Gunwale – The upper edge or planking of the side of a boat. The piece of wood or metal at the very edge of a boat that prevents water from running onto the deck, or into a boat.

Heel, Heeling – When a ship leans to one side owing to the pressure of the wind or an uneven load.

Helmsman – A person who steers a ship or boat.

Larboard – An old term for the left side of a ship as a person faces the front. The word now used for the left side of a ship is "port." Seamen stopped using the term larboard because it sounded too much like starboard (the right side of a ship) when yelled in a high wind or storm, or during a battle.

Longboat – A boat carried by a sailing ship on its deck. It is normally launched from the larger sailing ship and used for transport from ship to shore. Longboats were sturdy, seaworthy, and valued by the crews of the British navy.

Luff – To steer a sailing ship into the wind, causing the sails to flap and slowing the ship.

Main – Refers to the term Spanish Main. This term described the lands of Florida, Mexico, Central America, Northern South America, and the islands of the Caribbean, and the waters surrounding those lands. Spain controlled this area in varying degrees from the 1500s until the early 1800s.

Midwatch – The time between midnight and four in the morning, when a sailor might be required to stand watch.

Philip – (spelled with one "L") refers to Philip V, King of Spain. He was born in France and ascended to the throne of Spain in 1700. He ruled until 1746.

Porridge – In this usage, a hot breakfast dish of barley slowly boiled in water. It is eaten from a bowl with a spoon and is the consistency of a thin pudding or a modern-day bowl of oatmeal.

Powder monkey – Usually a quick and agile boy or small seaman. During a naval battle, the powder monkey would race from the powder magazine to the gun deck to deliver gunpowder to the cannon.

Quarterdeck – A raised deck at the rear of a ship usually reserved for officers and the men steering and directing the ship. This is the area designated as the command post of a sailing ship. The officers and important passengers usually lived below this deck.

Sloop – A single-masted sailing ship with one main triangular sail and one jib. The two sails are typically set running parallel to the sides of the ship with one sail in front of the mast and the other to the rear.

Speaking trumpet – The old term for a megaphone such as the ones used by modern-day cheerleaders.

Starboard – The right side of a ship as a person faces the front.

Swivel gun – A small cannon mounted on a post, usually located on the rail of a sailing ship. The swivel allowed the gun to have a wide range of motion. It could be loaded with a single shot or various smaller projectiles. Like a big shotgun.

Tack – To change course by turning a sailing boat's head into and through the wind. To make a series of such changes in course while sailing. To sail in the general direction the wind is coming from.

Tiller – A horizontal bar fitted to the head of a boat's rudder and used for steering.

Topgallant, mizzen, foreroyal – Various masts and sails on a square-rigged sailing ship.

Union Jack – The national flag of the United Kingdom, formed by combining the flags of St. George, St. Andrew, and St. Patrick.

Chapter 1

The Dome

The breeze caused only ripples, and the sunlight shimmered on the gentle swells. Where the dolphins circled, the water foamed. Bumping, rubbing, and jostling each other, nearly a thousand dolphins sped around the submerged crystal dome. Some skimmed the surface while others jumped and spun in the air. Many more sprang from the sea in low leaps to gain speed. They whistled, clicked, and brainspoke.

Shards of light danced on the ivory bottom sand and twinkled against the glass panels of the dome. The teachers stood on the catwalks inside the dome and watched the spectacle as the dolphins swirled above in an ever-contracting and -expanding circle of writhing energy. The teachers laughed and pointed as the dolphins, moving as one mass of flesh, spun the water above the dome into a vortex.

The youngest dolphins now possessed the power. The older dolphins knew they should conserve their body fuel, but none could resist the centuries-old tradition. An inner feeling prodded a pod of dolphins to peel away from the circle; other pods began to turn away, and the celebration waned. The migration back to their home waters would take many of these dolphins to the other side of the world. The sea calmed, and the dome sat empty and quiet.

Chapter 2

Helping Hands

Over the last few weeks, deep sleep had eluded Claire. Dolphins were always in her dreams. She could never remember what the dreams were about, but the dolphins never left her subconscious. Lately something peculiar had begun happening to Claire. As sleep washed over her, strange words would fill her mind. She could never understand the words, but it was as if someone was hovering over her and whispering in her ear. On this early morning the almost-words prodded her out of bed. Her mother stirred and mumbled, "Good God, it's early. What are you doing?"

"I'm going to the kitchen."

Grunting and mumbling in the Old Irish, Mary Riley rolled over. Claire got dressed, threw her shawl around her shoulders, and walked out into the cold morning. She did not go to the manor house but turned toward the bay.

Claire started down the cobbled road. As she walked along, a sense of urgency came over her. She knew it had to be something to do with the dolphins. She began to trot through the sleeping village. She didn't know why, but she began to push herself as fast as she could. The scuffing of her shoes on the cobblestones and her heavy breathing disturbed the quiet of the fog-shrouded morning. Claire ran out of the village and down the uneven cart path. The whispers pulsed through her mind, taking on a stressful, frantic quality.

Claire climbed on the rocks near the place where she often saw the dolphins. Through the mist, she heard the unmistakable sound of dolphins breathing. The sound of blowing air came as the creatures' heads popped to the surface and they exhaled and inhaled in a blink. Five dolphins bobbed just past the rocks in shallow water.

Claire jumped down to a small stretch of muddy sand. She paced along the water's edge as the colors of dawn pushed away the shadows. She rubbed her forehead with the heel of her hand. Claire dropped her shawl, kicked off her shoes, and walked into the water. The water soaked her dress to mid thigh and she gasped. Some inexplicable force pulled her in, and she waded into deeper water. The ice cold water and a nervous anticipation gripped her. She peered into the black water. Dorsal fins cut past. Claire could feel the powerful swimmers glide by her. This was the first time she had been in the water with her friends.

Help us, Meara thought.

Why is she here? Another dolphin brainspoke.

She's our friend, said Meara. *She might be able to help.*

She came here. She must know, a mind said. *She must know there's trouble.*

Meara, Bannon, Cwen groaned. *Help, please help. I feel the baby, but it won't come. The pain, the pain is stronger than ever. Please help me.*

Bannon rubbed against Cwen. *We're trying. Hang on just a little longer. Maybe Claire can help.*

Claire now stood in water past her waist, and a dolphin came near and rolled over. Its bloated stomach came out of the water. The small fluke of a baby dolphin stuck out of an opening near the mother's tail. Claire waded to the mother, rubbed her belly, and felt the baby squirm. She flinched and pulled her hand back. Claire trembled as she slowly reached out and touched the little tail protruding from the birth canal. It moved and Claire snapped her hand back again. A trickle of blood seeped out of the mother.

Claire, help us. The baby won't come, Meara called.

I tried pushing on Cwen's stomach, Bannon said. *Shall I try again?*

No, wait, maybe Claire will do something.

My baby will die, Cwen moaned.

Claire's head throbbed as never before; partial words, moans, howls, and whistles swirled along with the buzzing in her head.

Meara swam over to Claire, nudging her closer to Cwen. Claire looked down at Meara and then at Cwen. "You want me to help? She's in trouble and you want me to help?"

Meara's head came out of the water and she let out a series of squeaks. She slapped her powerful tail fluke on the surface. The slap and splash startled Claire. The dolphin slid back under and bumped Claire again. Her forehead furrowed, and for a moment Claire thought that the dolphin must have understood her. Claire held the mother dolphin's dorsal fin and moved her to shallower water. "There, there, my lady."

The dolphin breathed quick and hard. Claire sat in the water as Cwen rolled to one side. Claire rubbed her huge belly and then she saw the distortion—another lump. The dolphin took a breath. Claire rubbed her belly and then gently tugged on the baby's protruding tail fluke. It didn't move. Claire began to panic. *What should I do? What can I do?* She sat there for a moment, rubbing the dolphin's stomach and shivering. Claire's hand ran over the mother's belly and the other lump. Claire nodded. *The baby is wedged inside you, isn't it? That lump has something to do with it.*

Claire tugged on the mother's pectoral fin and struggled to roll the dolphin over on her back in the shallow water. The dolphin was at least twice the size of Claire.

As she sat in the water, Claire planted her feet in the soft sand. She grasped the baby's tail fluke with one hand and pushed down on the lump with the other. Claire pushed and pulled but nothing happened. She pushed again; nothing happened. *What should I do? I should go get Ma. No, I can't leave. I just can't leave her.*

Claire had seen plenty of births around the manor. Horses, cows, and sheep gave birth at different times of the year and there was always a litter of puppies being born among his lordship's horde of hounds. One human birthing scene remained etched in

Claire's memory. Her mother and four others had gathered around the pregnant one. The women had talked about the first birth always being the most difficult. Claire vividly remembered the grimacing face of the sweating young woman as she groaned and squirmed on the sheet-covered table in the manor house kitchen. Her legs were spread and her knees were bent upward. Claire's mother held the woman's hands; stretching her arms over her head. Meg, the round, red-faced cook, used her forearm and all her weight to push down on the upper part of the bloated belly. Meg stepped back and then pushed again, but this time she practically pounced on the poor girl. It was a harsh act. The baby squirted out into a pair of waiting hands.

Claire got to her knees. She put her chest against the dolphin's belly and pushed. She could feel the baby moving inside the mother. Claire rose up. "Come on girl, you can do this. Mother Mary, help us." She bent back over and put all her weight against the belly, using her legs to pin the dolphin against the sand. "Come on, girl, come on, damn it. Claire hugged and pushed. She pulled on the little tail with all the strength she had.

The sound of the mother's anguished, shrill scream slammed into Claire's forehead as the baby wriggled into its watery world. Claire fell back and slowly turned onto her hands and knees. The mother dolphin splashed and pushed away from the shallow water.

He's on the surface.

I'm with him; he's breathing.

Claire moaned, clenching her teeth; the most excruciating pain she had ever felt coursed through her head and down her spine. She pushed herself up, wobbling as she stood. Claire grabbed her head with both hands. She staggered back; her eyelids fluttered, and she crumpled against the wet sand.

Is the baby hurt?

No, he's fine. A beautiful male.

And you?

I'm tired, but I don't think I'm injured. What about Claire?

Meara swam into shallower water. *I can feel her mind. It seems as if…I think she's in a deep sleep.*

———

Claire felt the cold, gentle surf lapping around her feet; the pain throbbed in her head. She opened her eyes. Puffy white clouds moved across the blue sky, and she squinted at the morning sun. Shivering, she wiped some sand away from her eyes and mouth. Claire could hear the sounds of the dolphins' breathing near her. The dizziness faded a little, but the pounding in her head continued. She rose on one elbow, sat up, and pushed herself away from the icy water's edge. She knew she couldn't stand just yet. She knew she had done a good thing and she knew the baby had reached the surface. Claire's eyes darted from side to side. She labored to breathe as her head throbbed.

A few feet away, dolphins moved about and a little baby dolphin swam next to its mother. Wincing, Claire pulled her wet hair away from her face.

Meara's black eye came out of the water. *She's moving. I wonder what happened.*

Claire's whole body flinched. She gasped. Sitting in the sand, she twisted around to look behind her.

Did you just hear me? Meara slapped her tail on the water. *You heard me.*

Claire's eyes bulged wide open—she twisted around again, but saw no one. The words swirled through her mind. No sound rang in her ear, but she understood the words; she had heard the words, as she had heard the scream. Shaken and shivering, Claire pointed out at the water with a trembling hand. "You, you wondered what happened."

You heard me. Meara spun and rose to her pectoral fins. *You heard me.*

"Yes, yes. My God. Yes, I can hear you."

Don't speak, Claire. Just think the words.

"What's happened? Who are you?"

You can hear my mind. I am Meara and I have been trying to speak to you for years.

"Trying to speak to me? How can you speak to me?"

You did it, Meara. You got through to her, Padin said.

"Another voice," Claire gasped, as she moved back from the water a little more. "Who is that?"

She hears me too, Padin said.

Try to stay calm, Meara said. *Don't use your voice—just think the words.*

"What do you mean, 'think the words'?"

Don't use your voice.

"Dear Lord, is this a miracle or some kind of sorcery? Am I going crazy? How can it be?" She sat stunned and shivering. Her mind reeled and the dizziness persisted.

Claire, my name is Meara and you are not going crazy. I can hear the words you are thinking.

Claire thought the words. *You can hear my thoughts. This is a miracle. How did you know my name? How could you know? Your name is Meara?*

In the past, we heard your name called out when you were near the water.

Why have you been coming around me? Why me?

I don't know. I always felt this special connection. I felt something in you.

Claire got to her knees and pushed herself up. Still wobbly, she leaned against the rocks. Her head ached. She steadied herself and began walking back and forth on the beach with her soaked dress dragging on the sand. *Every time you came near me, I felt something. For as long as I can remember, I could sense your coming. You were trying to talk to me. Why? And how can you speak to me?*

I told my family of the bond I felt with you, and now we have this, Meara said.

Cwen swam over with her new baby. *Claire, I am Cwen. You saved my baby's life and my life as well. I will never forget you.*

Cwen? A new voice? Do dolphins everywhere speak as you do?

In this bay, many of us have the power, Meara said.

How did you learn to speak?

A long time ago, the teachers gave our ancestors the ability to communicate with them. They taught us your language and other languages in the hope that someday this very thing would happen.

Tell me about these teachers. Where do they live?

We promised, if this day ever came, we would not reveal the identity of our teachers.

Why? Who are they?

We took an oath of silence. I should say no more.

I don't understand. Are there other people who speak to you?

I know of no other.

Why me?

I don't know.

The mother and the newborn hovered nearby. *How do you feel?* Claire asked.

I'm fine, and my baby is perfect, thanks to you.

More dolphins sped toward the small piece of beach. *Is it true?*

Yes, she can hear us, and we can hear her.

You've done it, Meara. You finally reached her—the first one.

I am Stark. The big dolphin swam close to the shore. *The teachers will be happy it is a person like you.*

The teachers? Please tell me.

Enough, Meara said. *This is a wonderful day, but we must be mindful of our oath.*

Claire sat on a rock. Her head still throbbed and she shivered. She did not want to stop brainspeaking. The thoughts of every dolphin in the pod swirled around Claire and her mind filled with jabbering. Finally, Meara announced, *We must go. Cwen has moved away to tend to her new one. We should go with her.*

Claire stood and stepped to the water's edge. *Don't go—wait. There is so much to talk about. How is this possible? Why me?*

We will be back tomorrow, Meara said. *Come to the rocks when the sun shines highest in the sky. Go and rest—go and rest your mind.*

Where will you go?

Out to deep water. We need to eat, said another dolphin.

As Claire watched, the dolphins turned away from the beach. Meara stayed back. *Claire, you must promise you will keep this a secret.*

Why?

The teachers foretold of danger, danger coming from other humans once we found a speaker. We believe that if other humans knew of our power, some would seek to capture us. You must keep our secret, and the teachers must remain hidden. For centuries, we have sworn to keep the teachers hidden.

I don't understand about these teachers, but I'll keep your secret. I swear.

Thank you, Claire. I know we can trust you. Meara submerged. Three dolphins leaped in unison, arched over, and pointed downward in perfect dives. Claire waved both her hands over her head.

A huge dolphin jumped and turned, end over end. Stark's brain called out, *Until tomorrow.* The dolphin splashed into the water, and the pod disappeared.

Claire stood squinting as a few dorsal fins broke the surface far out in the bay. Her heart pounded and her breathing heaved in her chest. Exhausted, she sat in the sand, leaned against the rocks, and shivered. *It started with the scream, the mother's scream. Why did I faint? God, my head hurts.*

———

Breakfast came and went early for the working people of the manor. As the long day of labor began, the big house grew quiet around midmorning. Unnoticed, Claire plodded to the door of her little cottage.

Claire took off her wet clothes and wrapped herself in a blanket. She wished she could talk to her mother about her ability to communicate with the dolphins, but she knew she could not. She had given her word to the dolphins. She did not understand about the great danger or the mysterious teachers, but she had made a promise—a promise she knew she must keep. With the pain continuing to pulse through her head, Claire curled up on her bed and closed her eyes. Exhaustion gripped her body, but her mind was energized by the strange and wonderful events of the morning, and by the questions without answers. Claire did not sleep.

————

The dolphins gathered and swam in a circle.

We must tell the teachers. We must go to the dome and tell them the news.

Stark swam into the center of the circle. *I'll go. I'm the strongest and fastest among us.*

It is a long journey, Meara said. *One of you young males should go with him.*

A dolphin, a bit smaller than Stark, swam into the circle. Stark rubbed up next to him. *This is good*, Stark said. *We'll eat in the open ocean.*

The two dolphins tuned and surged away. In long, low leaps they sped out into the Atlantic and then to the west and south.

Chapter 3

Fishing on Bantry Bay

The gulls had not yet begun their morning cries. Claire knelt in the dark and placed two small pieces of turf on the smoldering ashes. She held her hair back, leaned forward, and blew on the embers. The gentle stream of air coaxed the small fire back to life and the peat began to glow red with warmth. Claire shivered and began dressing near the hearth in the hope of catching a little bit of the heat. Her mother rose from her bed and lit the three candles on the mantle. "Who is it today?" her mother asked.

"Mr. McMearty."

"That grump of a man in the shack behind Mrs. Leary?"

"He's getting on, you know, and he's too proud to ask for help. Mrs. Leary thought I might lend him a hand."

Mary Riley said something in the Irish. When she talked to herself, she always used the Old Irish tongue of her childhood. Claire pursed her lips.

"And you're doing a fine thing. I just wish you wouldn't do so much of it. You'd be so much better off walking into the village in a pretty dress rather than wearing his fishing gear. You won't be turning the heads of any lads dressed like that."

Claire glared at her mother for a moment and started to say that she didn't care about the young men of Bantry, but she just sighed. This was not the first time her mother had prodded her, and it wouldn't be the last. Most of the men around her age fished long and drank hard. She thought there was something a little wrong with the way they lived. Claire always wanted to get closer to one or two of them. She searched for a common ground, and hoped she could find someone she could talk to about something other than the weather, fishing, the pubs, or the English. As of yet that young man was nowhere to be found in Bantry or anywhere in all of County Cork.

Standing in the middle of the room, Claire raised her hands over her head and let the heavy Aran sweater drape over her. Baggy woolen pants with the cuffs tucked into high-topped brogans completed the ensemble. Since she was taller than most of the girls and many of the men in the village, the sleeves and pants were about the right length. The man who had once worn them had had quite a bit more meat on his bones. Her copper-colored hair flew as Claire held out her arms and spun. "Well, Ma, what do you think?"

"You do remind me of him, that's for sure."

"Does it sadden you, Ma?"

Mary busied herself tidying up the room. "I'm over it."

Claire hugged her mom from behind in a big bear hug. "I promise, tomorrow I'll put on my nicest dress and go into the village. I have a lesson to tend to and I'll spend some time with Eileen."

Mary squirmed away with a smile, picked up the tattered oilskin coat, and pulled it around her daughter. "Go see Meg in the kitchen; she'll have a jug of tea and some scones for you."

Carrying a canvas bag draped over her shoulder, Claire walked down to the docks in the gray of the morning. She thought about the young men of the village more than she would ever admit. Claire wished a few of them had just a bit of an education. She tried so very hard, but she did not seem to be able to hold the interest of any one of them for more than a short while. Almost every man in Bantry fished. The sea made them strong but harsh. Claire found it curious that they never gave a second thought to the horrific waves and the howling winds of the North Atlantic, but many of the younger men seemed to be intimidated by her. When the lads avoided her, she hid the pangs of sadness, but she knew her face never concealed the contempt that welled up in her when one of them blustered his way around or over her talking. Claire had considered changing her manner, but she knew she couldn't. Anyway, for the last week she had spent every moment she could talking to the dolphins. She thought she might like to be around some of the lads, but with the Radstone boys to tend to, the classes, and now her wonderful and magical dolphins, she just didn't have the time. Since the breakthrough, Claire had been thinking about the dolphins constantly. Being near and talking to the dolphins obsessed her. Today she would be on the water and she knew the dolphins would come. She worried about it and wondered if she could hide her worry.

In her usual jaunty way, Eileen walked out of the Harp carrying a basket filled with small loaves and hunks of cheese. Eileen balanced the basket on her hip as she swung along. Eileen always exaggerated the swinging of her hips when she peddled to the men on the docks. Claire called out and ran toward her. Eileen turned and looked up and down at Claire with a mock frown. "Well, my ladyship, I see you're wearing your most lovely finery."

"You're a pain in my arse," Claire said.

"It's why God put me here, don't you know? Who you helping today?"

"McMearty."

"He needs it."

"You could help sometimes."

"With all me duties at the Harp? You know Fitzpatrick has the place open now from morning to midnight. And anyway, I'd only be going with the lads, and I'm sure we wouldn't be getting much fishing done." Eileen winked and smiled an exaggerated toothy smile. Claire rolled her eyes.

"I'll be meeting Kevin and a few of the others when they come in. Why don't you join us?"

"I can't. I have to get back to the manor and the boys."

"The boys, the reading, the lessons—a pint with a few of us wouldn't hurt you none."

"I promise I'll stop by the Harp when I get in. But just for a few minutes."

"I'll tie you to a chair. I've got to be going. Old lady Fitzpatrick will wail like a banshee if I don't sell every last one of these loaves."

Claire called after her. "Maybe tomorrow we'll work on your reading."

Eileen turned back. "Now you're being a pain in my arse."

Claire laughed, as a man stopped Eileen to buy some bread and cheese.

Claire started to look for Mr. McMearty along the crowded dock as the men readied themselves for the day's fishing. She walked toward a group of young fishermen, hoping to see Sean Dweyer. She steadied her voice. "Morning, lads. Any of you seen McMearty?"

Sean looked up and stepped toward Claire, smiling. Claire felt a little flutter in her stomach.

"He's down at the end of the dock."

Claire smiled. "Mrs. Leary told me he was having trouble and asked me to help him with the nets."

"To be sure, the crusty old thing would never admit that he can hardly pull up the nets with those twisted hands of his," Sean said.

A voice came from the crowd of men. "Hey, Sean. Enough flirting there; the tide is tugging at us." The word flirting made Claire blush.

Sean smiled and touched his hat. "I got to be going. A good day to you, Claire."

"And a good day to you, Sean." Claire smiled back at him, then turned and started down the dock, hoping she wasn't blushing too much, and wishing she'd said more.

Sean called out to her. "Claire, will we be seeing the dolphins today?"

The words sent a shock through Claire. She fought not to react. She turned, shrugged, smiled a bit, and then continued on her way.

Claire saw Mr. McMearty loading his boat. "A fine morning, Mr. McMearty," she called. She knew he was a little deaf.

He didn't look at Claire. "Mrs. Leary told me you'd be coming by. The old woman needs to be minding her own business. You know I don't need any help at all."

"I'm sure of it," Claire said, smiling. "I thought I would just come along and do a bit of sailing. It should be a pleasant day out on the water."

McMearty nodded. Faoide Island usually shielded the village of Bantry. On this gray morning the cold north winds buffeted the docks. It would *not* be a lovely day for sailing out on Bantry Bay, and they both knew it.

They got in the boat and set out. Claire hoisted the sail while Mr. McMearty sat at the tiller of the skiff.

"I brought along some tea and scones for us."

"That's a fine thing, but it would be better if you had a touch of the Irish somewhere in that sack—just enough to keep me belly warm, you know."

Claire reached into the pocket of her baggy trousers and pulled out a small pewter flask. She winked at the old man. "I drew it out of a cask in the wine cellar last night. We'll have the tea and scones, and then you can have the flask on the way in."

McMearty's face lit up. "I always said you was a fine and thoughtful lass."

Following the fishing flotilla, they sailed out and around Faoide Island. "Do you think we'll have a catch today?" asked Claire.

"Only Saint Patrick knows for sure. But I do smell a little luck in the air. I told the boys at the pub last night you'd probably be along with me today, and they're all hoping the dolphins will be around. I mean, with you being out and all."

Claire held her emotions in check and filled McMearty's wooden cup. They sat in silence for a while. When the other boats were ready, Claire and the old man began putting out the nets. "So why did you say that about the dolphins?" Claire didn't look at McMearty and kept working the nets.

"Well, you know the dolphins have helped us with the catch before, and in the pubs folks are always talking about it. People say the dolphins would always come around when your mother would carry you down near the docks. Now it seems we rarely see the dolphins unless you're out with us or near the water." The old man grappled with the nets. "We'll see them today, for sure."

Claire didn't say anything. She knew the people of Bantry talked about her and the dolphins. She wanted to be near the dolphins every minute of the day. But today she hoped they would not come near.

McMearty and Claire sat and waited. A string of cork buoys, supporting the nets, meandered out in a line behind the skiff. Twenty other boats sat waiting in the windswept bay. Claire pulled her oilskin tighter in front of her.

A voice came from another boat. "Dolphins!" In the distance, ten to twelve dorsal fins broke the surface and then curved back under.

"They're coming to see you, my girl."

"I don't think so," Claire said.

"I do."

Claire said nothing more. She never looked back at McMearty, but watched as the dolphins swam nearer. Inside her head, the feelings began.

———

I can see the boats and the nets ahead of us, a dolphin brain sent.

I think she's out on one of the fishing boats, said another.

So she is. Have we all had enough?

The others agreed and knew what to do. The dolphins fanned out, squeaking, clicking, and whistling. The school of fish panicked, surged away from the noise, and swam into the nets.

I'm going over to that boat, Meara's mind sent.

Be careful. They'll begin hoisting the nets, Padin said. *Is it Claire?*

Yes, she's there. I can feel her mind.

Just be careful, Padin said.

———

The dolphin rolled to one side, and its black eye and pinhole ear came out of the water. McMearty pointed. "For sure, this dolphin has come to visit you."

A man in another boat waved and yelled, "Claire, Claire my lass, the dolphins have surely helped us this day."

Good morning to you, Claire, Meara's mind said.

I wish you hadn't come today.

Why?

It's just, well, people are talking.

Do any of them know? Have you told anyone?

No, I would never—I promised you I would keep your secret, and you can be sure I will. The village is small. People see you near me and they talk.

"Come on, girl," McMearty broke the silence. "Stop staring at that fish. The dolphins have pushed these fish into the nets, now we've got to get them up." The old man began hoisting the net.

Claire snapped out of her trance, grabbed the net, and started to pull. She watched Meara bobbing a few feet away.

I understand; come to the rocks tomorrow. I'll tell the others to be more careful. Meara sank below the surface and disappeared.

"Everyone thinks the dolphins do this because of you, my girl," McMearty said.

"I don't see how." Claire kept pulling on the net and watching the water.

———

Claire helped McMearty with the fish and the cleaning of the boat. He didn't look at her when he mumbled a thank you. She knew the words were heartfelt. Claire smiled, patted McMearty on the shoulder, and walked toward the Harp. As she came to the pub, Claire wondered why a dozen people stood outside near the entrance. She opened the door. The fishermen of Bantry and a good many of the villagers thronged the barroom. The mass of people jabbered and jostled about. A fog of smoke from every shape and manner of pipe hung in the rafters. Stepping into the crowd, Claire sniffed at the familiar smells of tobacco, whiskey, ale, and fish. The pubs of Bantry always had a whiff of fish about them. She waded into the room, and the crowd engulfed her. Standing on her toes, Claire looked over the heads and searched for Eileen.

A fisherman turned, and ale sloshed out of his glass. "It was a good catch today. You and McMearty brought in a good number."

"We were lucky," Claire said as she continued to look for Eileen. She saw her friend working her way through the crowd.

"Well now, your ladyship, stand right there and I'll get you a pint," Eileen said.

"No, no, Eileen, this is crazy," Claire pushed her way out the door with Eileen behind her.

"Stay for a while. Some of them will be going home soon. Have yourself a little fun," Eileen said.

"This is not really my idea of fun."

"I sometimes wonder what your idea of fun is."

Claire smiled at her friend and nodded. Eileen put her hand on Claire's shoulder. "Well then, we'll do it another day."

Liam Mulligan stumbled out of the Harp. "You're coming back in, are you? I need another pint."

"Looks to me like you've had about enough," Eileen said as she pushed past him back into the crowd.

Liam glared at Claire. "Are you coming in?"

"No, I've got to be getting back."

"Well then," Liam said, "I'll just walk you home."

"It's a short walk. Don't bother yourself."

He put his arm under hers. "A pretty girl always needs some company, and it'll be no bother at all." He smiled, winked, and the melody in his voice caused Claire to return a slight quick smile. The two started out of town and up toward Radstone manor. They walked down the next street and then turned onto a narrow lane leading up the hill. Liam pulled her close, spun her toward him, and grabbed her around the waist.

"What are you doing?"

"I've been watching you. I know you want to be kissed." His voice took on a guttural growling tone.

She turned her head away, and pushed him back. "You're drunk. I'd rather kiss a goat." Claire saw a wicked scowl come to Liam's face as he recovered and shoved her hard. Claire stumbled back against the stone wall that ran along the lane.

He grabbed her wrists and pinned her arms. She turned her head hard from side to side trying to avoid his face and mouth. Panic began to overtake her. The stale smell of soured ale filled her nostrils. He pushed himself against her body with all his weight. Claire froze and shivered with fear. She pursed her lips, scrunched her face, and kept her eyes shut tight. Claire whimpered as she felt his hot, moist breath on her face.

Claire heard the sound of running feet. Her eyes sprang wide open. A slab of polished dark-brown wood slapped into the side of Liam's face. Liam's head snapped back; his arms flung up, and he exhaled with a barely audible grunt as he crumpled to the cobblestones like a stringless puppet. In a snappy motion, a red-coated soldier flipped his musket around and pointed the bayonet inches from Liam's ribs. Two more soldiers skidded to a stop and pointed their bayonets at the still body. Liam's twisted arms and legs splayed in an unnatural pose. He never twitched. A fourth soldier trotted up. "Are you all right, Miss Riley?"

Claire, breathing heavily, looked down at Liam and then at the soldier who had said her name. She nodded and blinked her glassy eyes. She panted and didn't speak. Claire fought to hold back the tears as a single droplet fell on her cheek. The soldier who knew her name put his hand on her shoulder and gave her a comforting smile. "Easy lass, easy now, we're here with you."

Another tear fell. She didn't cry, but she breathed in short, quick, shivering gasps. Claire looked at Liam wondering if he was alive. A boot pressed down on Liam's chest and he groaned. Claire reached out to the soldier. "Please, please leave him be. He's a little drunk, is all."

The men looked back at their sergeant. "Leave him; we'll escort Miss Riley back to the manor." Claire picked up her canvas bag that now held the pieces of the tea jug. As they began walking away, Claire looked back. Liam had rolled over and was on his hands and knees. An odd feeling of remorse came to Claire.

"I'm Sergeant Webb, Miss Riley; I've seen you around the manor."

The short quick breaths of panic and fear began to leave her. "I'm glad you came along."

"Think nothing of it," the sergeant said. "We're happy to have been of service."

Claire and Sergeant Webb walked a few paces ahead of the other three soldiers. Claire wondered what would have happened if the soldiers had not come to her aid. "Sergeant, please don't say anything about this. It would worry my mother half to death, and I do have to live in this village. It would be better for me if we just forgot about this."

"I understand, miss. I'll make sure the men keep quiet about it. Just remember there is one other person who might tell the story." The sergeant smiled and cocked his head back over his shoulder. "That ruffian back there will not be forgetting the corporal's musket butt any time soon."

Claire had not considered what story Liam might concoct. She mused about how long it would take the story to get back to Radstone Manor. She knew this tale would blow through the village like a North Sea gale.

The sergeant stopped and touched his cap. "All right, miss. We'll leave you here to get yourself back."

The four soldiers started toward the village and the bay. Claire turned for home, relieved that things hadn't gone further. She turned back and called, "Thank you."

The men all waved. Claire thought about how she could minimize the incident when the story got back to her mother. She could only pray that Lord Radstone would not find out. Claire wondered if the young men of Bantry would consider walking her home to be a dangerous endeavor. She didn't care. Except for a few people in the writing and reading class, no one ever offered to walk her home.

Chapter 4

Caribbean Visitors

During the next few days, Claire's mind blurred as waves of excitement surged through her. On this particular day, she walked along the path toward the village to perform one of her favorite tasks. For years, Claire and her mother had set aside any extra food from the kitchen for the less fortunate people of the village. Each day, with Lady Radstone's blessing, Claire and her mother would rise early and wrap yesterday's uneaten food for Claire to take to the village. Claire enjoyed her visits with the villagers, and the walk there gave her time to think.

Today, she thought about the strange events that now surrounded her life. She considered herself very lucky to have grown up on Lord Radstone's estate. Lord and Lady Radstone had employed a series of tutors, beginning when their oldest son could barely learn his letters. Given the run of the property by her mother's generous employers, little Claire had quickly found her way to these fascinating—as she saw them—storytellers. For their part, none of the scholars had been able to resist such a quick and charming pupil. Lord Radstone approved, giving Claire access to the library after she learned to read in record time. With a little guidance and a wealth of books to explore, Claire had educated herself, especially on the subjects of literature and poetry.

It was two years ago when the boys' tutor had abruptly moved back to London, and Claire had been asked to supervise the lessons until a new tutor could be found. She embraced her new job with glee, vigor, and much seriousness. The youngest, Phillip, nine at the time, listened to her without question. Although James and Edward, at the ages of twelve and eleven, often challenged her, she proved her knowledge so often and so thoroughly that they soon respected her authority, even though she was only fifteen then. The boys came to enjoy Claire's cheerful and informal style, and the Radstones made her position as tutor official.

Claire's status enabled her to start a reading and writing class for the villagers. It began in a shed on the wharf with just a few women and children, and grew to include many of the fishing men of Bantry Bay. Claire relished the time she spent teaching the people of Bantry to read and write. She found it curious that adults and children filled her class, but no one close to her age, except for Eileen, ever attended. Eileen came and was always a bit disruptive with all her chatter. Claire knew Eileen was just covering up for being a bit slower than most of the others, but Claire was determined to help her along.

―――――

Claire walked past the row of neatly kept buildings across from the water. Three men sat in front of a shop, smoking their pipes. As she came closer, she realized the man sitting in the middle was Liam Mulligan. Her heart was in her throat, her breath quickened, and her pace slowed. She screwed up her courage and continued, her head held high. She wasn't about to give him the satisfaction of seeing her turn around or change course.

As she came to them, eyes forward, Liam spat on the ground in front of her. "Well, there she is boys, the English lapdog. I wonder how many laps she curls up on in a week." The other two kept sucking on their pipes.

Claire, embarrassed and infuriated, turned to face him. The side of his head was still misshapen and swollen; black-and-blue blotches covered half his face.

She took a deep breath and steadied herself. "The good men, and I do mean men, who come to my class truly enjoy learning to read and write, and they appreciate me coming down and teaching them. They know what happened. So, Mr. Liam Mulligan, if you ever put your dirty drunken hands on me again, the butt of an English musket will be the least of your worries. In fact, I'm surprised you're not already tiny bits of bait for the fishing fleet."

Claire turned and walked away, shaking with anger and fear. Tears welled up in her eyes, and she fought to hold herself erect and steady. She didn't look back; she wouldn't look back. The tears poured down her cheeks. She stopped, took a deep breath, wiped her eyes with her sleeve, and continued down the dock.

One of the two young men sitting there tapped the ashes out of his pipe on the side of the bench and snorted in a quiet laugh. "Well, Mulligan, I'd say you tangled with the wrong lass."

Liam Mulligan stood up. "Shut your yap," he growled, and stomped off toward the closest pub.

———

Meara's pod swam out at sea, west of Bantry Bay. The warm waters of the current flowing from the southern oceans always provided plenty of food. A few days passed as they waited.

Far out at sea, faint screeches and whistles pushed through the water. The males of the pod swam side by side in a line stretching out half a mile. They echolocated, searching for a school of fish. Swimming ahead of the pod, the males detected the far-off sounds and launched themselves into speed-swimming mode. The rest of the families followed.

Padin and his two companions broadcast out their identifying squeaks and whistles as their pod converged with another. As they came closer, their minds connected.

A new mind beamed out, *We have traveled from the southern seas. I'm Nami.*

I'm Padin. Welcome. Welcome to our part of the ocean.

As they met, a few of them jumped and spun in the air. Both pods introduced themselves, rubbing and bumping against each other.

Is your young one here? Is he ready for the journey? Nami asked.

Yes, but first, there is exciting news.

The dolphins swam in circles, discussing the breakthrough of being able to communicate with a friendly human girl. Meara told them that the message of the breakthrough was on its way to the great dome. The combined group spread out in the usual way, sending out their echolocation clicks. Soon they saw a school of pilchards and converged on it. The Bantry Bay dolphins held back while the travelers ate first. Before long, all had eaten their fill, and they then sped into Bantry Bay toward the place where they would normally find Claire.

————

The boys began their lessons early these days. Today Claire ended the lesson sooner than expected. Finally free to answer the call she thought she had heard, she ran down to, and then out of, the village. The roadway narrowed to a cart path, then to a worn trace of a trail on the lush green carpet of Ireland. She raced to the rocks. No dorsal fins moved above the surface. The dolphins had told her they were going out to sea. Perhaps she'd just imagined the call.

Having not slept well at all lately, Claire felt her exhaustion as she sat against the rocks and, nearly in a trance, gazed at the water. Far out in the bay, telltale white splashes appeared. Claire watched them intently.

The bodies of the dolphins became visible as the pod sped toward Claire, some leaping while others skimmed the surface. Claire's heart pounded.

Hello, Claire, Meara shouted out. *We've brought friends to meet you.*

Friends?

Claire, I'm Nami. It's a great honor to meet you. You are the first. Dolphins have been waiting and hoping for hundreds of years and now it has happened. Some of us will soon be returning to the warm waters around the islands of the Caribbean. We are excited to be among the first to have met you. All the dolphins will already know about you and they will all be—

What islands? Claire's eyes widened.

The thousands of islands in the southern seas, Nami said.

You mean there are dolphins in the southern seas who can speak like you?

Oh, yes. More dolphins with the power live in the Caribbean than any other place on earth, Nami said.

Tell me about the islands and the people, Claire said. *I often wonder about faraway lands and the people who live there.*

Much of what happens on land is a mystery to us, Nami said. *The islands look pleasant enough. Most of the people are friendly and kind, but we encounter many evil humans on the sea.*

There are evil people everywhere in the world, Claire said.

There are sorrowful ships always coming from the east. The sailors on them throw many bodies of dark humans into the sea as they sail toward the islands.

Dark humans? Those ships are transporting slaves from Africa to the Americas. Some of the slaves must die during the journey, and they throw them overboard. I wonder how many people die during the crossing? A terrible thing and an evil that humanity should not allow.

The dolphins talked about the islands, life in Bantry Bay, and their families. Claire learned that Rafe and Bannon would be taking their son to the islands. He could not brainspeak now, but would come back to Bantry Bay with the power.

It's time for us to go, Meara said.

Yes, I should be on my way as well, Claire said. *Will I see you tomorrow?*

Of course, Meara said.

Tomorrow I will be occupied with literature lessons, and I am not sure when I'll be able to come.

Don't worry, Padin said. *We'll be out in the bay. We will sense when you come near and swim to you.*

Claire stood. *I'll be looking for you.*

27

The dolphins turned in unison toward the open water while Claire walked toward the village.

———

The Radstone boys had been born in close succession and Lady Radstone only regretted the absence of a girl in her brood. The oldest, fourteen-year-old James, had proclaimed himself the leader of the brotherhood in its earliest days. James sported a mop of dark brown hair, and everyone considered him an image of his father. At thirteen, Edward stood taller and leaner than his brothers. He had curly blond hair and the look of his mother. Eleven-year-old Phillip could have been James's twin. Edward possessed an affinity for learning. Neither James nor Phillip studied with the intensity or joy of Edward. James and Phillip studied because they had to; Edward studied because he loved to.

James slapped his book closed and sighed. "I think we should go sailing this afternoon."

Phillip broke his gaze out the window. "Without Claire?"

"We don't need Claire to go with us every time."

"Do you think one of them will give us a boat without Claire?"

"I'm sure they will; I've got a few coins in my pocket."

Phillip nudged Edward, who was still looking down at his book. "Come on, Edward."

Edward looked up. "I suppose we could finish all this in the morning."

"Let's slip down the back stairs and out through the garden," James said.

Edward closed his book. "I want both of you to understand that the main reason I'm coming along is I know that if you two eejits sail out of sight of the village, you'll never find your way back. I would like to see both of you again." The boys all smiled at each other.

The wind from the North Sea blew down the long axis of the bay. The boys tacked the skiff against the wind. James sat at the tiller, Edward worked the boom line, and Phillip sat at the bow as the boat skimmed across the water to the windward side of Faoide Island. The skiff heeled to starboard.

"Pull her into the wind a little more," James said.

Edward pulled on the boom line.

"Phillip, move over to larboard. We can surely make her go faster," James said.

Phillip stumbled over to the side, put his hands on the gunwale, and leaned out a little. The boat bounced against a wave. Phillip's hands slipped off the rail, his midsection hit the gunwale, and he fell headlong into the bay.

"Phillip! Oh my God, Phillip!" Edward screamed.

"Throw him a line!"

"He's too far back. Come about, damn it! Come about!"

Phillip flailed at the water and screamed for help. He went under and bobbed back up. His woolen coat and heavy sweater sucked up the water and he sank into the cold darkness of Bantry Bay. James pushed the tiller and the bow of the skiff turned into the wind. The sail luffed and the boom swung to the other side; the sail snapped as it caught the wind, and the skiff turned back. Phillip was nowhere to be seen.

"Phillip! Phillip!" Edward screamed. The two boys looked at each other, their faces twisted with fear and panic; they scanned the water for any sign of him.

"Straight ahead!" Edward pointed. "Straight ahead!"

"Where?"

Edward pointed at nothing.

"There! I see him!" James yelled.

Just ahead of them and to starboard Phillip broke the surface. He didn't slap at the water. He hugged a gray dorsal fin. Phillip wrapped his arms around the fin as he straddled the dolphin's head, facing its tail. Two more dolphins came up on either side of the one carrying Phillip.

"My God, look at that," James said.

"A miracle. It's a miracle," Edward said.

The dolphins waited for the boat to pass them and then swam next to it. James let go of the tiller and helped Edward pull in their brother. Phillip gagged and water spewed out of his nose and mouth. The dolphins disappeared.

"Phillip, are you all right?" Edward asked, as he slapped him on the back.

More water poured out of Phillip as he gasped and coughed. "The dolphin—it swam between my legs, it pushed me up." Phillip could barely speak as he continued to retch and cough.

James got back to the tiller and headed back to the village. "What happened just now? I can't believe it. And where did they go?" he asked, looking over the water for signs of the dolphins.

"I don't know, I just don't know. It's too fantastic," Edward said. "How did they find him? Why would they do this?"

"To keep him from drowning, of course."

"But why?"

"We'll never know. Phillip, can you breathe?"

Phillip nodded.

"I wonder what Claire will think of this," Edward said.

"We can't tell anyone," James said. "If Mum or Dad were to find out about this, it would be the end of our sailing days."

Edward nodded. The boys agreed not to say anything to anyone about this amazing and very scary incident. Two fishermen helped the shivering wet dog of a boy up on the dock and laughed at his soggy situation. They knew the seriousness of the cold and took him to a smokehouse, where they warmed him and dried his clothes over a glowing turf fire.

Chapter 5

Staying or Leaving

The staff lined up in the courtyard of the manor house as the carriage wound its way up past the thatched roofs of the village below. The servants of the house and a few officers from the military garrison gathered in the courtyard. Claire and her mother stood with Lady Radstone and her three boys on the steps of the red brick and slate-gray stone manor.

Drawn by a matched pair of chestnuts and driven by two soldiers sitting at attention on the driver's bench, the open carriage clattered onto the cobblestoned courtyard. Lord Radstone stood up, opened the door, and jumped out as the driver pulled the horses to a stop. "My boys!" he shouted as he stretched open his arms. The two younger boys bolted away from their mother and into their father's arms, while James followed at a more adult pace.

"What did you bring us from London?" Phillip asked.

"Yes, Father," Edward said. "Did you bring us anything?"

"Did you see the new king?" James asked. "Did you speak to King George?"

"Indeed I did. The king asked me when you would be joining His Majesty's army." He turned to his wife, who stood smiling. "Elizabeth." He kissed her on the cheek. "I missed you."

She kissed his cheek. "We talked about you every day, my dear. We're all so happy you are home."

Lord Radstone thanked the staff for the welcome, and they began to return to their duties. Mary Riley and Claire lingered near the front door. Lord Radstone stopped. "Hello, Mrs. Riley, Claire, I hope you are well?"

"Very well, my lord." Mary and Claire curtsied.

"Ladies, I would like both of you to join Lady Radstone and me for dinner tonight. We shall be discussing a subject of great importance to all."

"Yes, my lord," Mary said.

"We shall see you both then at seven."

Both women gave a slight nod. Claire followed Mary as her mother moved through the house, inspecting the work of the other servants. Claire waited for her mother to bring it up. "I wonder what Lord Radstone wants to speak to us about," Mary said.

"I think I have an idea, Ma. I heard from some of the soldiers that the king would be giving Lord Radstone an excellent new position. They said he might be going to the Colonies to command the army. I also heard he might become the governor of some far-off possession."

"You think he might be going to America? I wonder if he'll ask us to go along."

"That would be exciting if he did, Ma. Just think of the adventures we'd have."

Claire noted her mother's silence. Mary finished her task and walked through the crowded kitchen, checking on preparations for the evening meal. They walked toward their little cottage to change.

"By the way, my *young lass*, keep away from the English soldiers. There will be nothing but trouble for you if you seek out the company of those men."

Claire stopped in her tracks and huffed. "Mother, why would you say such a thing?"

"My darling, I know you're a fine and good girl. Just remember, there is a world of difference between our fine Irish lads down in the village and that barracks full of Englishmen. There's not one of them redcoats that's worth a tinker's damn."

"Lord Radstone is an Englishman," Claire protested. She already knew her mother's response.

"And the finest gentleman we'll ever meet, but you couldn't fill a thimble up with the character in all the rest of them put together." Mary put her arm around her daughter's shoulder. "I do love you, Claire. Let's get changed and go hear what Lord Radstone has to say."

Claire mumbled, "Fine Irish lads, indeed."

At seven, Mary and Claire entered the house by the front door. They both wore plain cotton dresses, one blue and one green, faded by constant washing. They both covered their shoulders with identical shawls of natural wool knitted in the intricate Irish style.

"Mother, if Lord Radstone asks us to go with him, will you say yes?"

"I'm not so sure."

As the two women stood in the doorway of the formal dining room, Claire fidgeted. A long dining table, able to seat forty, filled the room with glistening mahogany. Red velvet–covered chairs, in perfect alignment, stretched down each side of the table. There was no china on the table, and Mary grumbled an Old Irish curse, as she wondered why her instructions for the table setting had not been carried out.

The Radstones came in through a far door, and Mary and Claire moved around the table. "Mary, Claire, thank you for coming. I think we shall enjoy an exciting evening together," Lord Radstone said.

"Good evening, sir." Mary curtsied.

"My lord, my lady." Claire bent at the knee in a quick curtsy.

"Oh, please." Elizabeth Radstone patted Claire on the shoulder. "None of that when we're alone. I spoke to cook and the servers, Mary. We'll dine in the family dining room. No need for us to use this big formal room." Lady Radstone motioned and everyone walked into the back room.

The smaller dining room glowed from the light of candles flickering in sconces at various heights on the walls of the room.

The crystal goblets and delicate bone china, ringed in lapis and trimmed in gold, looked beautiful on the snowy white cloth. Claire knew the correct use of each silver utensil—three forks, two knives, and two spoons—but always thought the use of so much silverware to be ostentatious.

"Where are the boys?" Claire asked.

"Oh, I allowed them to eat with Lieutenant Williams and the other soldiers in the barracks. They enjoy mingling with the soldiers," Lord Radstone said.

Lady Radstone shook her head.

Lord Radstone leaned over the table. "Mary, Claire, I have something important to tell you. I will be going to Jamaica as the new governor of that island and the surrounding territories in the Caribbean."

Under the table Claire's hand closed tight on the cloth of her dress. It was all she could do to keep herself from jumping up and screaming for joy. She thought of the dolphins. Could she connect with the dolphins in the islands? Of course she could. What if she couldn't? Claire put the thought out of her mind.

A moment of silence followed, broken when Mary asked, "When will you be taking on these new responsibilities, my lord?"

"I will be going very soon, in a week or two. Lady Radstone, the boys, and I hope both of you will join me as soon as another ship becomes available for your transportation."

"Oh, please, say yes," Lady Radstone pleaded. "The boys would be lost without you, Claire. And you, Mary, are my closest companion. I shall miss you both so much if you don't come." Lady Radstone passed a platter of roast beef and then a bowl of potatoes.

"You honor me, my lady." Mary smiled at Lady Radstone. "I must think carefully about this. Tending to Claire's future is most important to me. Bantry is our home and Jamaica is so very far away."

Lord Radstone put down his knife and fork, sitting back in his chair. "Ladies, listen to me. It is 1714, and the world is changing. Our new King George has decreed that England shall expand its

colonies around the world. It will be an exciting time for all of us."
There was an awkward moment of silence. Lord Radstone sat up
straight, looking at Mary. "I want you both to consider one other
thing—and please understand that the documents are signed and
the arrangements have been completed. If you come with us, I
shall give you and Claire a home of your own in Jamaica. A house
and land deeded to you, to be yours forever."

Claire and her mother looked at each other, eyes wide, then, as
if for confirmation, at Lord Radstone, and then back to each other
again.

"My lord," Mary said, "that is very generous and I—"

"Mary, you and your daughter are like family to Elizabeth and
me. If you decide to stay here, I will always see to your care and
comfort. My cousin, Lord Henry Smythe, will be assuming my post
here, and he has agreed to be the caretaker of Radstone Manor.
Your positions in the household will, of course, be maintained. If
you come with us, however, you will have a house and land of your
own, and adventures of fabulous proportions. I hope to hear your
answer soon."

"You will, my lord," Mary said.

Lord Radstone raised his glass. "To Jamaica." Glasses clinked
and everyone took a sip.

"Claire, what do you think?" Lady Radstone asked.

"It's a wonderful opportunity, my lady."

Elizabeth Radstone considered Claire for some time. "You
haven't eaten much this evening, my dear. Are you all right?"

"Oh yes, my lady, I have a slight headache, and I suppose the
excitement of this has affected my appetite."

Lord Radstone stood. "Let us retire then, and we'll talk of this
in the morning."

Claire knew she would not be sleeping much. As she and her
mother strolled back to their cottage after dinner, Claire asked the
question. "Well, Ma, what are you thinking?"

Mary stopped and grasped her daughter's arm. "Owning
a house and land of our own would never be possible for us in

Ireland. But living here on the grounds of Radstone Manor and with our positions is a great blessing for us."

"When the new lord comes, we might not be able to retain our positions. You know Lady Radstone loves the way you manage the house, and I know she is happy with how I have tutored the boys. Think about it, Ma. We keep our positions. We will have a house of our own, and we will be traveling to a new part of the world in the company of the Radstones. No one in County Cork would pass up this chance."

"How can we go?" Mary said. "Bantry has always been our home."

"Bah. Listen to you, Ma. There is little here for us to hold onto."

"You're well past seventeen now, and I thought you might find yourself a good lad here and settle down."

"You want me to marry one of these fishermen, gather mussels, and wait to see if he comes back in. I can't do it."

"I did it."

"Sure you did, and the sea sucked him down before I was old enough to remember him."

"Don't talk of your father in that tone."

"I know he was a good man. I told you last week I wanted to get away from here. I wanted to go to Dublin and maybe study literature. But even if you'd said yes, I might not have done it. I'm not sure I could have left you. Now we can be together and stay with the Radstones. The thought of this adventure has driven Dublin right out of my mind."

"So much could go wrong."

"Ma, nothing in life is certain. Having a house, land, a garden—those things will give you comfort and security forever. It's something you can grab hold of. What do you say, Ma? Is it off to Jamaica?"

Her mother looked at her long and hard. "Let's get some sleep, and we'll talk about it in the morning."

"But Ma—"

"No more tonight."

The two got ready for bed, and Mary blew out the candles. Claire stared up at the ceiling and wondered if she would live in this cold one-room cottage for all of her life. Claire listened to the scurrying and scratching noises that always began after darkness came. She thought about the field hands who slept in the barn. At least she had a warm blanket over her and she did have the dolphins.

"Are you awake?"

"Yes, Ma."

"Well, I've thought on it and I believe we've got to go."

"Do you mean it, Ma?"

"Of course, my girl, it's off to Jamaica. I'll tell his lordship in the morning."

"Ma, it will be the most wonderful time."

"I'm sure of it. Now will you try and get some sleep?"

Claire tingled with joy. She wanted to learn all she could from her mysterious friends in the bay, and now the thought of so many more in other seas intrigued her even more.

Mary's voice came through the darkness. "You know, I never did like gathering those damn mussels."

Claire smiled and rolled over. She thought of the Bantry dolphins and she thought about the dolphins in the Caribbean.

———

Stark and his companion clicked, squeaked, and whistled as they came into Bantry Bay. They soon found the pod.

You got back quickly, Padin said.

I'm the fastest dolphin in the sea. Did you have any doubt?

What of the teachers? Meara asked.

They're coming, Stark said, *or at least one is coming.*

How can that be? How will a teacher come? He won't come riding on the back of a whale.

I don't know, but they said they were sending someone from the dome to be near Claire and watch over her.

The pod swam around in an excited, swirling ball. Everyone talked and wondered.

Chapter 6

The Troubles

Claire and the three boys strolled across a windswept meadow, with the panorama of Bantry Bay spread out below. Claire and Edward both carried copies of Shakespeare's *Hamlet*. Phillip ran ahead and did some cartwheels. The boys chattered about Jamaica.

Phillip came back. "So, it's settled then. You're coming to Jamaica."

"That I am."

"That's wonderful," said Edward. "It will be the grandest of adventures."

"We'll be too busy for our lessons, I imagine," said James, with a twinkle in his eye.

"Your ma is one step ahead of you, James my lad. She has already talked to me about keeping up the lessons, even on the ship, and she's paying my passage, so you can be sure we'll all be working hard."

As they walked along the grassy hillside, young Phillip asked, "Are there Indians in Jamaica?"

"Of course there are," Edward said. "I've been reading the new book father brought us. It tells all about the islands and the people who live there."

"You don't know everything," Phillip said, shaking his head. Edward gave him a little shove.

"Actually, that's a book we should all be studying. Let's start reading it together tomorrow," Claire said.

"I heard father talking to one of the officers," James said with an air of authority. "He said pirate troubles are boiling up again in the Caribbean. Father said that King George wants to put an end to piracy."

"What if we run into pirates on the voyage there?" Edward said.

Phillip stopped and looked at them all, his eyes round with worry.

"Let's pray we don't encounter any pirates crossing the ocean," said Claire, who, seeing Phillip's worried look, decided she'd better change the subject. "Come, gentlemen, sit here under our favorite tree and let's read a bit more of *Hamlet*. Edward, it's your turn to read, and then we will discuss his ghastly and ghostly problems."

Claire sat down with her book. Phillip and James sat on either side of Edward and leaned in as Edward opened the other copy of *Hamlet* from the manor's library. As the boys read, Claire wondered if they would ever tell her the story of Phillip falling overboard. She, of course, could never tell the boys how she knew.

———

The boys, Lady Radstone, Lord Radstone, Claire, and Mary stood in front of the table behind the barracks. Six pistols sat lined up on the table. A few soldiers stood around the firing range. Lord Radstone addressed the group. "Lieutenant Williams will be instructing you on the loading and firing of these pistols. This afternoon, Lieutenant Thompson will start training the boys in the use of the saber. He is one of the finest swordsmen in the army. I want you all to know how to defend yourselves before your journey across the ocean."

"Really, Charles," Lady Radstone said. "I am none too happy with this talk of pirates and Indians and defending ourselves. First you tell us that Port Royal is a paradise surrounded by the English army and navy. Now we are practicing with pistols and swords. I'm beginning to worry about this adventure."

"Nothing to worry about, my dear; this is just a precaution."

"Next I suppose you'll be wanting *me* to carry a dagger."

"No, Elizabeth, you don't need a dagger. Your tongue is quite sharp enough."

"Hear, hear, Father," James said.

His mother turned to her son with a scowl that could have singed his hair if he were closer. "I beg your pardon, young man."

Lord Radstone had already begun to turn away. James realized he had better retreat as well. "Sorry, Mum."

The shooting went well; both Lady Radstone and Mary became adept at loading and firing. They even hit a target or two. Claire and the boys did much better. The straw targets were in the shape of men dressed in ragged clothes to represent pirates and savages—an image not appreciated by Lady Radstone, Mary, or Claire. The boys reveled in the thought. In the afternoon, Lieutenant Thompson worked with the boys using wooden training swords in the garden.

Phillip faced the lieutenant. James faced Edward.

"All right gentlemen, one more time. *En garde*. Edward, stiffen your wrist and raise your sword just a bit."

As Edward focused on the instructions, James yelled and thrust. He stabbed Edward below the left collarbone with his wooden sword. Edward staggered back, wildly swung his sword over his head, and slashed at James. Laughing, James stepped to the side. Edward's anger swelled and he swung with a backhand and struck James hard on the upper arm. James grimaced and raised his sword to parry Edward's next attack. Edward closed on James, got in close, grabbed his shirt, and slammed the hilt of his sword into James's face. James stumbled and fell on his back.

Lady Radstone yelled as she ran, "Stop it! Enough! Stop it!" She pushed Edward back. "Enough of this." James scrambled to his feet. Lady Radstone gave him a handkerchief to wipe the blood from his mouth. "Are you all right, James?"

"Yes, but *he* won't be." James pointed his wooden sword at Edward.

Edward held his sword with an anxious and surprised look on his face.

"I said, enough of this. Edward, James, put down those swords. Lieutenant Thompson, I expect you to control this madness. I will not have my sons slashing at each other in earnest with swords, even if they are wooden ones. And I don't care what Lord Radstone says."

The lieutenant bowed slightly, "My apologies, my lady. I'll make sure it doesn't happen again."

"Be absolutely sure of it." Lady Radstone glared at the lieutenant and turned to the boys. "Clean yourselves up, put on your jackets, and join me for tea."

Shaking her head, Lady Radstone turned and marched toward the house. The boys picked up their things and began to follow her. As James and Phillip moved ahead, Lieutenant Thompson touched Edward, and he stopped. "That was a good move with your hilt. I'll show you a few more ways to do that." Edward looked up at the lieutenant; his eyes gleamed and he smiled.

———

As morning broke over Bantry Bay, gulls called, and the British warship charged with carrying Lord Radstone to Jamaica buzzed with activity. A long line of Bantry men, each lugging a keg, box, or sack, trudged up the gangplank with the last of the provisions. Three masts towered above the black hull. A row of bright red gunport covers ran the length of the ship.

Everyone was in a state of excitement. Mary and Claire, along with most of the villagers, milled about as Lady Radstone and the boys walked down the gangway.

Claire strolled down the dock to where she could see out into the bay.

The shouted commands signaled the ship's departure; more men climbed the rigging. The gangplank slid aboard, taut lines fell loose, and the unfurled sails flapped in the light morning breeze.

Lord Radstone stood at the rail. "Adieu, my love. See you soon, boys."

"Safe trip, my dear," called Lady Radstone, wiping tears from her eyes.

"Good-bye, Father!" the boys called out.

The black hull inched away from the dock. More sails filled with wind, and the ship moved away at a faster pace. Claire stared out, not at the ship, but at the surface of the water. She could just make out a few dolphins following the ship. There was one lone skiff out in the bay. She turned away to join the others.

The villagers walked to their day's work as the ship sailed out toward the Atlantic. Lady Radstone, Mary, and the boys turned toward the waiting carriage.

The red-coated driver held the reins tight as the chestnuts pawed at the cobblestones. Phillip stopped to talk to two young boys from the village.

Lady Radstone sat in the carriage and watched the ship become smaller and smaller on the horizon. Mary sat across from her in the carriage. "Don't worry, my lady. He'll be fine, and we'll be together again soon enough."

"I shall pray for him every day."

"And I'll do the same, my lady."

"Thank you, Mary." Lady Radstone turned. "Phillip, come lad, we've got to be on our way."

Phillip jumped in the carriage.

Claire walked up to the carriage. "Mother, I must retrieve a book that I left for repairs." Claire's eyes wandered to the sea again.

"Is it that book of poems?" James asked with a grin.

"Yes, one of them."

"Your favorite—we knew you'd wear it out someday," Edward teased as the boys laughed.

"Be back in time for tea," Mary said.

"I'll be back in plenty of time."

The carriage lurched forward and then trundled away. Claire stood there and watched the carriage turn out of sight. She walked through the village. She didn't need to pick up her book, though she stopped by the harness maker's shop where she was having the leather binding repaired. She wanted to talk to the dolphins.

She walked to the rocks, sat down, and gazed at the bay—no dorsal fins in sight. She opened her book and flipped through her favorite sonnets, reading as she watched. Far in the distance, Claire spied fins speeding toward her. She turned to one of her very favorite sonnets. The dolphins would not be there for a minute or two.

> *Love alters not with his brief hours and weeks,*
> *But bears it out even to the edge of doom.*
> *If this be error and upon me proved.*
> *I never writ nor no man ever loved.*

Claire closed the book as a splash erupted near her. Meara swung around and rose out of the water, balancing on her churning tail. *Please don't stop; those are beautiful words.*

You can hear me as I read?

Yes, every day your mind grows stronger. As you read, you think the words and we hear them. Read more of those beautiful words. Whose words are they?

A man named William Shakespeare wrote them.

She read to the dolphins into the afternoon.

Claire walked back to the village and around to the back of the Harp. She peeked into her friend's room. "Eileen, are you there?"

"I'm in here."

Claire walked through Eileen's room. The room held a bed with a straw mattress, a chamber pot, and, at one end, a small hearth only large enough to hold two or three pieces of turf. What little bit of clothing Eileen owned hung from pegs on one wall. Most of the garments came from Claire and from around the manor. The whole affair was smaller than the linen closet at the manor house. Eileen worked at sweeping the floor among the boxes, sacks, and barrels.

"Did you see the ship leave?" Claire asked.

"Of course I did. Listen to them out front. The men who loaded the ship are drinking up the money they earned. So tell me, what happened?"

"Nothing much. Lord Radstone gave Lady Radstone a kiss on the cheek and off he went."

Eileen picked up a candle, smiled, and motioned to Claire. "Come on."

The girls walked down uneven stone steps into a damp dark cellar full of barrels and kegs. Eileen patted a small keg sitting atop the others. "Fitzpatrick just put it down here. He says it's the finest whiskey in all of Ireland."

Eileen took two metal cups off a peg, turned the spigot, and poured out the whiskey. The two girls clinked the cups. Eileen took a sip. "Mother's milk."

Claire took a sip and scrunched up her face. "Fitzpatrick will beat you raw if he catches you."

"Don't worry yourself. Fitzpatrick will never miss a few drops. I'll put a little water back in the keg."

Footsteps came into the storeroom. Eileen snuffed out the candle and gulped down the whiskey. She grabbed Claire's cup and tossed her whiskey in the corner. Eileen scurried like a mouse, hung the cups back on the pegs, and pushed Claire behind the barrels.

"Anyone back here?" A strange voice asked.

"Look around for yourself," Fitzpatrick said.

A man walked down a few of the cellar steps. The girls cowered in the darkness. He turned back.

"What in the hell happened?" another stranger's voice asked.

"I dropped off me box. Six marines were standing about. There was no way I could slip down to the magazine at all," a third stranger said. "Before I could move about, they were pushing off."

"Another ship is on the way. Half the garrison is being relieved," Fitzpatrick said.

"I'm sorry we missed Radstone, but I won't mind sending a company of redcoats to the bottom of the bay," a stranger said.

"Just remember to make sure you're well out in the bay before you light that fuse. Those English ships carry plenty of powder. I don't want you blowing up the dock or the Harp."

"Jaysus, Fitzpatrick, stop your worrying. I know what I'm doing. I'll have plenty of fuse tucked under me coat. Soon as I light it, I'll be up through the decks like a powder monkey, and over the side before anyone can touch me. It'll be an explosion heard all over Ireland. Without a doubt, it is past the time for it. First our land, and now over in Wexford, they're trying to keep people from going to mass."

"Dirty bastards," Fitzpatrick said. "Come on, lads, let's have a drink."

The girls sat wide-eyed. The footsteps moved into the pub. Eileen motioned and the girls   crept up and out the back door. They broke into a run down the alley.

They stopped, winded. "What should we do?" Claire said.

"Nothing."

"What do you mean nothing?"

"Nothing. We do nothing. Remember, you're Irish. You live in the manor, but you're Irish."

"But, Eileen. They were going to blow up the ship. They were going to kill Lord Radstone."

Eileen grabbed Claire by the shoulders. "Promise me you'll keep quiet. Do it for me and for Ireland. And one other thing you had best remember—if those men were to find out we heard them, they'd slit our throats for sure."

The two girls looked into each other's eyes. Claire hesitated, then nodded and hugged her friend. "All right, I didn't hear a thing."

"God bless you, Claire."

They walked for a while. Eileen had to get back to the Harp, and Claire started for the manor, deep in thought about what they had just heard. She had never had a problem with the English. No one ever tried to stop her from going to mass. She considered Eileen's thinking to have been twisted by listening to too much pub talk. What would the dolphins think? Would they even know the difference between a Catholic and a Protestant or an Irishman and an Englishman? The dolphins wouldn't care who owned the land. They didn't own anything and they seemed happy. Eileen was right about one thing—she was Irish.

Claire sat in the garden on a stone bench for a long time. She stood, took a deep breath, and walked into the house. She found Lady Radstone in her sitting room, reading. Looking about, Claire walked across the room. Kneeling down next to the chair, Claire touched Lady Radstone's arm, and began whispering as if going to confession. Claire knew Eileen and everyone in the village including the priest would consider what she was doing to be a despicable and traitorous act. Lady Radstone nodded and she patted Claire's hand. Claire rose, looked around for the all-seeing eyes of the manor, and walked out of the room. She walked much too quickly out into the garden, thankful that she had not run into any of the household staff. Claire slowed down and pretended to be looking at the roses. Her nervous breathing began to subside. Claire knew she had done the right thing. She knew she could not harbor that evil. She knew she had cleansed her soul.

Chapter 7

Declan Flynn

With the replacement ceremony completed, the redcoat infantry marched through the village to the beating of a single snare drum, and the British soldiers boarded the ship. The carriage stopped down the street. Lady Radstone stepped out and walked toward the ship. As she passed the Harp, Eileen stood and gave a halfhearted curtsy. Fitzpatrick and another man stood in the doorway. "Good morning to you, my lady. What brings you down here?"

"Good morning, Mr. Fitzpatrick. With my husband gone, I have come to bid these fine soldiers a bon voyage."

"It'll be a good day for sailing."

"I believe it will be." Lady Radstone turned away.

Under his breath, but loud enough for Lady Radstone to hear, Fitzpatrick said, "Fine soldiers, my arse. It'll be a great day when all of them get the hell out of here and take *her* with them, don't you know." The other man snickered.

Lady Radstone stopped, turned, and walked back to within six inches of Fitzpatrick. "I dare say those soldiers have never done you any harm. Many of them have certainly spent money in your pub, and because of them Bantry is a pleasant and peaceful place."

"To be sure, they've spent plenty in here, but most of the people around County Cork would rather not have any of their peacemaking, if you please—my lady."

Lady Radstone didn't blink as she looked at Fitzpatrick. "Don't think you can intimidate me, just because my husband is away, Fitzpatrick."

"I wouldn't think of it, my lady."

Lady Radstone turned and walked to the gangplank and up to the main deck. She talked with the officers and the captain and waved to the men. As she walked back to her carriage, she stared at Fitzpatrick.

A little later, Claire joined Eileen on a bench in front of the Harp.

"You missed Lady Radstone," Eileen said.

"I wonder why she was here," Claire said.

"She said she was saying good-bye to the troops."

"For sure, with Lord Radstone gone, the job would fall to her."

The girls sat in silence as the ship inched away from the dock and set sail.

"Did you see a stranger get on?" Claire asked.

"I think so."

"Did he come back off?"

"I'm not sure. I think he's below."

Claire's stomach felt sick and nervous. She leaned back against the wall and closed her eyes. Fitzpatrick leaned in the doorway watching the ship and the two girls. A small fishing boat sailed near the bigger ship as it moved out into the bay. The warship disappeared over the horizon, and there was nothing.

Claire whispered, "I wonder what happened."

Eileen looked at her with a piercing stare. "I don't know, Claire. Why don't *you* tell me what you think happened."

Claire fixed her eyes out to the bay. "I have no idea."

Eileen gave her a withering look, got up, and walked into the pub. Claire took a deep breath; her eyes became a little glassy.

One evening, several weeks later, Elizabeth Radstone, the three boys, Mary, and Claire ate in the small dining room. Steaming bowls of lamb stew sat before each of them, while a basket heaped with bread graced the middle of the table.

Phillip reached for another piece of bread, tore it, and dipped one of the pieces in his bowl. As he brought the bread to his mouth, a glob of brown gravy dripped on his white shirt. He tried to wipe it off and smeared the blotch.

"Remember, Phillip," his mother said. "The only thing that separates us from the animals is our manners."

Phillip rolled his eyes, since he had heard that comment every few days since he was old enough to remember it. James shook his head and Edward snickered.

"I'd like to learn how to sail a big ship," said Phillip. "Do you think the captain will allow me to take the wheel?"

"You're too young," James said.

"And you're old enough, I suppose?" Phillip shot back.

"Older than you are."

"I want to climb way up in the rigging and look all around from there. I hope they show us how," Edward said.

"No need to show me," Phillip said. "It's just like climbing a tree."

"Boys, there'll be no climbing in the rigging," their mother said.

"And you, Claire?" asked James. "What will you do at sea?"

"I think I'll just enjoy the beauty of the ocean—and read and write, of course. My lady, when we load the library on board, it would be good if we could get to the books."

"I am sure I can arrange that with the captain."

"You know, Mum," Phillip said. "We've been studying about the Caribbean. I can name many of the islands. The book has maps and charts and drawings of fruits and the strangest animals and birds you can ever imagine."

"We'll pack it last, so we can find it right away when we get to Jamaica," Claire said.

In the darkness, the dolphins moved out of Bantry Bay toward the open sea. As usual, the males swam out ahead of the others, echolocating. A hint of moonlight shone into the water, but the almost total darkness meant nothing to dolphins. Soon a huge school of pilchards appeared on their natural sonar, and the two pods sped toward the target.

The dolphins orbited the school in tightening circles. The countless fish bunched ever closer together in a seething, squirming, silvery ball that flashed and sparkled as they swam about, going nowhere at a frantic pace. Taking turns, the dolphins darted into the ball snapping up as many of the fish as they wished to eat.

Enough. I can eat no more, Rafe called out. *And look at Emmet there, his fat belly may very well sink him.*

The two families meandered and bobbed about.

Time to begin, Nami announced. *There's no need to go back into the bay. This food will last us for a few days.*

What about Claire? We didn't say good-bye to Claire, Stark said.

Bannon swam next to Rafe. *Emmet is ready for the journey. It's time for him to meet the teachers.*

We'll tell Claire you began your journey, said Meara.

Tell her the dolphins of the Caribbean will call out to every ship that comes our way until we find her.

How will we go? Rafe asked.

We shall swim to the east of the warm current, Nami said. *There are always schools of fish along the edge of the current, and we may find some of the gray whales to follow.*

Rafe and Stark took the lead in their normal manner.

The travelers settled into a fast pace. The leaders broadcast their clicking sounds, searching for food and threats. No fish escaped their search, and rarely did danger surprise a vigilant pod. They alternated between a quick pace and a slower swimming speed. The pod moved on relentlessly. They talked, ate, and even slept as they swam. They never stopped.

Morning always came too slowly for Claire. Today, as usual, she awoke and dressed before dawn. Since the first day of speaking to the dolphins, she had slept in fits and starts. She lay in bed, calling out to them. They never answered when she called from the cottage. In the predawn, she sat in the garden with the village and the black bay stretching out below her. Candlelight flickered in the house as the servants began to stir. Claire waited awhile before wandering into the kitchen.

Meg stood at the stove. Claire always tried to say as little as possible to her and still be polite. She knew anything said to Meg would, within minutes, spill out of her mouth. Most of the staff at Radstone Manor loved to gossip. Claire found it amusing that when the level of confidentiality around a bit of news rose, the speed at which the information traveled from lip to ear and ear to lip increased as well. Gossip, sworn to *absolute* secrecy, flitted to every corner of the house, as if carried on the wings of a swarm of tattling fairies. Mary Riley never participated in the gossiping. Claire thought it great fun to share the stories of the manor with Eileen, but lately Eileen had become distant.

"You know, my girl, the working folks in this house and the whole village are purple with envy—a house of your very own. It's a grand thing." Meg said.

Claire sipped the tea, took a piece of the bread, and started for the door. "Tell my mother I've gone down to the village for a while, will you, Meg?"

"That I will, Claire. Will you be visiting with the dolphins today?"

Claire stopped at the door. She turned slowly and gave Meg a hint of a puzzled smile.

Claire walked out the door, quickening her pace as she headed toward the bay. *Should I tell the dolphins about Meg's comments? They might think I told someone. The villagers can't know anything. They just can't. The dolphins said I am the only one. Maybe someone else can hear us.*

Claire stopped by the fishermen's wharf, peeking in the barrels. They held a few fish, salted for storage. As she strolled along, people waved and acknowledged her.

The door to the whitewashed cottage stood half-open. Claire poked her head in. "Hello, Mrs. Leary. Are you home?"

"I'm making a pot of tea. I'll put a cup on the table for you."

"Thanks, no. I've had my fill today." Claire sat at the table with the old woman. "I've brought you a handful of pilchards, a herring, and a loaf of bread from Meg."

"And what a lovely loaf it is. I'll share it with the others. We'll miss you, Claire. When will you be going?"

"Lord Radstone sailed almost two months ago. I believe it'll be soon."

"You have a kind soul, my girl. Thank you for thinking of me and the others."

"Say nothing of it, Mrs. Leary." Claire rose. "We'll talk again before I go."

Claire walked out of the village toward the rocks and the beach. She wondered if the eyes of Bantry followed her. Claire sat on the rocks as the sun warmed her. Soon sleek gray forms broke the surface far out in the bay and rolled under in perfect synchronization. They came out of the water together and went back under at exactly the same time. Claire shook her head in amazement.

The dolphins gathered at the rocks.

You swam together perfectly. You came to the surface at the same time—a beautiful sight. Why do you do that?

Sometimes when we move at a fast pace, we do it to help each other along, Padin said.

It gives us a feeling of togetherness, Meara added.

Did you bring any fish today? Cwen asked.

No, no fish again today. A week of empty nets—it's a bad time for the village.

Plenty of fish swim in this bay. We'll send some their way again soon, Padin said.

That would be a good thing. You know I'll be leaving soon.

We'll miss you, Meara said.

I just hope the southern dolphins will find me.

Stop worrying, Meara said. *We've told you so many times—if you're on or near the water, they'll feel your mind and reach out to you. We can feel your mind from farther out at sea than before, and we sense the power of your mind growing.*

I can't feel your mind unless you're swimming very close to me. Why?

We're not sure. You are the first, Meara said. *Just remember, when you sail toward Jamaica, reach out with your thoughts. Dolphins will be waiting and listening.*

As usual, Claire read to them. Today she read a passage from *Romeo and Juliet.*

The group talked for a while, and then the dolphins announced hunting time had come. Claire noticed a few fishing boats scattered in the bay. She wondered if the men could see her with the dolphins. She thought they might be too far away.

"Well, young lass."

Claire spun toward the voice.

"It seems the dolphins do enjoy your company."

A tall, lean man walked toward her. He wore a brown wool slouch hat, and his clothes announced this stranger to be a poor wandering man. There were plenty of rovers around Ireland in these hard days, and Claire knew many of them turned to being highwaymen just to keep a little bread on the table. Claire stood on the rocks, a little nervous. "Yes, and I enjoy them as well."

He stepped near her. "Well, that is a fine thing. I'm Declan Flynn." He bowed slightly.

"And I, sir, am Claire Riley." Claire turned her head for a quick moment, looking for the dolphins. They were gone.

Declan sat down and Claire perched herself against a rock. None of Declan's clothes seemed to fit him. Bits of grass and leaves covered his tattered gray coat, and the cuffs of his pants rode well above his dusty brown shoes. He carried a canvas sack over his shoulder, which, Claire surmised, contained this fellow's worldly possessions.

Declan Flynn gazed out across the bay. "Where do you think the dolphins went? I hope I didn't scare them away."

"I wouldn't know, Mr. Flynn." Claire did wonder if he had frightened them; she continued to be wary of this stranger.

"So you're the girl everyone in County Cork talks about."

She snickered. "I doubt that it's *all* of County Cork, and what, in heaven's name, would they be talking about?"

Flynn smiled and looked at the water. "Do you think the dolphins are attracted to you for any particular reason?"

"I couldn't tell you. They seem to come around when I'm near the water. I do feed them a few fish from time to time."

"Yes, to be sure, it's the fish."

Then Claire noticed the man's hands; a curious lump protruded from the side of each hand. The strange growth started at the base of his small finger and bulged out to near the wrist.

They both sat without talking for a while.

Claire broke the silence. "What brings you to Bantry?"

"I'm the most excellent blacksmith and carpenter in all of Ireland, and I've heard there is plenty of work around Bantry Bay," he said with a broad smile. "Fixing up the fishing boats around here would seem to be a fine business. I've seen some of them, and it's a wonder they float."

"I've thought that same thing on many a day." Claire smiled and thought better of the man. They sat in a more comfortable silence, looking out at the bay.

"Well, Miss Riley, I don't think the dolphins are coming back anytime soon." Declan stood. "I'll be off now, and I hope to see you again. Top of the morning to you." He tipped his hat, and started down the rocky path away from the village.

"Good-bye, sir."

He gave her a slight wave over his shoulder. Claire thought him to be a pleasant fellow, but a strange feeling about this man nagged at her. What of the odd shape of his hands? Then there were his eyes—eyes that almost glowed with an iridescent bright blue. And he never did say where he was from. She hoped she would see him again. He seemed to be kind. He also seemed to know something—something about her.

The next morning, as usual, Claire strolled down to the wharf and the sheds where the men stored their catch. As she walked toward the first shed, she heard a lot of commotion. Claire pushed open the heavy wooden door. Everywhere, piles of pilchards spilled across the floor. Baskets full of fish teetered, stacked on top of one another. The baskets above crushed the baskets below, the haphazard affair on the verge of toppling over. Men rolled barrels about while twenty or so men, knives flashing, stood side by side at two long tables, cleaning the larger fish and packing the smaller ones in salt.

Claire stood astonished for a moment.

"Top of the morning, Claire," Mr. Donovan called out.

"Mr. Donovan. Holy Mother, look at the fish."

"None of us can remember a bigger catch, to be sure." He wiped his face with a dirty rag. "A blessing from God it is. We've been salting them right through the night. Your dolphins drove this huge school of pilchards right into our nets."

"They're not *my* dolphins, Mr. Donovan. Why do you call them my dolphins?"

"Well, I don't give a damn what anybody calls them. For reasons known only to God and Saint Patrick himself, the dolphins pushed the fish toward us as never before. This may be the greatest number of fish ever caught in Bantry Bay."

"May I take a few, Mr. Donovan?"

"Surely, Claire, take more than a few. Those old women will be needing some, and today we have plenty."

They smiled at each other. Claire filled her basket with salted fish. She gathered a good twenty pounds of fresh, unsalted fish in a burlap sack, hoisted it over her shoulder, and set off. Claire stopped at cottage after cottage, delivering the fish to the neediest of Bantry, as she worked her way out of the village and toward the rocks.

Claire and the dolphins talked as she tossed fish to them.

You did a kind thing yesterday.

Think nothing of it, Padin said. *We ate our fill before we drove the fish into the nets.*

But the people are talking. They think I had something to do with it.

Tell them you can't swim that fast. Padin laughed along with the rest of the pod. Claire smiled broadly.

Chapter 8

HMS *Brilliant*

The boys sat close together at one end of a heavy oak table in the library. They hovered over an oversized book about the Americas. James turned the heavy pages. Every day the boys talked about their impending adventure. Every day they wondered when the adventure would begin.

Voices from the garden seeped through the leaded glass. Phillip walked to the window, and looked down at the group of servants gathered below. He looked up and saw the British man-of-war in the bay. "A ship! It's here, it's here!" His brothers scrambled to the window.

"Look at it. It's a fantastic ship," Edward said.

The boys, followed by Claire, ran out into the garden. Most of the servants gathered with Claire and the boys to watch the spectacle. All of the ships' sails had been furled except for one of the main sails. That sail caught the slight wind, and the ship moved ever so slowly toward the dock. The Union Jack hanging from the flagstaff looked too big even for this mighty warship. The breeze barely moved the flag and as it hung in repose it looked as if it might touch the water. The tall ship towered above the village as the crew furled the last sail and tightened the lines securing her to the dock.

Elizabeth Radstone walked toward the gathering.

Mary pointed. "It looks as if our transport has arrived, my lady."

"A beautiful sight. It is about time we were on our way. A good night of sleep has escaped me ever since Lord Radstone sailed away."

Mary looked at her friend, nodded, and smiled.

What seemed to be a tangled web of lines stretched from the masts and spars to a bewildering number of blocks and pulleys. The light-blond planking of the deck contrasted with the black hull.

"Mary, Claire, bring the boys and join me in the sitting room a bit later. I'll send the carriage down to the village and inquire of the captain. I'm sure he will be along to visit with us. Mary, please have the kitchen prepare some tea and cakes."

"Of course, my lady."

The captain wore his finest blue dress uniform as he strode into the sitting room. A servant announced the captain. "Lady Radstone, Captain Robert Lowe."

The captain, with his plumed hat under one arm, bowed. "Lady Radstone, I'm Captain Robert Lowe, commander of HMS *Brilliant*, at your service."

"It's a pleasure to meet you, Captain. Allow me to present my three sons—James, Edward, and Phillip."

"Fine strong lads. You young gentlemen can help us sail to Jamaica."

Phillip's face brightened in an expression of joy. "Can we really, Captain?"

"Of course you can. The *Brilliant* can always use a few more able seamen."

The boys looked very pleased at this.

"Captain," Lady Radstone gestured. "May I also present Mary Riley and her daughter, Claire. They are my closest companions and will be accompanying us."

The captain nodded toward Mary and Claire. "I was informed that these lovely ladies would be along. We've made preparations for you as best we can."

"Thank you, Captain." Lady Radstone said.

"My lady, there will be a delay. The *Brilliant* sustained a slight bit of damage in a storm off the French coast. We will be seeking lumber and a few skilled carpenters to aid in the repairs."

"There are plenty of capable carpenters in Bantry," Lady Radstone said.

"I'm sure. I would like to start loading your household items the day after tomorrow and be ready to set sail in three days."

"Whenever you're ready, Captain. We're anxious to be on our way. The boys and I would very much like to be with Lord Radstone as soon as possible."

"Well then, ladies, young gentlemen, I shall see you on board in a few days, or sooner, if possible. I'll send word when we are ready to receive you."

The captain turned and briskly walked out.

"Boys, Mary, Claire, we should pack our last things tomorrow."

"Did you hear, Mum?" Phillip grabbed his mother's hand. "We'll be able to help the captain."

"My dear, I am quite sure this will be an exciting and wonderful time." Lady Radstone hugged her son and looked over his head at Mary. Claire noticed Lady Radstone's doleful gaze.

———

Claire came around the corner and hesitated. A large gathering of villagers, and some people she did not recognize, stood around the rickety shed of a classroom. Claire walked into the crowd and they parted. She nodded to a few people in recognition and mumbled a few quiet hellos as her eyes darted from side to side. No one spoke. She made her way to the front of the packed classroom. Not even the littlest ones, sitting with their mothers, made a peep. She stood in front of them. They sat on the benches, each with a wooden board, painted black, resting on their laps. The room bulged with her students, and the people outside had opened the shutters, leaning and squeezing into the glassless window openings. A cool ocean breeze wafted through the room and brought with it the smells of the sea and fish. The place always smelled of fish. "As you all know, this is the last time we will be together for a while." Her voice cracked. "I don't know when I shall see you again. Many of you can read with ease, and I leave it to you to continue to help the others."

"Claire," a large rough-hewn man in the back of the room spoke up. "Don't fret. You've done right by us. We can all write our names and much more. Many of us can read, and it's all because of you. Just promise us you'll be returning some day and help us with Mr. Shakespeare's books. It's sometimes hard to know what the darling man was trying to say."

"I promise you I'll come back. Some of my happiest times have been in this room with you," She knew that fate might keep her from coming back. Claire wondered if her students could see that she was straining to smile. They chatted away the afternoon—hugging, crying, and shaking hands. After the room emptied, Claire sat alone. Eileen had not come, and Claire thought that she might never see her friend again. She thought about all that had happened in her classroom, and fussed with the well-worn books she would leave behind. As dusk began to darken the room, Claire lit a few candles. She wanted to linger in her classroom.

The door creaked, and that large man who had spoken from the back peeped in. Patrick Keenan walked toward Claire. "Sit down and talk to me for a moment"

Claire sat on a bench, and the big fisherman sat on the next bench facing her. He leaned over with his hands on his knees. "I don't want you to promise that you'll be back. I want you to *swear, swear* to Mother Mary that you will return."

"But I don't—"

"Hear me out. It's not because of your happy times here, and it certainly isn't about Shakespeare. It is about you helping the people living in this little corner of Ireland to free themselves from the bondage of ignorance."

Claire sat up straighter, her eyes widened, and she nodded.

Keenan leaned closer. "The English grip Ireland by the throat and keep us in poverty. Too many people in this country do nothing more than grow potatoes, fish, make babies, and drink far too much. You have shined a light, and the folks around here are beginning to see. I'm sure you noticed many of those people who crowded around this building today were not your students."

"I wondered about that."

"They are just some of the people who *now* want to learn how to read. You remember this, Claire Riley, when the majority of the poor country folks gain the knowledge of books, Ireland will be free."

Claire blinked and remained quiet for a moment. "You're a fine man, Pat Keenan. I don't believe I've ever heard anything that made more sense or was said in a more eloquent fashion. I swear to the Mother of Christ, to Saint Patrick, and to *you* that I will be back."

Kennan stood and put his hand on Claire's shoulder. "Well then, I'll walk you home."

"No need, I'll be just fine."

"Come on lass, we don't want any of those idiots in the pubs accosting you. It wouldn't be a good last memory of Bantry, and I really don't want to have to cut one of them up for bait."

Claire grinned. They snuffed out the candles, shuttered the windows, and began walking toward the manor in the dwindling light of the early evening.

The dolphins swam in slow circles.

Tomorrow morning the ship sails. I am excited, but sad.

We're happy that you were the first to talk to us. You are a gentle, kind, and thoughtful human, said Padin. *We can feel the kindness in your mind.*

Cwen swam over and slid her head onto a rock. *I owe you my life and the life of Clairin. I will always remember you.*

We will see you again, said Padin. *Remember that every time a young one is born into the pod, we eventually take the calf to the islands and to the teachers.*

Since I'm going to the islands, perhaps I'll meet these teachers.

Remember our words, Meara said. *They will reveal themselves only if they choose to.*

Meara turned. *Come, let's go out to deep water. There'll be no one bringing us fish.*

We will be near you tomorrow as you sail, Padin called back. The pod said good-bye, then faded into the distance. Six dolphins jumped out of the water in perfect unison, arched over, and hit the water at the same time. Again, they blasted skyward with the same amazing precision. One of the largest dolphins flew out of the water, flipping end over end and then flopping down.

As she shook her head in amazement, Claire turned and walked away.

Chapter 9

Bound for Jamaica

Claire and her mother sat with Phillip in the carriage, across from Lady Radstone and the older boys. Two soldiers sat stiffly on the driver's bench. The horses' breath hung in the cool morning air as they snorted and pulled away from Radstone Manor. The servants of the house waved and some of the women cried.

Phillip squirmed in his seat. "I want to look at the cannons."

"We'll have plenty of time for that," James said.

Phillip snorted at his brother.

"I'll go with you to look at them as soon as we get on board," Edward said.

Lady Radstone looked back at the manor and fidgeted with the bow on the hatbox she carried. In the distance, the ship towered above the village.

Mary held her daughter's hand. "The most exciting time of our lives is about to begin," she said. Claire's excitement about seeing new lands and meeting the dolphins of the Caribbean was tinged with a little apprehension about possible dangers at sea.

It seemed as if the entire village had gathered on the dock to bid them farewell. The bright-red Union Jack did not move in the still morning air. As the carriage eased into the crowd at the dock, Lady Radstone said, "*Brilliant* is an appropriate name for this ship."

A golden, swirling braid of wood ran along the outside of the uppermost railing of the ship from bow to stern. The gilded molding served no purpose other than to highlight the massive blackness of the hull; Claire thought it a beautiful, yet peculiar, embellishment for a ship of war.

The boys squirmed in their seats. Phillip stood in anticipation, ready to leap as the carriage came to a stop. He cried out, "They're ready to go!"

"Hurry, Mum," Edward said as the boys tumbled out of the carriage. "Come on. I'm sure they're only waiting for us."

The boys ran through the crowd to the gangplank, where a marine wearing a bright-red tunic stood guard. The marine blocked the way with no expression.

"May we go aboard, sir?" Edward asked.

"I think you might wait for your mum and the others."

Phillip frowned. James pulled Phillip aside. The boys waited, scanning the ship with excitement.

Their mother, Mary, and Claire talked and hugged their way through the crowd. Claire searched the crowd for suspicious-looking men, men not from Bantry. The three women assembled at the bottom of the ramp, and the marine stepped aside. The boys hurried up the ramp, followed by their mother and Mary. Claire stayed at the bottom of the gangplank for a moment, looking into the faces of each of the men carrying their last few items. She walked up the ramp and stood next to Lady Radstone, who leaned over. "Don't worry; the captain has taken every precaution."

A tall, good-looking young officer with tanned skin and a shock of blond hair walked over to the group. Gold buttons glistened on his dark-blue coat. He took off his hat and put it under his arm.

"Lady Radstone, young gentlemen, welcome aboard His Majesty's ship *Brilliant*." He turned to Mary and Claire. "And you must be Mrs. Riley and your lovely daughter Claire." He looked into Claire's eyes and gave a slight bow. "Lieutenant Charles Garrison, at your service. Captain Lowe is about his duties, and he asked me to show you to your quarters."

Claire knew she was blushing at this good-looking officer's special attentions.

"Thank you, Lieutenant," Lady Radstone said.

"This way, please—and please watch your step."

The young officer put his hat on, walked aft, and led them down a flight of stairs, which he called a "ladder." At the bottom of the ladder, a heavy wooden door faced them. Behind the ladder, the open gun deck stretched the length of the ship. The bracing above the gun deck made this area cramped; a tall man would need to bend over a little to avoid thumping his head on the thick beams. Two rows of black cannon pointed toward the sides of the ship, waiting to be rolled into firing position.

Lieutenant Garrison noticed the boys staring in wide-eyed amazement. "We call this the gun deck. I'll show you the whole ship once we get under way." The lieutenant opened the door. "The crew prepared this cabin for you and your party, my lady. You may find your accommodations a little cramped. In His Majesty's navy, we put every inch of space to use and this is the largest space available; be assured, my lady, we will do our best to see to your comfort."

Lady Radstone bowed slightly. "Thank you, Lieutenant."

"I am at your service, ma'am." The young man turned at the door. "As soon as we get out into open water, the captain will be along. You may want to come topside and bid Bantry farewell. Just stay near the railing, as there will be much going on." He closed the door.

"All of us in one room? Well, this will certainly be a cozy affair," Lady Radstone said with a frown, placing her hatbox on the round wooden table dominating the center of the small cabin. "My husband told me we would be at sea for thirty to forty days. Let's hope we're not at each other's throats before the end of this voyage. Boys, do try to stay out of this cabin as much as you can."

"Don't worry about that, Mum. We'll be spending our time exploring the ship," said James.

Triple-tiered bunk beds and one single bed lined the starboard side of the cabin. Two single beds fit end to end against the larboard side. The beds were so situated that one could hang a hand out a window while sleeping. Each bed resembled a large shallow box with the feather mattress resting inside.

James sat on the edge of the lowest bunk and fell into the bed. He grabbed the sides. "It'll be hard to get out of this bed in the morning."

"But almost impossible to fall out of it in rough seas," said Claire.

Heavy blue velvet curtains hung bunched at both ends of the room. When drawn, they would separate the sleeping areas. Across the rear of the room and down both sides, thick-leaded windows swung out to the sea. Thin wooden dowels held the windows open. The cool morning air and the cries of gulls filled the room.

A row of low bins ran under the rear windows, designed for seating as well as storage. Claire sat down at the window.

"The guns are just out there," Edward said to his brothers, as the three of them headed for the door.

"You boys stay here and help us put away our things," their mother commanded.

They reluctantly headed back to pitch in.

The women set to work, storing their things. The boys half-heartedly helped. The sounds of men moving above and shouting orders filled the cabin as the ship creaked and barely moved. The journey had begun.

"All right, boys," Lady Radstone said, "Let's all go on deck and bid farewell to Bantry." The boys raced to the ladder with Claire behind them. Lady Radstone held Mary back for a moment. "Where did you put the pistols and sabers?"

"They're all packed in the bottom of a trunk that is down in the hold."

"Do the boys know where they are?"

"They may, my lady, but I don't think they can get to them."

"Good, Mary. Very good."

The ship gradually pulled away from the dock. The boys, Lady Radstone, Mary, and Claire stood together and waved at the crowd below. Then Claire saw a row of villagers back behind the crowd. Eighteen members of her class stood, side by side, holding the black wooden boards against their chests. Each board had one letter written on it in white chalk. They spelled out F-A-R-E-W-E-L G-O-D B-L-E-S-S Y-O-U. Claire started to yell down and tell them they needed one more person. She stopped herself and waved.

Meg shouted, "Mary, Claire, God be with you! Write to me!"

Claire knew Meg couldn't read and didn't care to learn.

"I'll miss you!" Mary called. Claire kept looking for Eileen in the crowd. She could see the Harp from the ship and hoped Eileen would be standing in the doorway or at a window. She was nowhere to be seen.

Men scrambled among the lines, pulling at bundles of canvas, untying and unfurling the sails as they balanced themselves on thin lines. The sailors defied gravity, moving among the ropes like monkeys in jungle trees. The boys watched in silent wonder. Lines led from the bow to a pair of longboats filled with sailors. The men pulled and strained at their oars, inching the *Brilliant* away from the dock. Patrick Keenan stood in the back of the crowd. Claire thought she caught his eye. She waved and he waved back. His words were etched in her memory.

As officers yelled out strange seafaring commands using words such as topgallant, mizzen, and foreroyal, the deck buzzed with activity. Claire enjoyed watching the wide-eyed boys taking it all in, and she tingled with excitement thinking of the new experiences awaiting them all. She also shared Lady Radstone's and her mother's evident nervousness about leaving the comfort and safety of their home to embark on a voyage in rough seas with unknown dangers toward a new country.

As the morning progressed, billowing sails captured a breeze, the longboats were hoisted aboard with much hubbub but great efficiency, and the village of Bantry and Faoide Island disappeared behind them. The ship passed by the lush, green Irish countryside, sailing close to the southern side of the bay.

Claire leaned on the rail to catch the last glimpses of Ireland. *Will I ever see Ireland again? Will I see and hear the magical dolphins of Bantry Bay again?* She fought a feeling of melancholy.

Claire, Meara's mind called out.

Meara? Is that you?

We will swim along with you for a while.

It's good of you to see me off, Meara. I'll surely miss you.

Edward stood next to Claire. "The dolphins have come to bid you farewell. Do you think they'll follow you to Jamaica?"

Claire looked at Edward and smiled. "I haven't an idea, but I don't think so."

The dolphin pod swam closer, paralleling the ship. A few of them leaped forward in perfect synchronization, and then slowed to enable the ship to overtake them. Men in the rigging saw the dolphins and yelled down to their shipmates. A number of the ship's company came to the rail to watch the spectacle. Lady Radstone and Mary joined the group.

"Dolphins—a good omen for our voyage," Captain Lowe said from just behind his passengers.

Lady Radstone turned. "Good day, Captain."

"My lady, dolphins near a ship mean calm seas, fair skies, and a steady wind. Will you and your party join me on the quarterdeck?" The captain pointed to the raised area at the rear of the ship, allowing them to walk ahead of him.

On the quarterdeck, a few officers walked about, giving an occasional command and watching the sails.

Claire walked away from the gathering to the railing. *Meara, are you there?*

We're here, but it is time for us to leave you. Remember, call out with your mind; dolphins will always be close when you're near the sea.

That thought comforts me. Until we meet again, good-bye, my friends.

The sounds, the feelings, and the words of the dolphins' brains faded in Claire's mind as they moved away from the ship.

Claire leaned against the railing. Lieutenant Garrison walked up behind her. "You know, Miss Riley...," Claire turned to face him. "The officers have all remarked that the *Brilliant* has never had a lovelier passenger."

Claire blushed, searching for the right words to reply. Nothing came to mind except "Thank you."

"It should be a pleasant voyage at this time of year," the lieutenant said.

Claire composed herself. "Today is certainly a lovely day for the beginning."

"It's a fine day, indeed. Have you been with the Radstones for a long time?"

"We've lived in the Radstone house since I was a baby."

"Lady Radstone is—"

"Claire!" Mary called, and motioned to her daughter to come and rejoin them.

"Excuse me, Lieutenant." Claire walked over to her mother's side. Lieutenant Garrison followed along.

"I see you've met our Lieutenant Garrison, Miss Riley," the captain said.

"Yes, sir," Claire said.

Mary Riley gave the lieutenant a quick, cool, askance look. Claire caught it along with the inevitable Old Irish mumble. Claire smiled at her mother. She knew it was her mother's disdain for the English, especially young English men, bubbling up in her. Claire was not about to scorn the young lieutenant. He was a fine-looking man and he had a pleasant, gentlemanly air about him. She mused that it was going to be a long voyage and the attentions of the lieutenant would not be a bad thing.

"I have a few requests of you. Please treat my comments with the utmost seriousness," the captain said. "When we are training, or hoisting or lowering the sails, confine yourselves to the quarterdeck or below. We work at a feverish—and sometimes dangerous—pace. If we encounter foul weather and rough seas, you should remain in your cabin. You lads should not walk around the ship alone, and, at night, it is important that you be even more cautious. If one of you were to fall overboard, we might not discover it for some time and you would be lost." The captain slapped James on the shoulder. "I don't believe your father would think kindly of me if we sailed into Port Royal missing one of you."

"We understand, sir," James said.

"I can assure you," said Lady Radstone, "we will follow your instructions. Boys, please make sure you stay together."

"Don't worry, Mum, I'll see to it," James said. Edward and Phillip looked at their brother with obvious scorn.

"We'll be careful," Edward said. He turned to Phillip. "Who put his lordship in charge?" Phillip rolled his eyes.

"Can we help you fire the cannons?" Phillip asked.

"No, lad, it's far too dangerous. We will, however, make all three of you grommets of the ship."

"What's a grommet?" Edward asked.

"It's an apprentice seaman."

The boys looked pleased at this.

"When will we become grommets?" Phillip asked.

"There's a swearing-in ceremony and training. It will be soon enough."

James smirked at his youngest brother. Edward slapped Phillip on the back. "Grommets in His Majesty's navy—I think father will be proud of us."

That evening, the captain invited his passengers to join him and the officers on the quarterdeck for dinner. The sun turned into a reddish ball and then dipped into the sea, extinguishing itself. Oil lamps hung from poles at the corners of the deck. The lamps swayed gently and lit very little of the quarterdeck. Short, fat candles flickered in glass cylinders that shielded the flame from the sea breeze. The candles ran down the middle of a table fashioned from long planks resting on kegs. Dressed in blue coats with varying degrees of gold braid, the officers gathered on the deck. The midshipmen, some of them younger than Claire, huddled in a corner around a patch of light.

When Lady Radstone and her party arrived, the officers and their guests stood in silence for a brief moment. Claire glanced away, not wishing to confront the eyes of the gaggle of young officers. The captain motioned for the officers to come closer. "Allow me to introduce the ship's officers to you."

The captain recited their names, ranks, and duties, and Lady Radstone made sure to introduce Mary and Claire to each officer as her closest friends and companions.

"Our meal should be served shortly. Shall we sit down?" The captain gestured toward the table. The captain sat at the head of the table with Lady Radstone to his right and Mary, Claire, and the boys to his left. The captain lifted his glass. "Ladies and gentlemen, to a safe and pleasant voyage."

The starry sky sparkled and the shielded candles bathed the table in a yellow glow. Dinner-table chatter and laughter filled the quarterdeck as the enjoyable evening moved along. The officers passed around platters piled high with pieces of corned beef, potatoes, carrots, and a basket filled with big chunks of crusty bread. A sailor poured wine from a pitcher into pewter goblets. Claire noticed that her mother and Lady Radstone both looked a little nauseous from the constant movement of the ship.

"The service may be a little rough," the captain leaned toward Lady Radstone, "but, then, these men are seamen."

"Everything is fine, Captain, and my boys are having the most glorious time. I am sure they will not sleep much tonight."

"Excuse me, Captain, but my brothers and I were wondering if we would see any pirates on this voyage?" asked James.

"Not likely, my lad. They know they are no match for a warship of the British navy." Captain Lowe sat back and addressed the table. "One of the differences between the British navy and the pirates who ply the waters of the Caribbean is the rum, you know. They have a powerful taste for it and stay at it from dawn until midnight. It makes for sloppy and disorderly sailing. Now, there's nothing wrong with a bit of rum. It is a comfort to the men and it helps them to keep up their blood, but you'll never see anyone on a British navy ship half washed over in the middle of the day. I can most certainly tell you that this ship will always have an advantage over any pirate rabble because of the judicious use of rum."

Captain Lowe smiled broadly and raised an eyebrow. "Of course, it also helps that our men are quick and fearless in the rigging, and able to load and fire a twenty-four pounder in less than a minute."

The officers nodded. "Hear, hear," they said, and raised their goblets.

After dinner, the officers not on duty said good night. A few stayed on the upper deck directing the ship.

Lady Radstone seemed a little green with seasickness. She and the boys went below. Claire and her mother stood near the aft rail looking out at the black sea.

"I hope my stomach settles soon," said Mary.

"I'm sure it will, Ma. Soon you'll have your sea legs. There's no going back now."

"True, my dear. I pray we're doing the right thing, leaving Ireland, and Bantry, and all."

Claire put her arm around her mother's shoulders and hugged her. "We're together, and we're with the Radstones; we'll be just fine, Ma."

A few lanterns remained lit, producing spots of dull yellow light here and there along the length of the ship. As the ship rocked, the lanterns swayed; the light moved across the deck and the rigging. Shadows moved in, out, and around the lines and the canvas. The sails rustled in the wind and the sea lapped against the hull. Someone sitting in the dark toward the bow played a gay, jaunty tune on a fiddle.

The two women slipped into the dark cabin and groped their way to their beds, then fell into them. The coolness of the night poured over Claire; the rolling of the ship pushed her toward much-needed sleep. Dolphins swam in her dreams.

Chapter 10

Strange Seas

Claire's eyes popped open wide as a familiar smell crept into her nostrils. "Porridge?" Claire rolled out of bed and dressed in the darkness. She followed the smells and found a large hole in the gun deck where a circular ladder twisted below. She took a few steps, and bending, peered down to the deck below. Two men stood in the cramped ship's galley in front of an iron stove where black pots steamed. One man sat on a keg while the other worked at the stove. Pots and pans hung from the rafters, clanging and banging as the ship rolled. Boxes, bags, and barrels filled the space, leaving little room to move about in the galley.

She took a few more steps down. "May I come down? It smells grand."

The man sitting on the keg turned. "Please come and join us, Miss Riley."

Claire stopped on the ladder, puzzled. She recognized the voice and stepped down into the room. "Mr. Flynn? What are you doing here?"

"Just Declan to you, Claire. These English sailors needed another skilled ship's carpenter, and, since I am that, they asked me to join them. They offered better pay than anything I could find in Bantry, so I decided to sign on."

The man stirring the pots handed Claire a wooden bowl of steaming porridge. "Here you go, miss. And none of us in this navy have ever seen a finer ship's carpenter."

"Thank you," Claire said. She took the bowl, sat on a small cask, and began to eat. She liked her porridge with a little milk poured over it but knew there would be no milk on this voyage. She did think the added pieces of apple were a nice touch.

"I saw you when you came aboard," said Declan. "I didn't know you worked for Lady Radstone."

"I'm the governess…well, they're a little old for that. I tutor the three boys in literature and writing."

"To be a tutor at your young age—isn't that a fine thing, now."

"The position fell to me. I do enjoy the work."

"Are you excited to be going?"

"I surely am. My ma is a little worried," Claire said. "But when we get to Jamaica, Lord Radstone will give us a house of our very own."

"A house—that'll be grand—grand, indeed. If you'll be needing any carpentry work when we get there, I'll be glad to be of service."

"Thank you, Mr. Flynn. Thank you."

"Just Declan, miss." Declan touched the brim of his slouch hat. "Me carpentry work is calling. I believe it'll be a lovely day, and I'm sure I'll be seeing you around the ship."

Claire finished her porridge and walked on the deck. She watched the rolling blue sea as the ship plowed through the gentle swells. Her mind called out to the dolphins. Nothing came back.

———

A week passed, and life aboard the *Brilliant* became routine. Lady Radstone and Mary finally overcame their seasickness and were able to eat a little something. Eating bestowed no great blessing or benefit to the travelers, other than basic nourishment. The meals of dried fish and salted meats became more than just monotonous. There were a few animals brought along for eventual use and Claire found herself praying for the day when the little lamb, bleating and tethered near the galley, would meet with its demise. Claire found a few nooks where she could hide away with a book. She used the cabin or a corner of the quarterdeck to instruct the boys on the works of Geoffrey Chaucer, William Shakespeare, Daniel Defoe, and John Milton. It was a bit of a challenge to keep their minds on the books, with all the goings-on around them.

It was a bright, warm day and a brisk wind pushed the *Brilliant* to the southwest. The three boys stood, stripped to the waist and barefoot, before the entire crew. An older seaman stood in front of them wearing an old plumed officer's hat that had seen better days, whose once-fluffy feather drooped. He wore a cape made of sailcloth and carried a cutlass.

"Now then, swear a seaman's oath," the officiating sailor commanded, "that you will obey the Articles of the Able Seaman, and that you will do more work than you are asked to do, and that you will always, always, never fail to share your rum when asked to do so by a fellow seaman. Do you so swear?"

The boys said in unison, "I do swear."

"Then, by the power vested in me by Neptune, His Majesty, and the many thousands of able seamen resting beneath the waves, I now pronounce you grommets of HMS *Brilliant*."

Sailors stood behind the three boys, pulling their hair back away from their foreheads. The seaman in the hat and cloak dipped his thumb in a bucket of gooey tar, and, with all the seriousness he could muster, rubbed a black, oozing smudge on each boy's forehead.

"Heed my words and beware, for you are now marked with the seaman's black spot. Break your oath and face the wrath of Davey Jones."

The men cheered, and the boom of a single cannon firing startled the boys. Some of the men shook the boys' hands and others patted them on the shoulders before moving back to their duties.

The boys scrubbed their foreheads for three days before they got the smudges off. They were official grommets of HMS *Brilliant*, a title they cherished. James piloted the ship in the open sea. He stood at the wheel for hours, exhibiting a very serious demeanor, under the watchful eye of a seaman or the bos'un and an officer.

After their induction, the boys argued that they didn't have time for lessons with Claire, as the completion of their duties was necessary to the defense of the ship, the safety of the passengers and crew, and the successful completion of the voyage. Their mother insisted that their schoolwork shouldn't be neglected, so Claire still managed to get the boys to read, write, and discuss literature every day.

Claire enjoyed rising before sunrise. She would take her bowl of porridge or piece of bread, and enjoy her breakfast as the sky lightened. Crewmen passing her in the course of their duties always greeted her with a smile and the tip of a hat. The ever-present Declan Flynn constantly hammered and sawed at the never-ending supply of repair work. During the early days of the voyage, Claire would watch the sailors work with the web of lines and would regularly ask a seaman to explain the purpose of a particular line or tackle block. Before long, she and the boys had learned quite a bit about how the warship moved about the seas.

For the six passengers, the most exciting happening aboard the *Brilliant* came when the crew performed their gun drills. The cannon thundered and belched out white and gray smoke as the crews practiced firing their guns in rapid succession.

Even more exciting for Claire were her talks with Lieutenant Garrison. During the day, and sometimes in the cool evenings, he sought her out. Although he was a bit older, she gradually grew more comfortable around him. When not busy performing his duties, the lieutenant managed to attend to her as she wandered on deck. His eager attention and kindness enchanted her. They never talked for long, as he always had to get back to his duties. They did manage to talk about his adventures in the navy, her life in Bantry, and the authors they both enjoyed. Other than Lord Radstone, Lieutenant Garrison was the most educated man she had ever met. Claire reveled in the idea of someone to talk with about so many topics, and was amazed with the lieutenant's knowledge of literature.

One morning, Claire curled herself like a contented cat on the canvas stretching over the longboat on the deck.

"Morning, Claire. You certainly look comfortable there."

Claire snapped the book closed and swung her feet over the side of the longboat. "Oh, good morning, Lieutenant. That I am."

"Claire, if you don't start calling me Charles, I'm going to hurl myself into the sea." He spun, grabbed the rail, and looked down.

"Well, we certainly wouldn't want that, Charles." She laughed.

He turned back. "And what are you reading this fine morning?"

"Oh, just a few of my favorite Shakespearean sonnets."

"You'll have them committed to memory before we sail into Port Royal."

"I do know a few by heart."

"Maybe you'll recite them to me one day?"

Claire's stomach fluttered, and her pulse quickened. She smiled at him. "I'd like that."

"Well, Claire, I'd better head off—my duties call. I'll visit with you again later." He tipped his hat, smiled at her, and strode off.

———

The *Brilliant* began sailing in a more southerly direction. Claire and the boys learned much by keeping their ears open. The officers often talked about their heading and location. They had explained that the ship had started out on a westerly bearing, but now headed due south, keeping the coast of the colonies and the Americas off to the west.

Dawn had just begun to temper the darkness, and Claire gazed out at the horizon as she ate her porridge. The sky slowly turned from black to gray and blue, as the sun began to rise. A sailor walked by, and Claire caught his attention. "Excuse me. Have you seen Lieutenant Garrison on deck this morning?"

"No, miss. I believe the lieutenant stood the midwatch and is probably sleeping now."

As the sun rose, Claire held her face to the coolness and let it blow back her hair. She enjoyed the winds in these southern climes. They were so much kinder than the biting gusts of the North Atlantic that blew across Bantry Bay. Claire constantly thought about the dolphins. *Where are they? Meara said they would be near me whenever I ventured on the sea. I wish they could hear my mind.*

We can hear you.

The sound jolted her and Claire flinched. She dropped the bowl, flipping it down into the sea.

We're coming.

I can hear you. I can hear you.

Claire. Claire from Bantry Bay. We have been waiting for you.

Where are you?

We're jumping toward you from the east. We'll be there soon.

Claire shielded her eyes from the sun. There they were, swimming in unison. They broke the sea at the same time, leaping close to the surface. The group of six dolphins sped toward the ship and then turned south, slowed, and swam alongside.

Who is it? I think I know your voice.

It's Nami. My family lives in these waters and in the seas to the south. We meet again. My pod wanted to be the first to talk with you.

Nami. Nami, how wonderful. Any news from Bantry?

No. We'll tell you when we hear something.

How long until we reach Jamaica?

Your ship is slow, but it shouldn't be too much longer. You're nearing the islands of the Bahamas. We'll swim along with you until you reach Jamaica.

Claire, another voice, a male voice, came to her mind. *My name is Sanjay. I am Nami's mate. There are two ships coming this way. They're coming from the east. They fly no country's flag.*

Could they be pirates? Claire asked.

We cannot be sure.

Are they close by?

No, the ships are far to the east. You may never see them, and they may never see you.

Remember, we'll always be with you, Nami said.

How many of you—?

"Hello, Claire." She spun around. There stood Lieutenant Garrison. "You're up bright and early as usual."

She was pleased to see him, as always. "Oh, hello, Charles. You startled me. Yes, I do love these mornings on the open sea." She looked out at the sea.

"Mornings and the sea—two more loves we share, Claire. It seems we have a lot in common—literature, the sea, new adventures." He touched her hand resting on the railing and a shock ran through her. "You're the most interesting girl I've ever met—smart, knowledgeable, adventurous, and beautiful as well. I'm very glad you and your mother decided to take this voyage. Otherwise, I might never have met you."

Claire's heart quickened. She thought of the coarse, uneducated lads at home, who had been her only choices for a beau until now. She couldn't believe her luck that this sophisticated officer fancied her. *He actually likes me.* "I'm so happy to have met you as well, Charles." She noted that his hand had not moved and was still on top of hers. They smiled at each other.

The lieutenant looked out at the sea. "Out there, dolphins."

"Yes, I've been watching them this morning."

"They too are beautiful and fascinating creatures," Charles said. "I can see why you'd be interested in them, Claire." He looked at her and she blushed.

"I do find the dolphins fascinating. They are very special creatures." She took a breath, and then broached the subject that was on her mind. "Tell me, Charles, should we be encountering any other ships along the way?"

"We could see a ship or two, heading to or from the islands or the Americas. There are a large number of merchant ships plying these waters."

"What about pirates?"

Charles chuckled a bit. "Pirates would avoid us as if we carried the plague. You're quite safe."

"What if there was more than one pirate ship?"

"They normally sail alone, and usually use small, fast sloops that would never be able to carry the guns they would need to—"

"Mr. Garrison," the captain's voice boomed from the quarterdeck. Charles pulled his hand away from Claire's.

The lieutenant acknowledged the captain and then tipped his hat to Claire. "He wants my report."

He turned, climbing the ladder two steps at a time toward the captain. At a more leisurely pace, Claire wandered toward the quarterdeck.

The captain looked from the lieutenant, then to Claire and back again, his face serious. The lieutenant stood a little straighter, as if expecting a reprimand. The captain's eyes twinkled. "Anything to report, Mr. Garrison?"

"All is well, sir. We are continuing due south in a brisk wind. By our last reckoning, we are off the coast of Spanish Florida at approximately twenty nine degrees north and seventy nine degrees west."

"Very well, Mr. Garrison."

———

The day wore on in an uneventful fashion. The boys ran around the ship, and Claire followed them. She stopped now and then to communicate with Nami and her family. They spoke of Jamaica and the islands. They also talked about the two ships to the east.

At the edge of the horizon, a sail reflected the light of the setting sun.

"Ship ahoy!" cried the lookout, who was always perched high on the mainmast.

Captain Lowe yelled, "In what quarter?"

"To larboard, sir." The man hanging on the mast pointed east.

Claire walked over below the quarterdeck, standing out of the way. The officers on the quarterdeck gathered around the captain and Lieutenant Garrison as the two men pointed their spyglasses to the east. A few minutes later, another sail became visible.

Lieutenant Garrison pulled his gaze from the horizon. "What do you think, Captain?"

The captain snapped his long spyglass shut and thought for a moment. "Probably two merchant ships, sailing together for safety." He turned to the group of officers. "Gentlemen, begin moving off a little to the west; this evening we shall run without lanterns. Tonight double the watch. Tomorrow morning, awaken the men before first light, and feed them a hearty meal. If those two are still in sight, beat to quarters."

The small contingent of officers saluted. Lieutenant Garrison walked down the ladder to where Claire and the boys waited.

"What's happening, Charles?"

"Nothing to worry about; the captain is a skillful seaman and a competent officer. He is being cautious."

Claire gathered the boys. "We should get below. It will be dark in a few hours, and the captain announced that there would be no lanterns tonight. I think we should go to our cabin and do a little reading before nightfall." They bid Lieutenant Garrison goodnight and headed below.

Later, as they huddled in the darkness of their cabin, Mary asked, "What do you think of this?"

"I don't know," Lady Radstone said, "but I'm sure the captain knows what he's doing."

"I heard the captain tell his men to beat to quarters just before the morning light," said James.

Claire sat staring out an open window. "With no moon, those ships may not be able to find us. We might slip away."

"They might just be on their way to America and not even be coming toward us," Mary said.

"I'm sure you're right, Ma."

"I don't want you boys wandering around the ship in the morning. Stay in this cabin," Lady Radstone said. No one responded. "Do you hear me?"

"Yes, Mum," Edward said.

Everyone went to sleep, but Claire lay awake, concerned about the two ships. She decided to concentrate hard to try to contact the dolphins.

Nami, are you close by?

Yes, Claire.

Our lookout saw those ships. Can you tell me if they're any closer?

Two powerful members of our family are swimming toward them. When they come back, we'll tell you.

How will the two dolphins find the ships in the dark and find their way back?

We send out sounds in the water, and when the sounds echo back to us, we're able to see things. The sound allows us to see, and we can hear sounds in the water from very far away.

The sound lets you see? How can that be?

I'll explain another day. Try to sleep. We'll wake you when we know something.

Claire lay back. She could hear the measured breathing from the others.

In the middle of the night, Claire was awakened by persistent thoughts.

Claire, can you hear me? Nami called out.

Yes, yes I can. Claire pulled herself out of her bunk and sat under one of the windows.

The two ships are moving closer. They are smaller and faster than your ship. If you saw them, then they probably saw you before dusk.

When will they be near us?

Not before midday.

Chapter 11

Pirates

Well before morning, Claire heard men moving about the ship. She got out of her bunk and dressed quietly.

"Where are you going?" Edward whispered from the lowest bunk.

"Quiet. Stay here. I'll be back in a moment." Claire headed to the main deck, where the entire ship's company worked at a feverish pace preparing for the day.

Declan Flynn leaned on the rail next to her. "Hello, Declan. I'm worried. What do you think?"

"Today could be a dangerous day, Miss Claire. You had better stay below."

"Why would you say 'dangerous,' and why should I stay below?"

"It's just an odd feeling."

"If there's any trouble, maybe I could be of some help."

Declan touched her shoulder. "We're protected by a well-trained crew, my dear. Stay close to your ma, Lady Radstone, and the boys. Remember, you are the most special of people."

Claire stared at Declan as he walked away. *The most special of people? Why did he say that?*

A snare drum sounded its beat and every member of the crew moved about the deck. Lieutenant Garrison rushed past. "Claire. What are you doing here?" he shouted. "Go below, now."

Claire stood just below the quarterdeck as the blackness of night lifted. She walked from one side of the ship to the other. The two mystery ships sailed behind and to each side of the *Brilliant*.

A marine approached Claire. "Go below, Miss Riley; you should not be here."

"Yes, I will. I was hoping to speak to Lieutenant Garrison."

"Stay right here for just a few minutes and then go below." The marine turned and hurried away.

The two ships chasing the *Brilliant* came closer.

"They fly the skull and crossbones," Captain Lowe announced as he snapped his spyglass closed. "I believe, gentlemen, the foolhardy bastards intend to tangle with the *Brilliant*. Be steady and crisp in tending to your duties; keep the men at the ready."

Smoke billowed out from the bows of the two pursuing ships, and the reports of four cannon echoed across the sea. The shots whistled through the air, splashing into the sea behind the *Brilliant*.

The rear-facing guns on the *Brilliant*'s quarterdeck belched out an answer.

"Mr. Garrison," the captain barked, "we'll be in range of them soon. They have four guns facing us and we have only two facing aft. We've got to get more of our guns into action."

"Aye, sir."

"Go tell the gunnery officers to be ready and be quick. I shall turn her sharply to the west and bring our broadside guns against these idiots. Give the order to fire as we cut across the bow of that rat-infested scow on our starboard. If she turns with us, our second broadside will be even more effective. We'll be turning away from that one on our larboard; we'll deal with her after we pound this first one."

"Aye, Captain." The lieutenant raced down to the main deck, bumping into Claire. "Claire, why are you still here? Get below—now." He grabbed her arm and escorted Claire to the door of the cabin. "Stay in there."

"I can help."

"Not now, Claire." The lieutenant dashed down the length of the gun deck.

Mary, Claire, Elizabeth, and the boys huddled together, watching through their cabin windows as the *Brilliant* turned. One of the pirate ships turned as well. The *Brilliant*'s guns boomed. Near-misses sent foaming splashes soaring, but splintered planks flipped and flew skyward as some of the shells slammed into the pirate ship. The pirates continued to turn until the two ships ran parallel to each other. Smoke and flashes spewed from the pirate ship as it unleashed its broadside guns. Shots whistled overhead, and towering columns of water burst from the ocean to rain down on the deck of the *Brilliant*. One shell fell just below the aft cabin. A deluge of water splashed through the windows. Elizabeth and Mary screamed and grabbed the boys, pulling them to the floor on the far side of the room. Soaked, Claire watched the battle.

"Claire, get away from that window!" Mary screamed. "Claire!" Mary jumped up and yanked Claire to the floor.

The sounds of cracking timbers and screaming men filled the ship, accompanied by the sulfuric smell of burned gunpowder.

"Claire, you and the boys stay down. No one move," Lady Radstone yelled as she opened the door.

A seaman with his leg ripped open lay writhing near the first cannon. Mary and Lady Radstone pulled him away from the toppled gun. Mary tore a piece from her petticoat, wrapped it around the sailor's upper leg, and twisted it hard. The sailor, barely conscious, clutched the knot.

Broken timbers hung down, cannon lay askew across the gun deck, and smoke filled the room. The guns of the *Brilliant* roared again. One of the pirate ship's masts toppled over as more shells blasted gaping holes in her side. Mortally wounded, the pirate ship fired back. Another ball hit the gun deck; men and pieces of men flew in the cramped space.

A cannon lay atop one sailor, crushing him. Elizabeth held the man's head. He stared at her, but never spoke. Mary ran into the smoke, toward the screaming. The boys and Claire huddled together, frozen with terror.

Claire, are you safe? Are you hurt? Nami's brain called out.

My God—the blood, the screaming.

Are you hurt? Nami's brain yelled.

No, no—I'm not. Men are dying. May God protect us.

Jump into the sea, a dolphin said. *We'll keep you floating. We can take you to safety on our backs.*

I can't leave my mother, and I have the boys.

Bring them with you. We'll save them. The danger grows—please come.

I can't leave. She hugged Phillip, who shook uncontrollably.

The cannon of the *Brilliant* fired again and again.

The return fire from the pirate ship waned. It fired a few more times, but no shots hit the *Brilliant*. The battle had raged for only a few violent minutes, and the *Brilliant* had mauled the first pirate ship. Its splintered, toppled masts dipped into the sea; the whole ship listed precariously on her larboard side. The men of the *Brilliant* continued to fire at their now helpless foe.

Claire stood in the middle of the cabin while the boys huddled in the lower bunk. "Don't any of you move," she cried. Smoke hung heavy on the gun deck, and now poured into the cabin. Claire coughed as she stood in the doorway, peering into the haze.

She called out, "Mother, Elizabeth!"

Then men above on the quarterdeck screamed. The aft-facing cannon on the quarterdeck fired.

Claire turned to see the side of a ship and the muzzles of black guns just outside the aft windows. She dove into the bunk on top of the boys, pushing their heads down. The second pirate ship had turned behind the Brilliant and now was within a few feet of the *Brilliant*'s stern. The pirate's guns could not miss. Smoke, fire, and deadly shot exploded into the aft section of the *Brilliant*. The first shells hit the quarterdeck. The deck and the cabin's ceiling shattered as heavy timbers collapsed around Claire and the boys. The boys screamed above the terrifying noise.

Claire lay on top of the boys and held them tight, pushing them down into the box-like bottom bunk. The top bunk fell on them but held up some of the shattered beams. A shot blasted away the stern window frame, cutting a deadly furrow down the length of the ship. A hail of glass shards and splinters of wood hissed and zipped through the air as if a devilish swarm of hornets had been unleashed to kill everything they might touch. The sides of the bed and the fallen timbers protected Claire and the boys from being torn apart by the whirling glass, wood, and steel. The fighting men of the *Brilliant* had no such protection. James tried to squirm out from under his brothers and Claire. "I can help. Let me up." With a deafening thunderclap, another cannonball crashed through the opening and down the gun deck, then another and another. A splinter of wood jammed into James's arm. He grimaced and fell back in the bunk. Claire gritted her teeth as something sharp cut across her back. Screams, the stench of burnt gunpowder, smoke, and blood mixed in a hellish caldron that had been, a few minutes earlier, the orderly gun deck of the *Brilliant*.

Claire could see blue sky through the shattered ceiling. Blood seeped down from the torn planking of the quarterdeck and spattered on the floor. The boys stopped crying out, except for Phillip, who sobbed. Claire could hear them breathing.

"Where's Mum?" Edward asked.

"I don't know," Claire said.

Only a few of the *Brilliant's* guns fired. "To the stern, to the stern!" marines and sailors yelled.

Claire looked up and through the side window. Grappling hooks and lines now held the two ships together. The pirates from the second ship jumped and climbed aboard the *Brilliant*. They poured over the ship like rats swarming from a nest. As Claire and the boys lay frozen in fear, men cheered and cursed as they shot and stabbed at each other.

When the sounds of the hand-to-hand fighting subsided, Claire could hear the wounded. Men groaned and cried, calling out to God, their mothers, and their wives as the throes of death overcame them.

Claire, Claire, are you injured? Are you alive?

Yes, we're safe.

Jump in the ocean. We can help you.

No, not now. My mother—I must find my mother.

An exhausted Elizabeth Radstone staggered into the shattered living space. Blood stained her dress, face, and hands. Phillip cried out, "Mum."

"Is anyone injured?"

"No," Claire said. "Where is my mother?"

"She's on the gun deck somewhere; I lost sight of her. The pirates have control of the ship."

Lady Radstone stumbled over the fallen timbers to her bed. She fell to her knees and pulled the hatbox from under the bed. She tossed the hat aside, took the pistol, and clicked back the hammer. She walked back to the center of the devastated room.

Lady Radstone stood steadily as a sweat-soaked, blood-smeared pirate carrying a cutlass stumbled toward her. He grinned a black-toothed grin as he grabbed her hair. She lifted the pistol. Her arm recoiled as the shot blasted out, flinging the man away from her. He sprawled on his back; crimson spread as wisps of smoke curled up from the ring of black powder marks on his blouse. "Mum, Mum, are you hurt?" The boys held her as she staggered back. Claire took the pistol from her hand and stuffed it into the bedding of the bottom bunk.

The sounds of the battle ended, and Claire could hear men talking and shouting. Large things splashed in the sea.

"What is that?" Phillip asked.

James went to a starboard window and looked out. "My God. They're throwing dead bodies overboard." The two other brothers climbed over the rubble and looked out.

"Boys, get back here and stand behind me," Lady Radstone said.

Three men appeared in the doorway. Lady Radstone stood in front of the boys and Claire.

"I am Lady Elizabeth Radstone," she announced, her voice loud, confident, and unwavering, "wife of Lord Charles Radstone, governor of Jamaica, and these are my four children. If you harm us, you will pay with your lives."

The three men laughed. "Go get the *capitaine*," one of the pirates said in French.

Lady Radstone turned to her children and pulled them close to her. "Boys, be quiet, and listen to me. Claire is your sister." She looked at Claire. "You are my daughter."

"But my mother—I must find her."

"Listen to me. You're a lovely young woman and you would never be safe among these men if they thought you were other than my daughter."

"I don't care. My mother—"

Lady Radstone grabbed Claire's shoulders. "It will do you and your mother no good if these men realize you are not my daughter. Your mother will want you to be safe."

Claire said nothing, staring over Lady Radstone's shoulder at the carnage on the gun deck.

Lady Radstone shook Claire. "Do you understand?"

"Yes." Claire looked down the gun deck, hoping to see her mother and Lieutenant Garrison.

Six grizzled, bloodied men gathered at the shattered opening of the cabin, glaring at the women and the boys. Then they stepped aside. The pirate captain wore a long, bloodstained blue coat and baggy red breeches. Four pistols hung at his hips from a pair of richly embroidered baldrics, and he carried a cutlass with a gold hilt. A red bandana held back his long, slick black hair. Behind him stood a huge olive-skinned man stripped to the waist.

"I am *Capitaine* Bouchet."

Lady Radstone stepped forward. "I am Lady Elizabeth Radstone, wife of Lord Charles Radstone, governor of—"

"Yes, yes, so I heard." The captain came close to her. "Madame, you and your children are my prisoners." Captain Bouchet turned to his men behind him and spoke loudly. "No one is to touch the woman or her children. These may be the richest prizes we have ever taken. Lady Radstone, give me your word that you will not attempt to escape, and I will not chain you and your children below."

"I give you my word, Captain."

The captain reached down, pulled a knife from his boot, and held it to Claire's face. "If you break your word, I'll cut off a few of your children's fingers, or maybe an ear." The captain touched the blade to Claire's cheek. Claire stared into the captain's eyes without flinching. She could smell his stale breath and the sourness of his sweating body. Claire fought to control herself, though she wanted to run down the gun deck, screaming for her mother. The captain's eyes narrowed as he looked at her. "A very beautiful—and a very brave girl."

Elizabeth put an arm around Claire's shoulder. With the other hand, she gently and slowly pushed the blade away from Claire's face. "There will be no need for this, Captain; we understand. You have our word. My companion, Mary, is somewhere on board. Please bring her to us."

"You there, go find the woman. Kadar, stay here and let no one come near them." The big, shirtless man said nothing. Bouchet snatched the gold locket from around Lady Radstone's neck. He reached down and took her hand. Edward grabbed his mother's arm and tried to pull it away.

"Leave her alone."

Bouchet held the hand tight. "Easy, boy," he said, as he worked the ruby ring off her finger. "You won't be needing this." He jerked his head at two of the pirates. "You two, take the trunks and their belongings to the quarterdeck. Do you have any other jewels on your person?"

"No."

"You are a woman of wealth. If I find no other jewels in your trunks, I will take great pleasure in searching you, your boys, and your lovely daughter."

"All of my jewels are in a small box in that trunk."

Bouchet whispered something to Kadar and then turned and walked through the rubble.

Kadar's massive, muscled body made him easily twice the size of any normal man, and his bushy black hair stuck out in every direction. A black mustache drooped down around the edges of his mouth and off his chin. He carried a curved sword with a broad blade.

Claire stood behind a fallen beam, hoping for some sign of her mother. *Where is she? She would never leave me alone. Please, God, keep my mother safe. Where is she? She might be tending to the wounded. Please, God.*

Claire, what's happening? Are you safe? Nami's brain called out.

I'm all right. My mother is missing.

Jump in the water and we'll help you escape, a dolphin said.

I cannot. I don't know where my mother is, and I can't leave my friends.

Move away from the ship, Sanjay announced to the pod.

Don't leave me, Claire pleaded.

We'll be close by, Nami said. *The blood in the water has drawn the sharks. They're already swimming about, and they will soon become frenzied. Don't worry. We'll return soon.*

A pirate yelled down from the quarterdeck through the jagged opening in the ceiling. "The other woman is dead. We threw her body into the sea."

Claire fell to her knees, shaking. "No. Please, God. No," she sobbed, as Lady Radstone knelt beside her, and the boys gathered close. Claire felt her stomach spasm and tasted the sour fluid filling her mouth. She pushed away and stumbled to the jagged hole in the aft. Claire hung out the window and retched. Everything in her stomach spewed out of her mouth and nose.

Elizabeth held Claire's shoulders. "Steady, Claire, be steady." She hugged Claire. "Weep for your mother. Quietly, my dear, quietly." Lady Radstone pulled Claire in. Breathing deeply, Claire tried not to vomit again as she wiped her face with the hem of her dress.

"She died alone; I was not there for her, God forgive me. She died alone."

"Nothing could have been done." Elizabeth squeezed her even harder. "May God help her and help us all."

The boys stood around Claire, silent tears running down their faces. Claire's hands dropped to the floor, her head drooping as the tears puddled below her. She crawled, sobbing, to the shattered aft window, and heaved again. Her empty stomach yielded nothing. She saw the dorsal fin of a huge shark as it sliced through the water behind the ship. Claire stood, pushed past Elizabeth, and ran toward the big man. He grabbed her as she tried to run past him. "Let me go. I must pull her from the sea." Claire punched at the man. He laughed.

"I have to hold her in my arms. The sharks. The sharks have my mo—"

"Claire!" Elizabeth pulled her and spun her away from the man. "No, Claire, quiet. She's gone. There's nothing any of us can do."

Claire's eyes sparked with panic and her face contorted in anger. "The sharks. We can't let the sharks tear at her."

"What's this?" Bouchet appeared next to Kadar.

Claire turned toward him; James took her arm. "Quiet, Claire. Stay quiet."

"The woman who died was very dear to us. We wanted to bid her farewell and say a few prayers over her body," Elizabeth said.

"You're a little late for that." Bouchet smirked. "Pieces of her are in the bellies of some very fat sharks."

Claire spat at Bouchet. "Filthy pig."

Bouchet examined the spittle on his tunic. The pointed dirk appeared in his hand as he stepped toward Claire. "Be careful, girl. The only thing keeping me from pulling this knife across your pretty throat is the thought of the gold your father will pay me for you."

Lady Radstone stepped in front of Claire.

Bouchet pointed the knife at Lady Radstone. "Understand what I say to you. Your husband might pay me the same amount of gold for the three boys as he would for all of you." He put his dagger in his boot, pushed Lady Radstone aside, and grabbed Claire by the hair. Claire stood firm and winced as he tightened his grip and pulled harder. He wiped the spit off his jacket, and deliberately and slowly rubbed it across the front of Claire's blouse. Bouchet smiled a sinister smile, let go of her hair, and turned away. Claire shivered at the violation, but never flinched. Not fear, but fury swelled in her. At that moment, Claire knew she would never allow herself to be frightened again. She vowed to avenge her mother.

Bouchet turned to Kadar before he left the cabin. "I want only you to be down here with them until we get home."

Kadar walked down the gun deck a few paces and sat on the floor leaning against a cannon.

Lady Radstone stayed close, whispering in her ear. "Claire, your mother would want you to be safe. She would want you to live. Never do anything like that again. Do you understand?"

The tears ran down Claire's cheeks as she nodded.

Lady Radstone looked at her boys. "Our survival will depend upon us staying together and keeping our wits about us."

"We could've helped more if we had our pistols and sabers," Edward said.

"Mum, where are they?" James asked.

Lady Radstone glared at the boys. "Don't any of you even think about those weapons. What good would a few pistols and swords do against this band of cutthroats?"

"I would've killed Bouchet when he grabbed your hand," Phillip said.

"And now you would be dead, my son. No more talk of this. Where is the pistol?"

"I have it," Claire said.

"When the time is right, put it back in the hatbox. If any of you touch it, I will rip it away from you and throw it into the sea." Elizabeth stood. "I should throw it into the sea now."

James stood in front of her. "Mum, we will surely need it."

"Enough—quiet."

Claire's face hardened. "We must get away."

"I gave my word," Elizabeth said.

"Your word? Your word means nothing to these animals. Honor means nothing to this lot. Whether or not we try to escape, this captain will enjoy cutting off some of our fingers and ears. There is murder in his heart."

The boys murmured, wide-eyed, their fear palpable. Elizabeth Radstone remained quiet. They watched from their cabin as the first pirate ship succumbed to the earlier blows from the *Brilliant* and, still smoking, sank by the afternoon. The surviving men rowed toward the *Brilliant*. Tied together, the *Brilliant* and the remaining pirate ship drifted on the gently rolling sea. Captain Bouchet yelled down to the other pirate captain, "LeBeau, I wondered if you had survived."

"We lost many a good man today. It was a foolhardy thing to attack such a powerful ship," LeBeau called.

"You're wrong, LeBeau. Today we hold a great prize in our hands."

LeBeau climbed aboard. He was a short, squat man known as Captain Scar, although none of his men would dare call him that to his face. The disfiguring slash ran from his hairline straight down across his left eye and then down his cheek. The useless eye, a lifeless blob of milky white, never moved. "It was one ship for another," LeBeau said. "This one is more powerful, but slower. The British will hunt us down."

"LeBeau, LeBeau." Bouchet grabbed both his shoulders. "The ship means nothing, but she carries a great prize. The wife and four children of Lord Radstone, the governor of Jamaica, sit just below us."

LeBeau grinned and slapped his partner's shoulder. "They will bring us a mountain of gold."

Bouchet raised his voice. "A mountain of gold and much more!"

The men cheered.

As night came, Claire and Elizabeth listened as the captains sat on the nearby quarterdeck, drinking rum and discussing their plans.

"It's settled," Bouchet said. "We use the remaining English crew to make repairs. Then we head for home. We'll put the Englishmen in the longboats and send them on their way to Jamaica with a message for his lordship, setting the ransom. If he seeks us out, we kill his family."

The pirates slept and Lady Radstone huddled with her boys on one of the beds. Claire sat on the bench, staring out at the sea through the jagged opening the cannonballs had ripped into the *Brilliant*. She wept quietly and bitterly. She prayed for her mother and swore vengeance. She vowed that she would see these men brought to justice, or she would kill them herself.

Claire, we've come back, Sanjay said.

Where are you?

I'm just behind the ship. I am with my son, Bolo.

Most of the sharks are gone, Bolo said, *and the few that are near we can drive away. We'll stay with you until you're free.*

Listen to me, Sanjay said. *These ships will likely sail to the south and they'll pass the islands and the waters where hundreds of us live. It's then that you should jump into the sea.*

Yes, Claire, Bolo said. *Then we could take you to an island where you would be safe.*

I can't leave Lady Radstone and the boys. If I escaped alone, these pirates would harm the rest of them. Escaping together is the only answer. When we do, these men must never find us again.

We understand, Sanjay said. *We'll help you all escape. We'll stay with you until you decide what to do.*

All the dolphins will come together and help you plan your escape, Bolo said.

Remember, Claire. If these men take you ashore and move you inland, we will not be able to help you, Sanjay said.

I understand.

The sky grew lighter. Lady Radstone stood next to Claire and whispered, "Claire, I loved your mother. I loved her so dearly."

Claire sobbed, "I cannot stop thinking about her dying alone." The tears poured down. "And the sharks tearing at her body. The thought of that will never leave me. My stomach is sick and my heart aches."

"Mine as well, Claire, but we must all stick together and try to get through this. We are truly your family now. We have always been your family, but now it is more important than ever before. You can be sure my husband will save us and avenge the death of your mother and the brave men of the *Brilliant*."

Claire looked at her with red, swollen eyes. "Thank you, my lady."

"Remember to call me 'Mum,'" Lady Radstone said, smiling through her tears.

"I tell you this…Mum. If Lord Radstone fails to bring these men to justice, I will find a way to avenge my mother." Claire bent closer to Lady Radstone. "My lady, we must try to escape as soon as we can. I doubt these men intend to release us."

"You heard Bouchet. If we attempt to escape and we fail…."

"We have no choice," Claire said.

The huge sentinel with the black moustache slept on the floor, blocking the entrance to the cabin. He stirred.

"We'll speak of this later," Lady Radstone whispered. "Always remember, you are my daughter."

Chapter 12

Hidden Harbor

The sounds of hammering and sawing filled both ships. They sat grappled together and heaving in the gentle swells. The captured crew of the *Brilliant* worked under the pirates' not-so-friendly prodding. Some of the wounded were still recovering, while the men who were able grunted and heaved away with blocks and tackle to remount the cannon and get them into working order.

Pods of dolphins gathered around the ships. They wanted to talk to Claire, and many dolphin brains beamed their thoughts to her at the same time. Her head ached with the cacophony of words. She finally asked them to control the din of questions. The dolphins agreed, and decided that only two or three dolphins should talk to Claire at any one time.

Declan Flynn set his wooden toolbox down outside the cabin. "Kadar, the captain wants me to repair the quarterdeck. I need to remove the damaged beams from this cabin."

Kadar stepped away from the entrance to the room. Claire's eyes lit up. "Declan, you're alive. I'm so happy to see you."

Lady Radstone grabbed Flynn's arm. "Mr. Flynn."

"Lady Radstone, we're all happy that you and the boys are well. Claire, I prayed for your ma. I'm sure God is holding her in the palm of his hand."

Claire said nothing. Lady Radstone beckoned Declan and Claire to go with her to the far side of the cabin.

"Mr. Flynn," she said, "I've told these men that Claire is my daughter. I believe it's the only way to protect her."

"Yes, my lady. I agree. You did the right thing."

"Please make it very clear to the rest of the crew."

"I'll make sure they understand, my lady."

"How many of the crew survived?"

"There is Lieutenant Garrison and two of the gunnery officers, the purser, three midshipmen, and thirty-six seamen, six of whom have grave injuries and may not survive. Forty-three in all. Captain Lowe died early in the battle."

"My God, what a terrible loss of life." Lady Radstone closed her eyes. "God help us."

Kadar watched them intently.

Declan spoke loudly enough for Kadar to hear, "Well, boys, would you care to help me repair this mess of a cabin?"

"Sure, we'll be glad to, Mr. Flynn," James said. His brothers nodded in agreement.

"Excellent. Bring me toolbox over here and we'll begin."

Work continued on the two ships around the clock. At midday of the next day, Edward, James, and Phillip worked on one side of the cabin, attempting to move some of the rubble that Declan had begun to cut away the day before. Elizabeth and Claire worked on the other side of the cabin. Kadar dozed against the ladder out on the gun deck. As a light rain fell, Edward sat resting on the windowsill. With the pirate ship tied to the *Brilliant*, he sat just feet from the other ship's hull. His eye caught a movement. Edward spotted a black hand and arm reaching out of a small hole in the pirate ship's hull. The cupped hand faced skyward for a few minutes, then disappeared back into the ship. A moment later, it came back out again.

Edward watched for a while. "James, Phillip, look at this."

The boys both looked down. "A slave," Phillip said. "He's trying to catch some rainwater." Edward jumped up, came back with a jug of water, and climbed out the window. He grabbed a line hanging from the pirate ship; with his feet wedged against the two hulls, he worked his way down to the hole as the two hulls moved and scraped together in the gentle swells.

Edward slowly leaned down and looked in. A black boy, no older than himself, peered back from inches away. "Hello, there. I've brought you some water." Only something as small as a boy's hand would fit through the hole. The boy held out his hand. Edward poured the water into the outstretched hand. The hand slowly and carefully moved back through the hole and Edward heard the boy slurping the little bit of water. The hand came back out and Edward poured again. Edward finished pouring the water and looked in the hole. The boy's dark eyes, surrounded by glistening white and outlined by his dark face, peered back. He wore an iron ring as thick as a thumb around his neck with a chain attached to it. The boy nodded once, almost a bow, and said, "*Oshe.*"

Elizabeth and Claire noticed the boys and walked over to see what was so curious. Elizabeth gasped. "What are you doing?" she hissed. "Get up here. Get up here now."

Claire grabbed James and Phillip and pulled them away from the window. James gave her a defiant look and pulled away from her grasp. She looked over her shoulder to see if Kadar had been alerted. He was still napping. Edward climbed back to the window and his mother yanked him in.

"What are you doing? Have you gone mad?" She shook him by the shoulders. "You could have fallen between the hulls and been crushed. And you two, why did you let your brother go down there?"

"There is a slave down there. He wanted some water," James said. "All Edward did was give a thirsty slave some water."

"I would say he is about my age," Edward said.

"Why would you want us to stop him?" Phillip asked.

"Well," his mother paused. "We're all God's children, and we should always try to comfort those in need, but not now, not here. These pirates could have shot you, thinking that you were attempting to escape. Right now we must think of our own safety first."

As they ate hardtack biscuits and water in the dark, James said, "Could there have been slaves below on the pirate ship that sank?"

"I didn't see any black people row over here when it went down. The pirates could have just left them in the hold?" Edward said.

The group fell silent and stared at each other.

Elizabeth looked around the room, lit by only one small candle. "Only Satan himself must know how much evil lurks in the hearts of these men. Remember that, my lads."

Claire nodded. Before the meager meal was over, James and Phillip each slipped Edward a hardtack biscuit. During the night, while everyone slept, Edward climbed down and whispered into the hole. The boy's hand came out. Edward put the first piece of bread in his hand. The boy gave it to someone. The boy gave the second piece to another and then took the third biscuit. "*Oshe*," he said. Edward could hear him eating. Edward nodded, feeling better that he and his brothers were able to help in a small way.

The next morning, the crews prepared to separate the ships and set sail. The pirate captains ordered Lady Radstone, Claire, and the boys up to the quarterdeck.

Below them, Lieutenant Garrison and the remaining members of the *Brilliant*'s crew stood bunched together. Claire met the lieutenant's gaze. As she looked at him, she did not detect a look of worry or fear. His jaw was locked and his eyes squinted in a steadfast look of determination. The lieutenant wore no hat, but had a large bandage wrapped around his head with a little crimson seeping through the side. Now in command, he seemed to be making an effort to stay as positive as possible, given the situation. Lieutenant Garrison slowly moved his right hand to the middle of his chest and subtly raised his right thumb up. The thumbs-up gesture gave Claire a slight bit of comfort—as much comfort as one could have in this horrible situation. Bouchet came to the railing with LeBeau.

"English seamen," Bouchet announced, "as you can see, Lady Radstone and her children are safe and well. I'm releasing you to sail on to Jamaica. Except for the ship's master carpenter—he stays with us. You will carry this letter to Lord Radstone." He drew his cutlass and held it to Lady Radstone's throat. "If you seek us out and attack us, they will die."

A pirate handed Lieutenant Garrison the letter. "Captain, if you release Lady Radstone and the children now, I guarantee you Lord Radstone will treat you with mercy. You may retain all the officers as your captives, and we will pledge not to fight against you again," Garrison said.

"Mercy?" Bouchet said. "Did you hear that, men? He offers us 'mercy.' What do you say to that, LeBeau?"

"I think I would rather have a chest of his lordship's gold."

The pirates cheered and pushed the captive sailors toward the railing, where three longboats waited below. The sailors climbed down and scrambled aboard. Lieutenant Garrison stood at the rail supervising the lowering of the wounded men into the boats. The lieutenant called to the quarterdeck, "Captain Bouchet, you don't need to keep them to collect your ransom. Take me and the officers with you and release the children."

"Get down, Lieutenant, and head for Jamaica. I think I will keep his lordship's most valued possessions. Be hasty and deliver the letter to Lord Radstone."

Lieutenant Garrison turned to Lady Radstone and the four young people. "God keep you all safe until we return." The three small, heavily laden boats set their sails and moved away to the south. At the tiller of one of the boats, Lieutenant Garrison turned back for a final, long look at Claire, who stood there watching the departure. She gave the slightest wave, and he nodded solemnly. She realized he was someone she truly cherished. In the short time she had known him, she had found things in him she had never known existed in any other man: tenderness, strength, and intelligence.

What is happening? Nami asked.

The pirates are letting the British seamen go on to Jamaica. They're keeping us for ransom.

There are too many people in those boats, Sanjay said. *It will be a dangerous voyage.*

Help them, Claire said. *Help them find Port Royal.*

We'll send dolphins with them, Nami said. *We will try to guide them on their journey. Sometimes humans don't understand, but we will try.*

Claire prayed for the sailors in the longboats. She prayed that these men and Lieutenant Garrison would survive. *Please God, watch over them.*

The pirates waited until the three small boats disappeared, then unfurled the sails of both ships and set off to the south. Claire sat by the window the next day, watching as they sailed past a string of uninhabited islands.

———

I can't see any more islands, she said to the dolphins.

There are hundreds of islands near here.

I wonder where we're going.

You've turned to the west, southwest, Nami said. *In a day or two, if the ship remains on this course, you'll come to the land called Cuba.*

I heard what happened, a voice broke in. *I'm here to help.*

Claire recognized the voice from Bantry Bay.

Stark? Is that you, Stark?

It's me—the most powerful dolphin in all the seas.

Claire smiled. *It is you. What are you doing here?*

I left Bantry before you. I came here to find a mate.

And have you found one, my big friend?

No, not yet. We'll talk of that another day. Jump, and I'll take you to safety.

I can't; Nami will explain.

I'll stay near you.

Stark and the rest of the dolphins talked with Claire through the afternoon. Stark's voice rang with a bit of an Irish lilt; it made Claire think of Bantry, her little cottage, and, of course, her mother. She tried to fight off the melancholy pouring over her.

Phillip sat next to Claire. "You've been looking out at the sea all day."

"Just thinking."

"Father will come for us, don't worry."

Claire hugged Phillip and rested her head on top of his.

———

Dawn broke as the two ships sailed into a secluded bay. "I wonder if this harbor is their home port," James said, pointing out the window. A village of fifty or sixty thatched huts and cottages squatted under the lush trees. Palms reached out in every direction to catch the sun. Tucked against the hills surrounding the cove, the village remained hidden from the open sea; they had only seen it after sailing through the inlet. Dozens of pillars of smoke from breakfast cooking rose in the still morning air. A group of thirty or forty people stood and waved on the beach. The gathering grew as more people wandered down from the lush hillside. Claire could see native women, blacks, European women, plenty of children, and a few men casting fishing nets in the shallows. It looked like any village to her. Maybe a little different from the seaside villages she was accustomed to back along Bantry Bay, but a village just the same. Except for the two pairs of cannon placed on either side of the harbor's entrance, an ominous note to a setting of quiet paradise.

"Where do you think we are, Mum?" James asked.

"I'm not sure, son. An obscure island, or maybe we're on the coast of Florida. It seems like a large piece of land."

Bouchet walked into the cabin with four men. "Kadar, well done. Go ashore; these men will take over. Lady Radstone, a few men will be on board with you and your children until we sail again. The ship will be your very own private Tower of London."

"I gave you my word. We will not try to escape. My daughter and I would like a little privacy, and we certainly want to get off this ship."

"Yes, you gave me your word—damn your word. Men, make sure you stay awake, one outside this door and one on the deck above. Allow no one else on board unless I give the order. They may move about the ship in daylight, but watch them. These five are worth much gold to us."

"Aye, Captain," they said.

The captain stood inches from Lady Radstone. He reached over, grabbed her hand, and pulled his ever-ready knife from his boot. "You remember what I said I would do if you tried to escape." He pressed the knife against the top of her hand.

Lady Radstone tensed her hand, but Bouchet gripped it tight.

"Leave her alone," Claire said, as she grabbed Lady Radstone's arm.

Bouchet pointed the knife at Claire. "I may send another message to Port Royal. I may send one of your fingers—or maybe an ear. Your bravery does not impress me. Your bravery is stupid."

Claire stood inches from Bouchet. "I don't think of myself as brave. I do know you're a coward. We're helpless, and you enjoy terrifying us."

"A lion among sheep will always terrify the sheep." Bouchet smiled.

"A lion? More like a jackal."

The muscles of his face tightened, his eyes narrowed, and his face contorted into a scowl.

Lady Radstone pulled Claire back. "Enough of this, if you harm any of us, it will only serve to fill my husband with a more terrible resolve."

He looked at Claire. "You wag your tongue just a little more, girl, and I'll cut it out." He turned on his heels and stomped off.

When he was out of sight, Lady Radstone rounded on Claire. Her eyes bulged wide with anger and fear. "Claire, keep your mouth shut. Don't provoke these animals. We can only imagine what these lawless men might do. Boys, never, never speak to any of them."

Phillip hugged his mother. "Will father be able to find us here?"

"Yes, my dear, of course he will." She looked over her son's shoulder, and Claire could clearly see the doubt in her eyes.

That night, shadowy figures danced on the shore to fiddle music. Bonfires lit portions of the beach, and torches moved about the village. As the night wore on, the torches moved up into the hills, blinking out from under the thick canopy. Music, singing, laughter, and an occasional pistol shot echoed across the water.

The four pirate guards complained through the night. They worried about their share of the rum. The sounds coming from shore told them it would soon be gone.

In a few days, a new group of guards came aboard; the new men brought rum with them. They drank it sitting outside the cabin, their drunken gazes and sneering smiles fixed on Lady Radstone and Claire.

"I think the older one would be a bit feistier," one of the pirates said. They both laughed.

"Shut your filthy pig mouths," James said. The two laughed even louder. Elizabeth slowly put her hand on James's arm and squeezed it as tight as she could.

Captain Bouchet brought new men two days later, along with a woman who brought bread, roasted corn, and fruit, which they devoured ravenously. Lady Radstone protested, "Captain, these men drink too much rum, and I fear for my daughter and myself."

Bouchet laughed. "Remember—if you touch one of them, I'll order Kadar to tear out your heart with his bare hands. Do you hear me?"

"Aye, Captain," they said.

"Now, my lady," Bouchet said in a mocking tone, "are you satisfied?"

"No, I am not. Relieve these men of their rum."

Bouchet turned and walked away. "Did you hear that, men? She wants me to take your bumbo away from you."

The pirates laughed.

Chapter 13

Heeling

The pirates emptied the ship and distributed all of the Radstone's household goods and possessions. Claire begged them to let her keep her books—no one listened.

Day after day Claire walked the deck studying the hills surrounding the bay. She realized that making it to shore might not be that difficult, but surviving in the jungle would be impossible.

Days turned into weeks. Declan came and went as he continued to repair the *Brilliant's* battle scars. He gave Claire and the Radstones any information he gleaned from the pirates, and they began planning their escape. The dolphins always swam near the ship and Claire knew she must keep everyone close to the dolphins. She knew she must sail with the Radstones to freedom.

Claire stood at the railing listening to the macaws and parrots squawking in the canopy as the sky brightened. A longboat full of lumber and supplies moved away from the dock. The men cursed as Declan came aboard and ordered them to hoist the supplies on deck. Carrying his toolbox, Declan announced to the guards, "The captain ordered me to put a new door on this cabin. I finally got the blacksmith to make the hinges." Declan walked into the cabin and put down his tools. "A good day to all. It's a fine morning," he said, as if they were strolling down a street in Bantry.

"Good morning, Declan," Claire said.

"Mr. Flynn," Lady Radstone said, "I'm happy to see you."

"Madam." Declan touched his hat in acknowledgement and went to work. The guards moved to a table halfway down the gun deck, where they played cards. Declan hammered and sawed for a while. "Boys, help me here," he said. He motioned to Claire and Lady Radstone with his head. Edward, James, and Phillip came closer, pretending to focus on the work to be done. The two guards, across the gun deck, played their game.

He whispered, "Be ready—tomorrow night is the night."

Everyone leaned in as Declan spoke. "They think I am one of them, but I'm sure they don't completely trust me, you know. There is a strong English longboat with a fine mast and plenty of sail. I'll bring it to the far side of the ship tomorrow. We'll be shielded from view so that we can put up the mast, set the sail, and slip away in the night. They shouldn't discover what happened until morning and by then we'll be long gone. Claire, You'll be doing the sailing."

"I can sail her," Claire said. "Like I told you, the fishermen of Bantry taught me well."

"I can sail too," said James.

"Then tomorrow night we go," Declan said.

Elizabeth motioned toward the pirate guards. "What of them?"

"I'll bring them an extra cask of rum in the morning."

"But there are four of them," James said.

"Don't worry, lad," Declan said. "They'll have bellies full of rum. When I give the word, you boys move quickly. We will need to gather food, water, guns, powder, and shot—fill the longboat with as many provisions as she can hold. Do you understand?"

They all nodded.

"We've done a lot of exploring. We know where everything is aboard the ship," Edward said.

"That's perfect, lad."

"Mr. Flynn," said Elizabeth. "I'm worried about this plan. They cannot catch us. We must succeed in our escape."

"We'll succeed, my lady," Declan said. "I fear if you don't get away now, you'll never leave this place."

"Will you be able to overpower the guards and do it quietly?" Lady Radstone asked. "There can be no sound. What if someone fires a pistol?"

"Don't worry—I'm sure I'll be able to overpower them," Declan said.

"My husband will be searching for us. If we stay here, he could find us and secure our freedom."

"My lady, if he finds this place and there's a battle, you may very well die. And even if your husband pays the ransom, these men still may not release you."

Lady Radstone hugged Phillip, lowering her head in silence for a moment. "I believe you're right. We're left with no choice. God help us."

Declan turned away. "Now let me get to work. We don't want them to suspect anything. We'll talk in the morning."

Nami, are you there? Claire sent out.

Yes, Claire, we're in the bay.

Tomorrow night we are going to escape.

How will you go? Where will you go? Sanjay asked.

We'll be in a longboat, and I think we shall sail along this coast. When we get far enough away, we'll put in.

Remember, Nami said, *if you're on land, we cannot help you. You should sail to the north where there are hundreds of islands. We'll show you the way.*

Bolo joined in. *Claire, our family has lived around these islands for centuries. We know where fresh water runs into the sea. There are tall green islands in places where large ships can never go, but your boat will sail in the shallows. There are many small coves where you can hide. These men will never find you. We'll also be able to warn you if these ships come near. We cannot help if you are in the jungle.*

Yes, yes. You're right, Claire said. *I'll sail the longboat and follow you, but remember, these pirates must not overtake us once we make our escape.*

The places we describe are far to the north, so you must sail hard and fast. We'll go and bring more dolphins, Nami said. *When you slip away, get out to sea as quickly as you can. As long as you are over the horizon, we can swim between you and them and help you turn out of their path.*

I pray we get out of sight, Claire said. *Until tomorrow.* Claire watched through the window as the dolphins sped out of the bay.

None of them slept very much. The boys plotted through the night.

"Take muskets, pistols, powder, and shot. After we load what we need, we should throw the rest overboard," Edward suggested.

"We shouldn't waste time throwing things overboard," James said.

"Don't forget the flints," Phillip added.

"How long will we be at sea?" Edward asked.

"We'll need as much food and water as we can take," James said.

"Mostly water," Phillip said.

"Get some sleep, boys," Elizabeth said.

———

Before daybreak, Claire and Elizabeth sat at the window, talking in hushed tones.

"I'm frightened of this plan. If things go wrong, Bouchet's wrath could be terrible," Elizabeth said.

"To be sure, and be sure of this. Your husband may never find us. If he does, and he pays them the ransom, what then? These men will have no reason to keep us alive. Once they have the gold, they could set us adrift, or drop us on an uninhabited island, or worse. We must get away from them now."

"You're right. Pray that we succeed."

As morning broke, Claire and Elizabeth watched two men row the longboat toward them with Declan aboard. As they neared the *Brilliant*, they rowed around to the side of the ship facing away from the village. Elizabeth and Claire walked to the other side of the cabin and leaned out the window.

Declan yelled to the guards on the deck. "I didn't want the captain to see what I'm bringing you men." He tapped one of the kegs.

"Am I looking at two kegs of English navy rum?" one of the men called down.

"It is that indeed, and I've already mixed it into the finest bumbo you swabs have ever had. Now help me get these supplies and our rum on deck."

"You're a fine thief," a pirate said, as they loaded the rum on board.

"Since I did the stealing, you just make sure you protect my share. I'll be back out tonight to join you for a mug or two."

"You can be sure of that," one of the guards said as he slapped Declan on the back.

Declan and his two helpers worked through the day. Declan finally visited the cabin. "Are you ready, my lady?"

"Yes, Mr. Flynn. We know we must do this."

"There's no other choice." He turned to the boys. "Now, lads, time will be short, maybe an hour or two, so remember—get to the weapons locker first and bring plenty of them. Be quiet about it, and don't load Phillip down with too heavy a burden."

"I can carry as much as them," Phillip said.

"I'm sure you can. Ladies, collect a few water casks, extra canvas, and rope. We'll pile everything at the railing. We'll use the block and tackle to load the boat."

Declan returned to his two helpers and they finished their work on the gun deck. Topside, Declan called to his two comrades. "Leave the longboat—the skiff is much easier to row."

Claire watched as Declan and the others rowed toward the beach. "We'll begin when Declan returns after dark. Do you remember what each of you has to do?"

"Yes."

"Yes, we're ready."

"What if Declan can't overpower the guards?" James asked.

"We'll help him," Edward said.

"Boys," Lady Radstone stood in front of them. "You shall do no such thing. Stay away from those drunken monsters. Do you hear me?"

"But, Mother…" Edward said.

Lady Radstone held up her hand and glared at the boys, who wisely said nothing. They sat in the dark and waited.

Nami, Declan will be here soon. We'll load the boat and be off, Claire said.

We're ready, Nami said. *More of our family and friends joined us today.*

Some other dolphin minds greeted Claire.

As night fell, the sounds of merriment rose. The laughter and noise ashore subsided sometime after midnight. Claire watched from the window as a shadowy man walked out onto the dock and stepped down to the skiff. She pointed, "Declan."

He rowed out and again swung around to the far side of the *Brilliant.* "Ahoy," he called in a muffled tone.

"Ahoy, is that you, Flynn?" a slurred voice called.

"Aye, be quiet, man," he whispered.

"It's late. We saved you a bit of the bumbo," the voice said, hardly able to talk.

"I didn't trust you dogs, so I brought another cask. Bouchet should not be hoarding the best rum."

"You're right about that, Flynn."

Declan climbed aboard; almost immediately the captives heard a muffled cry, then an anguished moan from Flynn's next victim. The guard outside the cabin stumbled to the top of the ladder and crashed back down. He lay at the foot of the ladder in a crumpled, motionless heap.

"Quickly now," Declan said from outside the cabin door.

Elizabeth pushed the door open. Declan stood on the dark gun deck. "Boys, go to the weapons locker and bring every weapon you can carry—plenty of powder and shot. Bring everything to the larboard side. Be quick about it and be quiet. Remember, sound carries across the water. My lady, Claire—first water, then food." As Declan spoke, he tied the wrists of the man on the floor, lashed his feet to a cannon, and gagged him.

They scampered over the ship, and in an hour had collected tools, rope, extra canvas, and every weapon they could find. Declan brought them a sextant, a compass, and two spyglasses. As the boys worked together and used a block and tackle to lower the heavy casks, Elizabeth and Claire set the mast in the longboat, readied the sail, and packed the provisions away as best they could. Phillip came from the kitchen, pots clanging together as he walked.

"Quiet, Phillip," Declan whispered.

———

Kadar walked down the beach. He heard something, stopped, and peered out at the ships, then kept walking. When he reached the dock, he noticed that one of the skiffs and one of the longboats were missing. In the moonlight, he checked both ships; there was no skiff moored to either of them. He heard a familiar sound, and strained to hear it again. Kadar recognized the squeaking of the wheel in a block and tackle at work. He took off running toward Bouchet's hut. Before long, the captain and a few men stood on the dock.

"Ahoy!" Bouchet yelled. "Ahoy, *Brilliant*!"

Declan grabbed James by the shoulder. "Quickly now, you and your brothers, leave the rest. You'd best be getting down to the longboat."

Claire called softly, "Declan, what is it?"

Bouchet fired a pistol. "Ahoy!"

Declan glanced at the shore. He helped the boys over the side, watching them climb down to the longboat. "We're out of time. Set sail. Get on with it, now."

"Come on, Declan, get down here. Hurry."

"No, I'll stay and hold them off. Go."

"But Declan, you'll be—"

"I'll be fine, lass, don't worry. I'm sure I'll be seeing you again someday."

Claire began to climb back up. "I can't leave you here."

"We've been discovered. I'll delay them. It will be your only chance. Get going."

Claire looked down at the Radstones and back up at Declan. "God bless you, Declan." He disappeared and she jumped back down to the longboat. "Push away, boys. Then grab an oar and row. Pull—pull as hard as you can. Help me, Elizabeth."

A pistol shot rang out from the ship. "Ahoy, shore."

"Who goes there?" Bouchet called.

"It's Flynn, Captain, and all is well!"

"Very good, Flynn!" Bouchet yelled. He turned to Kadar. "I'm itchy with something amiss. What's he doing out there? And what happened to the guards? Get every man you can find into the longboats and get LeBeau. And hurry."

Bouchet jumped in a boat. "To arms, men, snap to it!"

Declan saw the flurry of activity on the shore and braced himself for the onslaught. Looking around, he could see the longboat's sail catching the wind. Claire sailed past the harbor entrance and out to the open silvery sea. He turned back, preparing himself for the battle.

Declan loaded a dozen muskets and a few pistols as the pirates began to row toward the *Brilliant*. First, he ran forward and fired the swivel gun. The shot splashed just in front of Bouchet's boat and the men stopped rowing. Declan switched to a musket, and an oarsman slumped over. Bouchet fired back, but Declan held the advantage. The pirates made easy targets and they knew it. Bouchet shouted orders as Declan kept firing.

More of the men in the boats fell as the shots hit home. The pirates fumbled with the oars of their wounded and dead comrades. Bouchet and his men backed away and waited. Soon two more boats rowed out, and they began their assault again. They circled to the stern and bow of the *Brilliant*. Declan fired, hitting a few more men as he ran from the quarterdeck to the fo'c'sle and back. Claire's longboat had disappeared. With the pirates climbing onto the ship at both ends, Declan picked his shot, taking out the first man aboard. The second man charged toward Declan, brandishing a cutlass above his head. Declan spun and shot him just as the blade began its downward arc. More men climbed over the rails. Declan dropped his spent pistols, ran, and jumped onto the railing, balancing himself. He looked back at his pursuers, smiled, and, as shots whizzed by him, dove into the black water.

The sound of gunfire rang out, echoing across the water. Claire sat at the tiller, focusing on the sail and her course. She feared the worst for Declan and said a silent prayer.

"What do you think happened to Declan?" Edward said.

"He held them off for us," James said.

"We didn't know him that well. He was your friend," Phillip said to Claire.

Elizabeth bowed her head. "Gentlemen, let us say a silent prayer for a man of true bravery and honor."

As the boat moved away from the black land, Claire cursed under her breath at the full tropical moon. Elizabeth sat next to Claire. "How well did you know this Declan Flynn?"

"Not well."

"Amazing, truly amazing. Are we sailing to Jamaica?"

"No, not yet."

"But Jamaica is our only sanctuary."

"The pirates will expect us to make a run for Jamaica, so I think they'll sail toward Port Royal. Lieutenant Garrison showed me the maps and charts as we sailed south; I believe the pirate harbor lies somewhere on the coast of Cuba, but I can't be sure. I'm sure of one thing—if we don't get over the horizon, Bouchet will surely run us down. This moonlight is no help to us, and daylight is only a few hours away. Tighten down the boom line, James," Claire said. "We must find every bit of speed the wind and this boat will give us."

"Where will we go?" Elizabeth asked.

"Thanks to Declan, we have a compass along. The sun should rise to our starboard and, if we keep on this northerly course, we should find those islands we passed coming south. I'm sure we can hide on one of them for a time."

Elizabeth touched Claire's arm. "Sail well, and may God help us."

Claire's expression did not change. She knew what she had to do.

Are you there?

Yes, Claire, Nami said. *We're out in front of you.*

Are we going in the right direction?

Yes. When light comes you'll see our dorsal fins. There'll be two of us ahead of you. Just follow us.

The big ships set sail, Sanjay said. *We'll follow them, swim back and forth, and tell you where they are.*

Are they coming this way?

We're not sure. We will know soon.

The dolphins started to speak among themselves.

Where shall we take Claire? Sanjay asked.

To the tall island where the water runs into the sea, Nami said.

The cave is there.

Yes.

Should we tell Claire?

Not now.

Claire sailed on through the night. Everyone worked at the lines and shifted the cargo. No one slept. The morning came and the wind strengthened. Claire leaned on the tiller. "She's heeled as far as we dare. Elizabeth, you and the boys sit over on the larboard side."

A huge dolphin swam parallel to the boat.

Edward pointed. "A dolphin."

"There are more ahead of us," James said.

One of the ships turned east. The other one sails in this direction, the big male messenger said.

Are they getting closer to us?

Yes, I think they are. Four of us are swimming between you and the ship. We'll be able to judge the distance soon.

The tropical sun beat down as Elizabeth used the spyglass every few minutes, searching the horizon. Spray flew back as the longboat cut through the growing waves. The boys remained serious and quiet as they worked the lines.

"Oh my God." Elizabeth dropped the spyglass from her eye. "A sail."

"Hold this." Claire gave Elizabeth the tiller and took the glass. "It has to be them." She snapped the glass closed. "If we can outrun them until dark, we can change course and slip away." Claire looked up at the clouded sky.

"Boys, move more of the load to larboard. We'll heel her over and keep the water just below the starboard gunwale. Move, boys," Claire ordered. "James, pull the sail as tight as you can." The boys shifted the supplies to the other side of the boat.

High above the *Brilliant*, the lookout called down, "Sail off the starboard bow!"

Bouchet ran forward with his spyglass and stood on the bowsprit. "There they are!" he yelled. "More sail! They can't outrun us!"

Nami, we can see a sail. Could it be one of the pirate ships? Claire asked.

Yes, it's the ship that brought you to the Caribbean.

We can see them. Do you think they can see us?

Let's hope they stay on their present course, Sanjay said. *They're coming north, but are moving a little to the east. In time, you will move further away from them.*

Perhaps we should move more to the west, Claire said.

Yes, Nami said. *A good idea. I'll tell our friends up ahead to point a little more to the west. We'll be able to take you to the islands, but in a different way.*

Don't worry, Claire, Sanjay said. *We won't let them take you.*

If they overtake us, you may not be able to stop them.

True, but many of us are far out in the sea, searching for help.

What help?

The whales, Nami said, *the great gray whales.*

The whales? They can speak with their minds as you do?

Yes, they roam the seas and bring back news from faraway places.

"They're coming closer," James said as he pulled back on the boom line.

The sails of the *Brilliant* rose higher and clearer on the horizon. "God help us. They're going to overtake us," Elizabeth cried.

"It's past midday," Claire said. "Let's pray these clouds stay with us. They may have a hard time seeing us tonight."

Edward sat straight up and squinted into the distance. "Whales."

White plumes of spray and steam shot skyward as the whales moved closer to the longboat. Huge tail flukes slowly lifted out of the rolling sea and slid back under.

"Look, there must be eight or ten of them," James said.

"Look, Mum. Over there." Phillip pointed.

"They could be dangerous. Claire, move away from them," Elizabeth said.

Although the mass of their bodies hid below the water, the area at the top of their heads just barely broke the surface. The boys stood and moved about, trying to get a better look at the whales.

Claire yelled, "Sit down, boys! Boys, sit down!"

Within a few feet of the boat, a mass of charcoal-gray flesh, dotted with spots of lighter gray and white barnacles, slowly rose out of the sea with barely a ripple. Its blowhole opened. The incredibly loud whooshing sound made by the mighty beast exhaling startled everyone, and the boys flinched back from the side of the boat. They could feel the whales' hot breath as droplets rained down on them.

Elizabeth drew back, while Claire concentrated on sailing the boat and moving away from the giants.

"Oh my God."

"Will it capsize us?"

"Look at the size of it."

"Amazing." Phillip lunged over to the starboard rail and reached out.

"Get back, Phillip!" his mother yelled.

"I just want to touch him."

"Get back," Claire said. "If you fall over and we have to stop and pick you up it'll be all over for us."

Phillip moved back to the larboard side. The creature rolled over until its glistening, saucer-sized eye came out of the water and inspected the boat. The hot steam burst out. The inhaled air rushed into the giant's lungs. *I am Brey.* A deep, bellowing voice echoed in Claire's mind.

Edward stood toward the aft of the longboat. "I can see its body. It's four or five times the size of our boat. "

The other boys stood, rocking the boat. "Sit down, boys," their mother ordered.

We have come to help you, Brey boomed.

How—what will you do?

We will do whatever we can to slow their ship. Brey submerged, moving away with the rest of the whales. No other words came from the huge creature.

Elizabeth sat next to Claire. "What kind of strangeness is this?"

Claire said nothing.

"They're gone," Phillip said.

"Look—over there to the south." Edward pointed at the telltale misty plumes of exhaled breath.

"First the dolphins, and now this." Elizabeth's eyes pierced into Claire. "What does this mean?"

"I don't know. James, pull the boom more into the wind. Boys, move everything you can to the larboard side. Let's try to heel her to starboard a bit more."

On the ship, Bouchet clicked his spyglass closed. "I can see her now. We're closing on them. When we get within range, we'll fire the bow chasers. Mind you, I don't want to hit them. They do us no good dead. We can't kill them—yet."

"Aye, Captain," a few of the crew said.

Three of the gray whales nudged against the starboard side of the *Brilliant*.

The helmsman felt a strange sensation at the wheel—a pressure against the rudder.

The sound of the whales breathing alerted the crew. The lookout aloft cried down, "Whales to the starboard!"

Men walked over and pointed down. Bouchet stood on the fo'c'sle and leaned over the side. Puzzled, he turned back and noticed that the ship's bowsprit, which had pointed directly at the escaping longboat, now pointed slightly to the west and away from its prey.

"What are you doing?" Bouchet yelled back at the helmsman. "To starboard, back to the east."

The helmsman said something. Bouchet did not understand what the man said. He walked back to the quarterdeck.

"She won't answer the helm, Captain. I can't turn her." The helmsman pulled at the wheel.

Irritated, Bouchet walked to the starboard rail, where much of the crew gathered, watching the spectacle.

A fourth whale joined in and they nosed into the bow of the ship. Their tails churned the water behind them into a boiling white froth. Bouchet checked for the sail of the longboat; it now lay well off to the east. He turned back to see the helmsman pulling hard on the wheel.

"Sorcery—very strange sorcery," he said to himself. Then Bouchet screamed, "Don't stand there watching, you fools—stop them! They're turning us away! To arms, you dogs!"

The men, snapped out of their trances, ran for their pistols and muskets.

The whales spouted as they pushed the *Brilliant* onto a westerly course. The sails luffed in the wind as the men began to shoot down at the mass of gray flesh. Pistol and musket shots hit the whales, but nothing seemed to faze them as they pushed.

The *Brilliant*'s bow soon faced directly west, and then began to swing toward the south. Bouchet screamed, "The pivot guns! Use the pivot guns!"

The small cannon fired down and blood poured out of a whale's back. The wounded whale sank out of sight and moved away. Another took its place.

"Reload! Fire again!" Bouchet screamed as he ran back to the quarterdeck. The *Brilliant*'s bowsprit now pointed to the south, heading in the opposite direction from the longboat.

"Back to the east, to the northeast!" he screamed at the helmsman.

"I can't, Captain."

Bouchet grabbed the wheel; the two men pulled with all they had. Some of the whales swung around to push on the larboard side of the ship in order to keep it pointed south. The pirates fired the swivel guns quickly and accurately; more blood poured from the gray backs. Every time a wounded whale fell back, another would join in and push.

Some of the men stopped firing. "Witchcraft," one of them said. "It is surely that," said another. The rest of them stopped firing.

Dusk came and the whales turned away from their task. The sail of the longboat had disappeared over the horizon by the time the *Brilliant* turned back onto a north-northeasterly course. Bouchet stood on the quarterdeck, trying to understand what had happened. He was furious, and no one dared speak to him. No one knew what to say or think. The crew remained quiet in the darkness.

"Why do you think they turned?" James asked.

"I don't know," said Claire. "But we're sailing north-northwest, now. If the pirates turn back toward us, they'll probably stay on their original course toward the east."

"Then maybe we'll be able to slip away," Edward said.

"Pray for that," Claire said.

"The dolphins are swimming on this westerly course and we're following them. Why would they turn to the west?" Elizabeth asked.

"It could be that they're following us."

Elizabeth stared at Claire for a long time.

"Get some sleep, lads, tomorrow will be long and hard," Claire said.

"Claire." Elizabeth took the tiller. "You get some sleep as well. You truly are a skillful sailor. Without you, we would have never escaped."

"Declan made our escape possible," said Claire. "I wonder what happened to him? I hope he's still alive."

"I pray he survived. He did a brave thing," Elizabeth said.

Claire rested her head against a keg. Brey's deep voice entered her mind. *It is done. They will not find you in the dark.*

What did you do?

We pushed on the hull and turned her off course. The pirates fired their guns, but they could not stop us. Whales died this day.

How many of you gave your lives for us?

I'm not sure. They died helping you. We consider it an honor to help you. Remember, you are the most special of people.

I shall pray for them and all of you, said Claire.

Pray for us. He paused. *I'm sure no one has ever done that. Prayer, a good thing.*

No more words came to Claire. Her body ached with exhaustion, but her mind spun. *"You are the most special of people." Someone else said something like that to me, not too long ago.* She finally fell asleep.

Chapter 14

Paradise Found

Elizabeth and Claire took turns in the night sleeping and keeping the longboat following the dolphins, while the boys slept. As morning came, with Elizabeth and the boys asleep, Claire spied low, green islands rising on the horizon. *Are we going to those islands?*

No, Nami said. *We'll guide you past these first few islands to the land hidden behind them. You can't yet see the land where we are taking you. Calm, clear waters surround the island, and there are many fish. Fresh water runs into the sea. You'll be safe there.*

It sounds perfect, Nami. Thank you.

Yes, and the water is shallow. There are reefs and sandbars everywhere. No big sailing ships will be able to come near the island.

Another dolphin mind spoke. *I bring news. The pirate ship sailed hard during the night, and now roams far to the east and even a little north of us.*

Then we're out of their reach—thanks to you and your family.

And the whales, Nami said.

The very brave whales. We owe our lives to them. The only thing larger than their bodies is their courage.

We shall tell this story for generations to come, said a dolphin.

The boys began to stir. "There are islands ahead." Claire pointed.

James rubbed his eyes, stood, took the spyglass, and scanned the horizon. "No sails."

"Which island shall we land on?" Edward asked.

"I'm not sure," said Claire. "We'll keep sailing for a while."

"The dolphins are still in front of us. Do you think they know which one of these islands would be the best one for us?" asked James.

Ignoring his question, Claire said, "Keep searching in every direction with the glass and make sure there are no sails on the horizon or people on these islands. We don't want to fall into the hands of another pack of scoundrels."

The longboat sailed on, passing close to a few of the low islands. Phillip leaned over the side. "I can see the bottom."

"No large ships will be able to come this way," Claire announced.

Claire, look ahead of you, Nami said. *The island with the tall land in the middle is where you should land your boat. We know nothing of this land, except that fresh water runs into the sea.*

James stood at the bow while Edward worked the line on the boom.

"James," Claire said. "Search the shoreline of the big hilly island ahead of us."

James peered through the spyglass for a long time. He pulled it down and stumbled aft. "I don't see any people, and there is a stream running down from the large hill in the middle."

"I can see the stream. We'll land near there," Claire said, as she swung the longboat toward the island. Lush greenery covered every inch of the land, which was bordered by a glistening white beach.

Still leaning over the side of the boat, Phillip said, "I can see fish everywhere."

The little craft slid to a stop, heeling over as the boys jumped in the water and ran onto the beach.

Elizabeth and Claire pulled down the sail as the boys ran toward the gully where the stream ran out of the tree line and over the beach.

Claire dug around in the cargo, found a belt with a cutlass, and cinched it around her waist. She stuck a pistol in the belt, then handed Elizabeth a belt, a knife, and a pistol. Elizabeth reached down, grabbed the hem of her long cotton dress, and pulled it between her legs, tucking the fabric into her belt. Claire watched her, smiling, then did the same.

The two women climbed over the side into the knee-deep water and waded ashore in their not very becoming, but very practical, baggy pantaloons.

"It's good to be standing on dry land," Elizabeth said.

Claire thought about her mother. She knew her mother would be proud. She also knew there would be much more to do.

James ran back to them. "The stream is cold and clear. We should explore the whole island."

"We shall," said Elizabeth, "but we will do it together."

Birds of every size and color dotted the thick jungle canopy. They flew above the group and scurried along the beach before them, their squawks and cries filling the air. Edward and Phillip stood in the gully, in knee-deep water, splashing about and laughing.

"I think we should make our camp near this stream, but inside the edge of the jungle. Our camp should be hidden from the sea," Claire said.

"What if they see the boat?" James asked. "We should try to hide it."

"You're right, James," Claire said. "It looks like these shallows stretch far out to the west, but someone could see us with a spyglass. The pirates will be searching for us in these waters."

"Let's all gather broken palm branches from the ground to cover the boat," Elizabeth said.

The boys darted in and out of the jungle gathering the palm fronds. They worked quickly, and in a matter of minutes had covered the boat. The group walked down the beach. The stretch of sand bent to the east until it ended next to a rock outcropping. Seabirds covered every inch of the cliff. A stone's throw across a channel, the cliff of another small, barren island faced them.

"There doesn't seem to be much over there." Elizabeth pointed to the other island.

"You're right," Claire said. "We should go over and explore it soon. Climbing to the top of these hills should give us a good view of the rest of this island."

"Come on, we can climb up there now," Edward said.

"Right now I think we should get the boat unloaded and decide where to set up our camp," their mother said, redirecting their energy.

They unloaded the longboat and carried the provisions to their new campground near the stream. Elizabeth took an inventory as the boys recovered the longboat. The evening sun painted the sky in pinks, grays, and blues.

"We've covered up the powder, shot, and weapons under a tarp over there," James announced.

"We didn't bring along very much in the way of food," Elizabeth said as she handed everyone a hardtack biscuit.

"We can catch some fish to eat," offered James.

"Should we build a fire?" Edward asked.

"No," his mother said. "Not tonight—I'm sure Captain Bouchet is still searching for us."

"How'll we know when he stops looking for us?" Edward asked.

"We won't. But thanks to Claire's seamanship, we can enjoy our liberty once again."

They slept huddled together on a piece of canvas spread out on the ground, with another piece of sailcloth hanging above them from ropes strung around four trees. No one slept well among the chirps, squawks, and rustles of the jungle.

The cries of gulls announced the arrival of morning well before first light. Claire awoke and walked down to the water's edge.

Are you out there? Claire's mind called.

Yes, we're here, Nami said.

This is a beautiful place. Thank you for leading us to this island.

It should be a perfect place for you to hide for a time.

What of the pirates?

They sailed far to the north. They have turned and are coming back this way. Members of our family are following them.

Will they pass by here?

We think they will, but remember, they must stay to the east of this land in deeper water.

That's good, but they could lower boats and come around to this side.

If they do that, we'll warn you and give you time to hide or sail away.

We'll be ready, Claire said.

Elizabeth and the boys woke up, and they ate a few more of their provisions.

"We should try to find some fresh food," Elizabeth said.

"Maybe we should hide the boat better," James added.

Just past the stream and up the beach to the north, a rocky outcropping curved to form a slight breakwater. After breakfast, they decided the first course of business for this morning would be to find a better hiding spot for the longboat.

After uncovering the longboat, everyone pushed and shoved to dislodge it from the beach. The boys rowed behind the rocks, and by midmorning had succeeded in hiding it.

"Well done, boys." Claire slapped James on the back. "We must keep her ready to sail at any moment. Make sure there's a keg of water in her at all times."

Everyone agreed.

"I think we should explore this island," James said.

Edward chimed in, "Come on, Mum, Claire. Let's climb to the top of the hills."

"Why don't we follow the stream? Then maybe we can find the source of the water," Claire said.

At times the lush jungle made it difficult to walk, but the boys ran ahead of the two women.

"Mum," Phillip called back. "Look at the strange fruit."

Elizabeth pulled a piece of the green fruit off the tree and sniffed it.

"What could it be?" Claire asked. "Do you think it's edible?"

"I think I remember it from one of the books we were reading before we left Ireland." Edward took a nibble. "It is very hard. I think if we let it ripen, it could be fine." Everyone smiled at Edward's analysis.

"That book you and the boys were studying had sketches of fruits and vegetables, as well as maps and charts. It's the one volume we should have brought with us," Elizabeth said.

"I thought of it last night. I left all my books as well. The Bard and his wonderful sonnets are in the hands of those animals. I'm sure none of those pigs can read; I hope they don't destroy the books. No matter now. I'm sure we can find plenty of things to eat on this island, though I don't think coconuts will sustain us," Claire said.

"Mum! Claire!" James yelled. "We found it! Come on!"

The women climbed onto a small plateau, where a gentle waterfall cascaded from a bubbling sapphire pool. Behind the pool, a grotto curved into the hillside, below the summit. Dark-green ferns and vines surrounded the entrance to the shallow cave. "This could be a perfect place to locate our camp," Edward said. "We could hide in the cave, and it would give us shelter from the rain."

"That's a good idea, Edward. But it was quite a climb to get here," Elizabeth said. "I think we'll be better off down near the beach."

"But this would be a good place to hide, or take shelter in a storm," Claire said.

The boys continued their climb to the summit. Phillip called down, "Mother, Claire, come quickly! A ship!"

"Get down, boys. Get out of sight," Claire hissed. They dropped down immediately.

Claire and Elizabeth crawled to the bare rocks at the top of the hill, where the boys lay flat on the ground. "Crawl over here," Claire said. "Were you standing in plain sight for long?"

"No, only for a moment," Phillip said.

"That was stupid," James said.

"Shut up, James. You would've been standing there too, if you had gotten up on the rocks before me."

"Remember, if it's Bouchet and his men, their spyglasses will be scanning these islands. We can't allow them to see any sign of us," Claire said.

Claire poked her head above the rocks. "It is the *Brilliant*. If she furls her sails, our plan will be to get to the longboat and sail west. Remember, boys, we must stay hidden until we're sure that any ship we see is a British warship. Only then should we reveal ourselves and signal them."

The *Brilliant* continued sailing to the south. They all breathed a sigh of relief.

James fashioned spears out of long pieces of bamboo, and the boys poked and stabbed their way all over the island in the next few days. Young Phillip became adept at shinnying to the tops of the coconut palms and dropping down the greenish-brown nuts. They searched the dense jungle, finding strange and wonderful fruits and berries. Hundreds of macaws and parrots, costumed in vivid blues, greens, yellows, and reds, squawked in a cacophony of sounds that pierced through the canopy covering the island. The boys, Elizabeth, and Claire followed the incessant noise.

"There they are," Claire pointed. "The parrots are eating the green fruit on those trees."

"If the birds are eating those, we should be able to eat them," Edward said.

"I'm not sure, but we should try," Claire said. "Shoo them away and let's pick some."

"The last thing I tried tasted bitter. I got a stomachache," Phillip said.

"I'll try it first this time," James said.

Back at their camp, the group sat around on a piece of canvas with the dozen or so strange fruits piled in front of them. Edward picked up a yellow fruit the size of his fist. "This one is part lime, part lemon, and part something else; the juice is sour but good."

Elizabeth pointed to another one. "That brown, fuzzy one there has a firm, sweet, and exotic-tasting meat inside. Maybe I can grow them in my garden one day." Everyone smiled.

Edward sliced the apple-sized green fruit in half. He sniffed it. Then he gently touched the tip of his tongue to the bright pink flesh as the group watched. He grinned, took a tiny nibble, then a bigger bite. They all took a taste and Edward named them "pink apples." The little green fruit became a favorite at every meal.

———

Claire walked the beach alone in the afternoon.

Good news, a dolphin called out. *One of our family just returned from Jamaica. The men in the three longboats arrived in Port Royal.*

That's wonderful news. I think of them every day. I'm sure Lord Radstone has begun searching for us. Of course, he doesn't know of our escape.

We'll tell you if he sails near here. The pirates that held you continue to sail in these waters. Some of our friends are following their ships, Nami said. *You must stay hidden.*

I understand, but we can't stay on this island forever. We must head for Jamaica as soon as it's safe.

I know, Nami said. *At least for now you're in a good place.*

Is there enough to eat? Sanjay asked.

We're fine. There's plenty of fruit, and we have caught crabs and lobsters in the rocks. Catching fish has been difficult.

Yes, we watched the boys with their spears, Bolo said. *They're not very quick, but we can help them. Tell them to stand at the water's edge tomorrow morning. We'll chase the fish to them.*

A huge male swam toward the beach, spun in the shallow water, and flipped a large, light-brown shell onto the beach.

Here, pry the flesh out of it. The islanders eat them. You can dive down in the shallow waters just off the beach, where they crawl on the bottom.

Claire inspected the coconut-sized, cone-shaped shell with a spiral pattern. She turned it over to reveal a flared slit where subtle colors of beige, white, and pink blended. A piece of grayish-brown flesh contracted deep inside. To Claire it looked like a giant snail. She took it back to the others.

"I found this near the rocks where the boat is." Claire plopped the shell down on the bamboo tabletop. "I think it might taste like a clam or an oyster, or maybe even a mussel from Bantry Bay."

"Mussels poached in white wine; I've dreamt of it," Elizabeth said with a longing look and a shake of her head.

"We'll be having them again soon enough," Claire said.

Boiled, then roasted, the chewy flesh made a tasty meal.

"We should find more of these tomorrow," James said. "Do you think they're near shore?"

"I don't know, but since it does remind me of Bantry mussels, we should try to find more," Claire said. "I saw the dolphins chasing fish near the shore. In the morning, bring your spears so we might catch something if the dolphins chase some fish into the shallows."

"We can try," Edward said, "and tomorrow we'll dive down and find more of these shelled creatures."

"I think they would make a very nice stew—if we could add a few carrots and onions to the pot," Elizabeth said.

"And potatoes," Claire added.

"Yes, a touch of Ireland wouldn't be so bad," said James.

By first light, the boys couldn't wait to get into the water to search for the sea snails. They found ten of them and piled them on the beach. Elizabeth gathered four in her arms and set off down the beach.

"Where are you going?" asked Edward.

"I'm going to put these in the tidal pool over among the rocks. If they stay there in the water and don't escape, we'll be able to pluck one up for dinner whenever we want."

"A smashing idea, Mum," James called.

Phillip pointed. "There they are. The dolphins." Gray dorsal fins cut through the surface, then curved back under.

"Quick, boys, get your spears," yelled Claire.

"What should we do?" asked James.

"I've seen the dolphins chase fish into the very shallow water until the fish cannot swim anymore and the dolphins grab them.

Stand just at the water's edge. If they chase a fish past you, spear it. Get one for dinner."

There's a fine school of mackerel out here. We'll drive some past you.

"Get ready, boys."

The dolphins swam away from the boys, then turned and pushed the fish toward the beach.

"We're in the wrong place." Edward ran down the beach.

"No, wait," Claire said.

The surface of the water boiled and seethed as the fish panicked. The dolphins turned back parallel to the beach, swimming faster and faster at a flat angle, maneuvering the fish toward the edge of the water.

The fish, in no more than six inches of water, scurried past the boys. The dolphins planed next to the fish, keeping them from escaping back to the deep and safety.

The boys jabbed, but no one found the mark.

"They're moving too fast," Phillip cried.

What happened? Sanjay asked.

The boys didn't realize how fast the fish would be coming. They missed. Can you try again?

I don't think the boys are very good at catching fish, Bolo said with a laugh.

The dolphins circled out into deeper water for a bit, and then they herded the fish back toward the shore. "I think they're going to do it again, lads. Be ready," Claire said.

First Phillip, then Edward and James stood in ankle-deep water, forming a line. Claire and Elizabeth, holding long wooden spears, joined in. "Here they come!" the boys shouted.

"Be quick now!" James yelled. Three, four, five wiggling fish darted by. They thrust their spears into the water and missed, except James.

"I got one! I got one!" A two-foot-long silver mackerel wiggled on the end of James's spear. They cheered as the fish flopped around on the sand.

"A fine, fat fish," Elizabeth said, grabbing it by the tail. "Well done, James."

That evening Elizabeth turned the spit as the fish roasted. The conversation turned to the dolphins.

"They helped us today, that's for sure," James said.

"And the whales, what about the whales?" Phillip asked.

"They were swimming near us," Edward said. "But I'm curious. The dolphins were always around you in Bantry, Claire, and now they're around you again. I wonder why?"

"I'm not sure, but they've helped all of us here. Maybe dolphins everywhere enjoy helping humans whenever they can."

James looked at Edward and then at Phillip. They all nodded in agreement.

"You're right," Phillip said. "Dolphins saved me from drowning."

Elizabeth stopped turning the spit and looked at Phillip, wide-eyed. "What? When?"

The boys told the story. As the tale unfolded, Lady Radstone's furrowed brow relaxed. Elizabeth took the fish off the fire.

"An amazing story," Claire said. "These playful creatures surely want to be our friends and maybe help us."

Everyone dug into the fish. Edward wanted to question Claire further, but decided to wait for another day.

Claire realized that her secret would only become more difficult to maintain. She wondered if she could ever explain the dolphins' behavior without breaking her word. She was relieved when the discussion shifted to another subject. After talking it over, the group agreed that they should develop a plan if they hoped to be rescued or to escape.

The next day, they gathered a six-foot-high pile of sticks and wood on the bare rocks on the highest hill. Every day they took turns standing watch with the spyglass, looking for a friendly ship to signal. No one was allowed to ignite the bonfire alone. There had to be unanimous agreement as to the ship's friendly nature; only then would they light the fire. From time to time, a call echoed down from the watch and everyone climbed to the crest of the hill. The few ships they did see either were too far away or did not fly a friendly flag.

Chapter 15

Spiny Things

These days Claire slept less than she had before. The dolphins had swum through her mind for the past few months and kept her from deep sleep; now the night sounds of the island made things worse. A vivid picture of her mother's body and the sharks came to her every night. Claire fought to keep her nightly weeping silent. She knew the lack of sleep and the sadness was wearing her down.

She watched Elizabeth roll out of her hammock and walk down the beach. Claire ducked out from under the canvas tarpaulin and stretched in the muted morning light.

She followed Elizabeth but stopped at the stream. As she threw water on her face, she heard a scream and then her name. She clambered across the gulley and ran toward the tidal pool. Soaking wet, Elizabeth screamed as she crawled across the algae-covered rocks. Claire grabbed her arms and pulled her over the slippery rocks.

"My foot. Oh God, my foot." Elizabeth's face contorted in agony as she took short, quick breaths. Claire saw blood running in the water. Claire gasped when she realized what had happened. A huge, round, black, spiny creature was stuck to the bottom of Elizabeth's foot, with the spines piercing through.

Elizabeth clenched her teeth in pain. "I slipped and stepped down with my full weight. God help me. Get it off."

Claire reached under Elizabeth's arms, pulling her over the rocks and onto the sand. "Boys! Boys! Help! Quickly!"

James flipped out of his hammock and ran down the beach. Edward and Phillip followed.

"What happened?" James saw the foot. "Mum."

Edward and Phillip, seeing the black spiny thing stuck in their mother's foot, slid to a stop in the sand.

They carried her back to camp and laid her on a piece of canvas. "Roll that cask over here and rest her leg on it," Claire said, as she sat on a cask facing the bleeding foot. "James, hold her leg steady. Phillip and Edward, hold your mother's arms. Elizabeth, I'm going to pry this thing off your foot. Hold on. Try and stay still."

Two of the spines, like black nails, drove through and stuck out the top of the foot. Claire took a long, thin knife, slid the flat blade against the bottom of Elizabeth's foot, and carefully pried off the black pincushion of a creature.

Elizabeth cried out in pain; her whole body tensed as the boys tightened their hold on her.

"Hang on, Elizabeth." Claire worked until the spiny thing fell away. "There are still four of these spines; two of them pushed through the top of your foot. This will hurt."

Elizabeth clenched her teeth and grimaced. Claire pulled and the black needles slid out as Elizabeth screamed. One of the spines broke as Claire tried to work it out, and she feared a piece of the spine remained deep in Elizabeth's foot. "James, get my petticoat and we will make bandages. Edward, get two cups of rum. Give one to your mother and hand me the other. Phillip, hold your mother."

Edward helped his mother drink the rum, while Claire dipped a cloth in the alcohol and tried to clean the wounds. She wrapped Elizabeth's foot and, with the boys' help, laid her in her hammock.

The boys hovered around their mother, who lay there wincing from the pain, as Claire walked to the stream to wash away some of the blood.

Claire, are you there? Nami called.

Yes, Nami.

We felt trouble in your mind.

My friend stepped on one of those black spiny creatures. She is badly hurt. I pulled the spines out of her foot. Are they poisonous?

Some of them are, Nami said.

I must tend to her.

We'll be nearby.

Elizabeth moaned, twitching and tossing in her hammock. "The rum has made her sleep. Come away from her for now; let her rest," Claire said.

"Will she be all right?" Phillip asked.

"I don't think we can do anything else for now. We'll try to keep her comfortable and I'll change the bandage every few hours."

The boys went to gather fruit, and Claire sat on a keg next to Elizabeth.

I won't tell them about the poison. Why worry them? Maybe there is no poison. She's sleeping—that's a good thing. Oh, Lord—she can't die. First my mother, and now this. Please, God, let there be no poison. She must survive. She can't die. But what if she dies?

Claire and the boys spent a sleepless night, taking turns sitting next to Elizabeth. Through the next day and night, Elizabeth tossed and turned, shivering with cold and burning with fever. Claire changed the bloody bandages. By the third day, blue and red skin stretched over the bloated foot, while dark, reddish-black pus oozed from the puncture holes.

Elizabeth raised her head. "How is it?"

"The bleeding has stopped, but it is very swollen," Claire said.

Elizabeth's head fell back into the hammock. "Phillip, I am so very hot. Can you get me some water?" A cool breeze blew across the beach and rustled the palms.

Claire walked down the beach. *Are you there?*

Yes, Claire, Sanjay said.

My friend is not doing well. I fear her wounds are infected. I believe she is in grave danger. Have you seen any British warships?

No, Nami said. *No one in our family has seen any ships flying the red flag in weeks. We have only seen pirates and slavers.*

I need to take her to a doctor.

You could go to Nassau, Bolo said.

Yes, Nassau. Many people live there and maybe there will be a ship in the harbor, Sanjay said.

It will take you two or three days, depending on the wind. We will guide you and warn you of any ships, Nami said.

I'll go. Claire walked back to the camp, gesturing to the boys to join her.

"Boys, the foot is looking bad. It's infected, and your mum could die from the infection. We've got to get her to a doctor."

Phillip started to cry, and the others looked shocked. "We should sail for Jamaica," James said.

"No. I'll take her to Nassau. It's the closest and safest place."

"We'll go with you," Edward said.

"No, I'd better go alone. If I run across Bouchet or some other pirate ship, at least you three will still be free, and your mother may survive."

"Where's Nassau? How will you find it?" James asked.

"Lieutenant Garrison showed me the charts as we sailed south. I'm sure it's to the north of us along these islands. I'll sail northward. Help me get the boat loaded; we've got to hurry."

James shook his head. "You can't know where we are, and you can't know where Nassau is."

"I'll find it, hurry."

They began to place things in the boat. James took Claire aside. "We should all go with you. It isn't right for you to do this alone. She's our mother."

"James, please. Stay here and stay alive."

"Then at least let me go with you. I can take care of Mum while you sail."

"We can't leave Edward and Phillip here alone. Enough—help me get this keg of water into the boat."

The boys completed the preparations by nightfall. Elizabeth lay in the bow of the boat in a stupor. "There will be a full moon, as good as daylight. Remember, boys, James is the oldest. I leave him in charge. Push us out."

Claire stepped into the longboat and hoisted the sail as the boys pushed the boat out into the gentle surf. The wind filled the sail as Claire took her seat at the tiller. "Take care of each other."

"Hurry back," James said. The boys waved.

"Godspeed!" Edward called.

Claire worked the sail and the tiller, turning north. She watched the boys walk down the beach as the tropical moon lit the landscape in a pearly glow. The boys stood at the northern point of the island and waved. Claire waved back.

Can you see us ahead of you? Nami asked.

Yes, I can see you and hear you.

Good, Sanjay said. *We will nudge your boat a little if we feel you moving off course. Members of our family are searching for ships.*

If you find a ship, you must tell me quickly and guide me to it. It doesn't matter what kind of a ship it is, just take me to it. It may be my friend's only chance. The dolphins said nothing.

From time to time Claire tied the tiller fast, moved forward, and sat with Elizabeth, cooling her face with a rag wet with seawater. At one point, Elizabeth roused from her stupor. Claire met her eyes, answering her unspoken question. "I am taking you to Nassau, where a doctor will help you."

She gazed at Claire through her delirium. "The boys...are the boys safe?"

"Yes. They're fine. We'll return for them once you are cared for."

"Claire, take care of the boys...Keep them safe."

"The boys will be fine, and you'll be taking care of them soon enough."

"Promise me you'll take care of the boys; promise me you'll take them to their father. Swear to me—please, swear to me."

"I swear; I swear the boys will see their father again."

Elizabeth lapsed back into a fitful sleep, moaning, her head moving from side to side. Claire felt her burning skin and knew she had only a short time to save her friend. She sailed into the next night, dozing off from time to time.

Claire heard from the dolphins again. *We sent a few of the fastest members of the pod ahead to Nassau to see if there are any ships there. They will be back by midday,* Sanjay said.

How much longer will it take me to sail to Nassau?

I think a day and a night, Nami said.

The sun rose, beating down on the little boat. Claire rigged a piece of tarp over a rope to shade Elizabeth. Bathed in sweat, Elizabeth faded further into delirium, and her eyes rarely opened. Claire got her to drink a little water and some rum mixed with sour juice. She hoped the rum would allow Elizabeth some restful sleep. It did not.

Her leg swelled past the knee, making the red, blue, and purple skin as tight as a snare drum. A sickening, putrid odor came from the oozing bandaged foot. The wind strengthened, and the longboat heeled to starboard. Claire thought the additional speed might give Elizabeth a chance.

Two big males leaped out of the water coming from the north. *Two ships rest in Nassau. One is docked with no one aboard. The other was readying itself to sail.*

What kind of ships? Claire asked.

The one ship has cannons and could be a pirate ship. The other ship carries slaves, a dolphin answered.

There would be no doctor on that ship, Nami said. *They are evil ships.*

Claire nodded. The day wore on and the sun beat down. Elizabeth fell deeper into unconsciousness. Claire watched her chest heave as she labored to breathe, panting and gasping. Mercifully, the sun set, but then the sail luffed and the longboat slowed. Claire secured the boom and tied the tiller. She went forward and sat holding Elizabeth's head in her lap.

"Elizabeth. I am so sorry. First my mother, and now you," Claire brushed the tangled hair away from the woman's sweating face. She wiped Elizabeth's brow and cheeks with a rag dampened with seawater. Tears ran down Claire's cheeks as she rocked, holding Elizabeth as the night wore on.

Sometime in the night, Elizabeth took another short, irregular breath and exhaled—then nothing. No other sound or motion or even a twitch came from Elizabeth. Claire cried and sobbed. Exhausted, Claire lowered the sail. The boat drifted just off a small cay and Claire fell asleep holding Elizabeth.

Claire woke with the sun in her face and the sounds of dolphins breathing and small waves lapping against a shore. The longboat had drifted onto a beach. Claire brushed Elizabeth's hair from her forehead. Her skin was cold. Claire had never touched a dead person before. She stood and jumped into the shallow water. Hoping the cool water would soothe her and wash some of the sweat and smell out of her clothes, Claire moved out into deeper water. The dolphins gathered around her.

We can feel your sadness, said Nami.

I'll take her back to the island and give her a proper burial.

She died at sea. You should put her in the sea, Sanjay said.

The boys should remember their mother in a better way, Nami said, *and it will take you almost two days to get back to the island.*

She deserves a proper grave, Claire said.

My mother is right, Bolo said. *The oceans of the world will be her grave. Any time you look at the ocean, you will think of your mother and your friend.*

Claire waded back to the boat. She took off her clothes and draped them over the bow. She pushed and the boat moved away from the sand. She jumped up and into the longboat. *Help me. Push me out into deeper water.*

The dolphins nudged the boat out. With tears streaming down her face, Claire struggled to roll Elizabeth's body out of the longboat. Sobbing, she let go and watched her second mother sink in the calm, clear water. Outlined against the white bottom, the body looked like a statue resting in the sand. Her arms seemed to be ready to hold a visitor in a welcoming embrace and her hair took on an exotic and beautiful look as the tendrils splayed out, moving with the gentle pulse of the sea.

Claire sat there for a while, watching her friend at rest. After a time, she knew she needed to set a course. She considered going on to Nassau, but, with Elizabeth gone, she saw no reason to risk capture. She returned to the tiller and swung the boat toward the south. Naked, she sat there thinking about her life. Her mother and Elizabeth were gone, and now she was solely responsible for the lives of the Radstone boys. She had no one to turn to. She thanked God that the dolphins were always nearby. She sailed all day, through the night, and all the next day. Her head bobbed as she fell asleep from time to time. The dolphins kept her on course.

Claire recognized the shape of the hills as she sailed up to their island. The boys gathered on the beach while Claire pointed the boat toward the shore, sailing it onto the sand. "We saw you coming from above. You've been out for three days. How is Mum?" asked James, as his hopeful yet desperate eyes bored into Claire.

Claire, her heart heavy, lowered the sail.

"Is Mother being cared for? Is she well?" Edward asked.

"When can we see her?" Phillip said.

A bit of panic came into James's voice. "Where is she? Where's Mum, Claire?"

The dread of this moment gripped her as Claire stepped out of the boat. She looked at them, tears rolling down her cheeks. "Your mother is gone."

Phillip cried, "What do you mean, gone? Where is she?"

"Your mother died yesterday and I buried her at sea. She died in my arms."

The boys gasped and sobbed. Claire reached out, pulling the boys to her and hugging them. James pushed away, tears streaming down his cheeks. "You dumped her into the sea? Why? You should've brought her back to us."

"She deserved a proper burial," Edward said.

Claire stepped back and stared at the three of them. "There was nothing else I could do." Claire and the three boys silently walked toward the camp.

They sat around the fire, and quiet sobbing mixed with the crackling of the flames. Claire broke the silence. "Boys, listen to me. Your mother died at sea and she rests with my mother. Every time you gaze upon this or any other beautiful ocean, you'll remember your mother." No one spoke.

In the morning, they gathered at the northern end of the island and waded out into the shallow water. Each held a single flower.

"Goodbye, Mum. I'll always love you." James threw his flower in the water.

"You're resting beneath the waves and you'll always rest in my heart," Edward said.

Phillip placed his pink hibiscus on the water. "Don't worry, Mum, I'll remember, 'the only thing that separates us from the animals is our manners.'"

Claire spoke a little louder than the boys. "Elizabeth, I know you and Mary are holding hands right now and looking down on us. I promise you, we'll be safe. We will survive, and the boys will be reunited with their father."

Far out, Sanjay's dorsal fin cut through the waves. *What are you doing?*

We're saying farewell to Elizabeth.

But she's already dead.

We're talking to her spirit, her soul.

You must tell me of this soul.

Someday.

Chapter 16

A New Alliance

The sun began to warm them. Claire held her and gently stroked her hair. Elizabeth's lifeless face rested peacefully on Claire's lap. The image haunted Claire. For the Radstones, however, grief gave way to the daily routine, and time wore away some of the sadness. The boys took more and more initiative to ensure their survival. They gathered food, explored the island, gradually got better at catching fish, and taught themselves how to swim in the surf. For swimming, the boys wore breeches that they raggedly cut off above the knee. Claire swam in a blouse with no sleeves, knotted in the front, and a pair of torn-off, shortened bloomers. The dolphins continued to help them catch fish and often swam with them, leaping and squeaking.

First Claire, then the boys learned to hold onto the dolphins' dorsal fins as the dolphins pulled them through the water at fantastic speeds. The laughter and happy shouts would go on for hours; the dolphins never tired of pulling the boys.

Claire enjoyed swimming with the dolphins, but she also spent time sitting on the rocks at the top of the hill looking out at the deep water. She prayed for a British ship to pass. Ships did sail by. Not one of them flew the Union Jack. James made sure someone always manned the lookout.

Most days, when not gathering food, Claire walked the beaches, thinking. This day, she sat on the beach, drew up her legs, and rested her head on her knees. She again thought about the twists and turns of her life. She had sworn to the Virgin Mary, Saint Patrick, *and* the surprisingly eloquent Patrick Keenan that she would return to Bantry. She wondered what her life in Bantry would be like without her mother and the Radstones. No matter, she mused, she had made a promise and she would keep it. Maybe the people of Bantry had already forgotten about her. Maybe no one cared if she returned. Claire decided to think about this another day. First she had to get off this island, and take the boys to safety. She stood up, took a deep breath, wiped her face, and began walking back to the camp.

Nami swam near the shore. *You are troubled.*

I am thinking about my life.

Remember, we are your friends, and we are here to help you.

Thank you, Nami.

———

"You've been very quiet lately." James looked at her across the glowing embers of the dying fire. Claire gazed back at their three faces, illuminated by the fading yellowish light. She stirred the coals with a stick, putting two more pieces of wood on the hot coals.

"I've been thinking about how we might leave this place. We can't stay here forever, and we never see a friendly sail on the horizon. Last week we only saw one ship; she carried plenty of cannons and flew no flag—a pirate ship, for sure."

"How long do you think we've been here?" Edward asked.

James said, "It has to be at least six months."

"It could be more than that," Claire said.

"I wonder if father thinks we're dead," Phillip said.

"I'm sure he's searching for us, and I know he's thinking about you lads every day," Claire said.

"It's a huge ocean with thousands of islands," said James. "He could search for us for years and never come close to this place."

Claire poked at the fire again with her knife. "You're right. That's why my thoughts keep turning toward sailing to Nassau, but I'm afraid if we put out to sea and come upon a pirate ship, we may not be as lucky as we were before. At least this island shields us—on the sea we are in full view."

"But you never made it to Nassau," James said. "Do you think you can find it?"

"I think so."

"If you go again, we should all go with you," James said.

"Yes, you'll need some protection. We have our pistols. We could hold off any pirates," Edward said.

James stood at the fire. "One of us should go with you. An extra pistol or two would be helpful."

"Maybe so, I just want to—"

She saw him in the flickering light. Just beyond the camp, he stood motionless behind the trunk of a coconut palm, though not hiding. The yellow, flickering fire revealed his dark body, which otherwise blended into the shadows of the jungle.

Claire raised her hand, palm out, and with the other hand, slowly picked up her pistol. "Lads, stay still."

"Why?" Edward asked.

"Gentlemen, be calm; we have a visitor."

James spun; the boys grabbed pistols and spears, scrambling to their feet. The dark man flinched. Claire walked past the boys and stopped. The boys fell in behind her. The young man stepped back, holding his spear upright.

"Pirates," Edward whispered.

"I don't think so. Be slow and easy, boys."

"Hello, there." Claire forced a smile. "I am Claire—Claire Riley. And who might you be?"

The flickering flames highlighted a string of bright white shells of every size and shape against the dark-brown chest of the man. From what she could make of his facial features, he was not an African, and he was certainly not a white man. Around his waist, tied with hide, was a piece of faded brown cloth, which hung down to the middle of his thighs. A broad-brimmed hat of woven palm leaves covered his head, hiding his eyes in shadow. His black hair fell to his shoulders.

A rustle in the darkness brought another quiet form into the faint light. Then another came from the other side. Claire's eyes cut back and forth. The two moved closer to the man in the straw hat.

James pulled back the hammer on the pistol he held at his side. The unmistakable click cracked the silence, and the dark people stepped back into the shadows.

Claire kept smiling. In a calm, commanding tone, she said, "James, there'll be no need for that. Step back and give our visitors a little more room."

The boys moved around the fire. Claire walked backward, beckoning the visitors closer. The young man, a younger girl, and a much older man stepped into the light of the camp. The two men wore hats woven of palm fronds and pieces of cloth hanging from their waists. The young girl wore a European-style cotton dress of very bright reds and blues. Her long, shiny black hair flowed almost to her waist.

Claire beckoned again. They took a few steps forward, but not close to the fire. Each of them carried a bow draped across one shoulder. For a while no one spoke. Claire motioned for them to come closer to the fire. No one moved. The two groups stared at each other as the fire dwindled.

"What should we do?" James said.

"Nothing," said Claire.

"I don't think they want to hurt us," Phillip said.

The old man said something; the three visitors backed into the darkness.

Claire moved toward them. "Wait, don't go."

"We will be back tomorrow," the young man said.

"You speak English?"

All three disappeared into the jungle.

The boys jabbered softly. "Who are they?"

"Indians, of course. Natives of these lands. Remember the book about the Americas?"

"They couldn't live here. We've searched every inch of this island."

"They must've just landed here."

"They saw our fire."

"I wonder where their boat is."

"We can try to find it in the morning."

"Enough, lads," said Claire. "I don't think they intend to harm us. They could have easily attacked us before we ever saw them. Let's be careful and keep a lookout through the night. James, you and Edward take the first watch. Wake Phillip and me later. Keep the fire burning, and keep a pistol near you."

The boys peered into the dark. No one slept much.

Morning came. Claire and the boys sat in camp, eating some pink apples for breakfast.

"Shall we go to our lookout post?" Phillip asked.

"No," Claire said, "not today. Let's keep together near the beach for now. As I said last night, I don't think they intend to harm us, but we should be ready." Claire put a pistol in her belt.

The noonday sun beat down, and Edward stood at the water's edge. He turned and ran toward the camp. "Here they come."

The three Indians walked along the beach toward them. The young man approached Claire. He walked straight up to her. Whatever shyness he might have had last night was gone. The others stood back a few paces. "I am Kataga. My sister is Ada. My grandfather is called Gani."

"Where are you from? Where did you learn English?"

"There are not too many of us and we move from island to island. Our people traded with white sailors for a long time. My sister and I learned from them."

"Please, sit and eat with us. This is James, Edward, and Phillip, and I am Claire."

They sat in the camp together.

"Does Gani speak English?" Claire asked.

"He understands much but does not speak your language. He does not trust white people. None of our people listened to him, and now most of them are dead or gone."

"What do you mean?" Claire asked.

"Pirates came to our island. They killed many of our people and took the rest away in chains."

"They burned our village; they killed my mother and father," Ada said.

"My God," Edward said. "Almost the same thing happened to us. Pirates attacked our ship and captured us. We escaped and found this place."

"We have the same enemy," Kataga said.

"Yes," said Claire. "The pirates killed my mother, too. We should join together, and be friends."

"Friends," Kataga said. He translated to his grandfather.

Gani pointed at James and said something to his grandson.

"My grandfather says he wants you to give us guns and teach us how to use them," Kataga said.

Claire reached over and picked up the pistol sitting on the keg next to James. "What are you doing?" James hissed.

"Quiet." Claire stood and, with two hands, handed the pistol to Gani.

Gani reached out and took the pistol. He held it as if he were holding a newborn baby. Then he rose and handed the pistol back to Claire. He spoke and the others stood.

"We will be back soon," Ada said, smiling.

———

Gani set about gathering palm fronds and pieces of bamboo. Phillip climbed trees with Ada and Kataga, cutting down a large number of palm fronds. Working together, they soon constructed three huts with peaked roofs. When the first rain came, much to the surprise of Claire and the boys, not a drop of water leaked in. The roofs, made of thick layers of palm fronds, dried to a light tan color over the next several weeks. With no walls in the huts to block it, the cool ocean breeze gently rocked the hammocks. Claire and Ada slept in one, Kataga and Gani shared the second, and the Radstone boys shared the third. They built a fourth hut for the storage of food and supplies.

Claire thought Kataga was probably slightly older than she was. Ada and James were about the same age. Ada was not a little girl anymore. No one could guess Gani's age. The old man's weathered skin attested to his advanced years, yet his nimbleness and stamina always amazed his young companions. Gani spoke little. He always worked and was happy to teach. The old man taught his new friends about wonderful medicines and dangerous poisons found in nature. He showed them where they could find many different things to eat and how to fashion the most intricate weavings for hats, baskets, and mats.

Kataga and Ada taught Claire and the boys how to swim and dive with greater skill. The boys loved to swim in the clear, warm ocean and did so almost every day. Claire often thought of the first time Ada pulled her dress over her head, threw it on the sand, and ran into the surf. The boys had stood in the water, eyes wide, gaping. She only wore a thin hide strip around her waist to which she had knotted a piece of cloth in the front, pulled it between her legs, and then tied it in the back. The patch of cloth did not conceal much, and Ada's long, black hair did little to cover the rest of her womanly body.

The boys never talked about Ada openly. Claire knew they whispered among themselves. Ada swam with the boys almost every day. Claire thought about discussing the concept of European female modesty with Ada, but never got around to it. Besides, she realized they were not in Europe now but in Ada's homeland. Claire soon exchanged her bulky bloomers for Ada's freer-style bottoms, although she used a larger piece of cloth and kept her sleeveless blouse for the top. Claire thought about doing away with the blouse. A smile tempered with a little sadness came to Claire as she thought of what her mother's reaction would have been to her running into the surf covered with only a patch of cloth. Claire concluded that in her new role as mother and leader, wearing the blouse was probably a good idea.

Gani made bows and fashioned dozens of arrows and spears. Claire and the boys practiced for hours, eventually becoming accomplished archers. They never became as good as Kataga or Ada, and could only dream of being as accurate as Gani. In the eyes of the boys, the old man's skill with a bow took on a mystical quality. Kataga, Ada, and Gani quickly mastered firing pistols and muskets. They cherished these weapons and kept them close. The old man always carried his bow and arrows.

On an early morning, Phillip and Gani walked down the beach. A large gathering of gulls stood ahead of them, curiously all facing in the same direction—out to sea. Gani pointed and then motioned toward his mouth with his hand. "Mmmm, good."

"I've never eaten a sea gull."

Gani held his hand out to Phillip, motioning him to stay back. He drew an arrow from his quiver and walked toward the gulls. The gulls fluttered and Gani fired. Feathers flew as the bird fell. Phillip ran to Gani wide-eyed. "You hit him on the fly. You shot a flying bird from the sky."

Gani smirked, picked up the bird, and handed it to Phillip.

That evening, six birds roasted on a spit turned by James.

"He must have hit them as they stood on the sand," Edward said.

"No, I tell you," Phillip said, "most of them were flying. He hit two of them above our heads. He only missed a few times. Go with him; you'll see."

"Amazing," Claire said.

"I think it tastes a little like pigeon," James said.

"Maybe a bit like duck," Edward said.

"Well, it's definitely good, but I think I prefer fish to these," Claire said. "And I do love the giant sea snails soaked in the sour juice. We would have never known about that if you hadn't shown us."

"The juice makes the meat tender," Ada said in her quiet way.

With Ada's help, Edward became the best at weaving palm fronds into very practical hats. He made tall hats and hats with wide brims. Claire cherished the pointed admiral's hat Edward made for her. The palm hats started out green, but faded to a light tan in the tropical sun.

Claire picked up a small basket, woven of bright-green fronds. "A nice piece of work. When you get to England, you could do very well for yourself making these things."

Edward stopped working on his basket. "For one thing, Claire, there are no palms in England...and I doubt we'll ever see Ireland or England again."

Claire got up from the keg she had been sitting on. "Listen to me, lads. We will see your father, and we will see Bantry. There will be a day of reckoning for the jackals that caused the deaths of your mother, my mother, and the good seamen of the *Brilliant*. I swore to your mother that you would see your father, and see your father you shall." Claire sat back down. The boys remained silent, weaving their palm fronds.

———

The first time Kataga, Ada, and Gani saw the dolphins chasing fish to the shore, they laughed and screamed. Gani ran along the beach, chattering in his native tongue.

"My grandfather says there is powerful magic between you and the dolphins," Ada said.

The boys and Claire struggled, but managed to spear a fish or two. When Gani stood in shallow water with his bow drawn, the success of the fishing changed. He never seemed to be concentrating—then, with a twitch, he would fire, and rarely miss. He hit a smallish mackerel, pulled his arrow out, and tossed the fish out into deep water as he yelled out across the waves.

"What did he say?" asked Edward.

"My grandfather thanks the dolphins for their help," said Kataga. "He said they must share in the catch."

The boys and Claire appreciated Gani's wisdom; they threw a few more fish out into the water.

That night they ate a delightful meal of roasted fish, along with some tropical fruits, nuts, berries, and roots. Edward sliced open a brown, fuzzy piece of fruit. "I really do like these; they taste like they're part apple and part pear, but softer and juicier. Mum liked them as well. She talked about bringing the seeds back to Ireland and planting them in…" Edward looked up to see three sad faces looking back at him.

Claire broke the silence. "We shall take the seeds back with us and grow them in her honor. They will probably need to be planted in the greenhouse. I don't think these tropical plants will do well in the cold."

Claire picked up a brownish piece of root and tried to change the subject. "This reminds me of potatoes back in Ireland."

"More like a parsnip, I think," James said.

"Tell me about Ireland," Ada said. "Where is Ireland?"

"Far to the north. It is beautiful and green like here, but much colder for about half the year," Claire said.

"Is it as cold as the night wind up on the hill?"

"Much colder than that—bitterly cold."

"I don't think I would like the cold."

"No, I don't think you would." Claire smiled. "I'm starting to realize I could do without the cold weather myself."

"My grandfather says the dolphins come because of you." Kataga pointed at Claire.

Claire said nothing. She stirred the fire, while Gani stared at her as the embers began to fade to darkness.

───

The dolphins always came close when their human friends swam. James and Claire sat on the beach as Phillip, Ada, and Edward bobbed out in the water.

"Slap down on the water again," Claire called out to them.

Kataga and his grandfather jogged up the beach.

Gani pointed and shouted.

"There they are," Kataga said.

The dolphins jumped as they sped toward them. Five dolphins came at them and circled, rubbing against the swimmers.

Are you going to come in? Nami asked.

No, not today, Claire said.

The boys and Ada grabbed onto the dorsal fins of the dolphins. They held on, screaming and laughing, as the powerful dolphins pulled them. The dolphins swam faster and faster; the yelling and cheering became louder and louder.

Ada swam out in deeper water. She waved. "Watch. Watch what I will do." She took a deep breath and disappeared under the water.

Nothing happened for a moment.

"Where did she go?" Kataga stood at the water's edge.

Ada burst out of the water with her body straight, her arms at her sides, and facing skyward.

The huge and powerful Stark thrust Ada up with his nose nuzzled against the bottom of one of her feet. The giant dolphin and the young woman flew as one with foam and spray falling away. As Stark leapt skyward and reached the apex, they separated. Stark turned and dove, hitting the water in the exact spot where he had emerged. Ada flew up a little higher, gracefully spun, arched over, and, with her black hair trailing behind, dove back into the ocean.

"Oh, my God." Claire clapped.

"Magnificent!" James yelled.

"I don't believe it," Claire said.

Gani danced on the beach, laughing.

Ada popped to the surface and waved. She took a breath, went under, and flew again. Stark laughed. *This one swims like us, and I can make her fly like a bird. She weighs no more than a good-sized mackerel.*

Phillip ran into the water. "Show me how, Ada. How did you get them to do that?"

"I'm not sure, but I'll show you what I did. Swim down deep, make your body stiff, and put your arms tight against your sides.

Cross your legs and make your foot flat and the dolphin will put his nose against your foot. The dolphins will do the rest."

Soon, the dolphins threw the boys into the air repeatedly. Ada and the powerful Stark always flew the highest. Claire and Kataga joined in, too, while Gani watched from the beach.

Chapter 17

Gold

C laire woke to the sound of the three boys talking on the beach.
"It's your turn, that's all," Edward said.

"I don't care. It's no use," said Phillip.

"Today could be the day," James said.

"None ever do come, or they sail too far away. Why bother going up there?" Phillip said.

"Don't act like that," James said. "Never mind—I'll go."

"Good."

Claire walked to them. "What's the problem, boys?"

"Phillip should be on spyglass duty this morning, and he doesn't want to go," Edward said.

"No British ship ever comes close to this island. If you want to go, here." Phillip threw the spyglass at James. James twitched as he tried to catch the spyglass. The brass cylinder fell in the sand.

"Pick that up," Claire said. "You need to go to your post and do your duty. We all have to do our part to get through this. Do you understand?"

Phillip grabbed the spyglass and stalked off.

"I'm going for a walk," Claire said.

Claire walked to the northern end of the island where the land came to a point and flattened out into the sea. Almost every day she came to this secluded place. Claire hung her tattered dress on a tree limb. She wore a piece of cloth fashioned the same as Ada's and a sleeveless shirt with the tails knotted in front. She floated face up in the water, listening to the gentle sound of the surf lapping against the beach.

Claire turned to see two dorsal fins curling back under.

Your mind feels troubled, Sanjay said.

It's time for us to leave this island, no matter what the risk.

You may not be safe at sea, said Sanjay. *We see the pirate and slave ships all the time. But we helped you before, and we will try to help you again.*

The longboat has been sitting in the water for some time now. We pulled it ashore, scraped the hull, and did our best to repair it. I fear if we wait much longer, it may not be seaworthy. I think I can sail it to Nassau. I am quite sure it would never make it to Jamaica. There should be a few good boats in Nassau.

Yes, a few small boats sit in the harbor and sometimes a larger ship or two. Ships visit there often, Nami said. *You could go there, hide, and wait. We could warn you if we found slave or pirate ships. It would be very dangerous.*

I think we must try. I only wish I had something to bargain with. Those swine took Lady Radstone's jewels.

The dolphin minds fell quiet.

That night, Claire gathered her band around the fire. "This morning, Phillip said something so very true. We may never get a ship to come here. We must go to Nassau, find a better boat, and somehow sail to Jamaica."

"How will we do that?" James asked.

"We might have to steal one."

"We'll go with you," Kataga said. "We'll sail our canoe along with you. My grandfather can show us the way."

"We can book passage on a ship in Nassau," Phillip said.

"How? We've got no money," Edward said.

"True, but if we told them who our father is, I'm sure a ship would take us," James said.

"Lads," Claire said, "you can't tell anyone your true identity. It's too dangerous. If we told men in Nassau the truth, we might become captives again."

They nodded. "I hadn't thought of that," said James.

That night Claire slept fitfully, thinking about the preparations and the dangers ahead.

Claire, Nami came to her mind. *Claire, wake up.*

I'm awake.

In the morning, come to the rocky end of the island. We want to show you something.

What is it?

Something to help you on your journey. Come alone tomorrow.

Claire did not sleep much. As the sky turned from black to gray, she walked toward the rocks at the southern end of the island. The dolphins swam in the cut between the two islands.

Nami, what do you want to show me?

Over there on the other island, in the rocks, there's a cave, Nami said.

I walked every inch of that island, Claire said. *I never saw a cave.*

The sea hides the entrance, Nami said. *The cave holds a great treasure.*

A treasure? Gold?

Yes, piles of chests, full of gold and silver.

Shall I show her, Mother?

Yes, go get one.

Bolo spun in the water and submerged at the rocks on the other side of the cut. He surfaced in front of Claire. She stepped in the water. Bolo rose and dropped a glittering piece from his mouth into her outstretched hand.

"Good Lord," she said. "A doubloon."

Those gold pieces cover the bottom of the cave.

Can I get in there?

Ride on my back. I'll take you in, Stark said. *The water doesn't fill the cave; you'll be able to breathe.*

Claire held on to Stark's dorsal fin as he swam across the cut. She drew a deep breath and they submerged. When they surfaced, Claire could see a broad, dry, sandy ledge at the far end of the cave. Decayed chests spilled their contents. Gold doubloons and silver pieces of eight carpeted the shelf. Claire swam over and crawled onto the ledge. A dark stone dome vaulted above. Light from the cave entrance made the water shine a crystalline blue. Wiggling white lines of illumination, reflected by the rippling water, danced on the black walls of the cave.

How did you find this place?

Our ancestors watched men put these chests in here long ago, Nami explained, as she surfaced in the cave. *Why they put this gold here, and who they were, has been lost in time.*

No human has been in this cave since those men sailed away. The dolphins who first saw them have long since gone, Sanjay added.

Why did you not tell me of this place before now?

The teachers told us that seeking gold and silver has always brought misery to humans.

How very true, but with this gold we have a chance to get to Jamaica.

Claire stood motionless for a moment as the coins blazed up at her, even in the imperfect light. She reached in, scooped up a handful, and watched them cascade back onto the pile.

With this gold, we could buy a fleet of ships.

You only need one, Nami said.

Claire removed the bandana she wore around her head, spread it out, and piled coins on it. She tied the corners of the cloth together and rode Stark back to the other side.

She sat against the rocks across from the barren island for some time, looking at the gold and thinking; then she began searching for a suitable hiding place. She found a loose stone leaning against the wall of rock, above the high tide line. She tugged on it and it fell away, revealing a hole. Claire got on her hands and knees and was able to squeeze into the hole. The hole narrowed to nothing a few feet in. A beetle ran over her hand; she flinched and bumped her head. Claire backed out of the hole, rubbed her head, and then dumped the coins in the opening, put the rock back, and ran back to the beach.

Stark, take me back to the cave.

What are you going to do? Nami asked.

I found a place to hide some of the gold. I want to put some more there. It'll be a way for me to explain how I found it. We'll keep the rest of the treasure hidden.

Back in the cave, Claire found some rotted leather bags and put some coins in them, to make it look like the gold had been in this new spot for a very long time. On her third trip from the cave, she filled her bandana again and carried a small wooden chest the size of a large loaf of bread. It was heavier than she first thought; she struggled with it, but managed to bring another one on her fourth trip.

The cavity glittered as Claire filled it with gold and silver coins. She put a few handfuls of coins in her bandana and maneuvered the stone to cover the opening. She stopped when the hiding place was just slightly uncovered.

The sun blazed high in the midday sky. Claire walked, and then started to run when she came in sight of the camp. Kataga tended to the cleaned fish hanging over a smoldering fire. Gani, Edward, and Phillip stood at the water's edge, spears in hand.

Claire yelled, "Come quickly!" She slid to her knees in the sand next to a woven mat.

"What?" Edward asked.

"Where's James?"

"Spyglass duty—Ada went with him," Edward said.

"Phillip, go get them."

"Why?"

Claire spilled the coins out on the mat. Edward dropped to his knees, grabbing a handful. "My God. Where did you find all this?"

"Phillip, go get them. Hurry."

James and Ada ran out from the jungle. James knelt down and picked up a coin. "A Spanish doubloon. This is a fortune."

"There's much more. Come on, I'll show you. Bring two or three baskets."

When they reached the rocks, Edward reached in and dug out a handful of the glittering gold. "Look, hundreds, maybe thousands of coins."

"I was sitting on these rocks and I put my foot on that stone and it moved. I pushed it away and looked inside. There it was, shining out at me."

The boys scooped up the coins and pulled the small chests out. Phillip crawled in as far as he could and picked every coin out of the sand. Gani never touched the gold; he just squatted nearby, never moving or making a sound. They carried the baskets of coins and the small chests back to the camp.

They talked into the night as their plan took shape. They agreed that with this gold, they could hide their identities and buy their way to Port Royal. The danger of encountering a pirate ship as they sailed the longboat to Nassau became a risk worth taking.

"Then it's settled," Claire said. She sat on a keg in front of baskets filled with gold and silver coins glowing in the firelight. "Tomorrow we'll gather our things and get the boat ready. The day after tomorrow we sail for Nassau."

"How much of the gold should we take?" Edward asked.

"I think one good-sized bag should be enough. It'll be more than we need to buy passage to Port Royal. If no one there will take us, we'll need enough to buy a better boat and provisions. Then we can take our chances and sail for Jamaica."

"Where should we hide the rest of the treasure?" Phillip asked.

"We'll decide tomorrow," Claire said.

Gani looked at the fire and spoke in a soft, measured tone.

Kataga translated. "My grandfather says you should throw the gold and silver into the sea. He says gold and silver make white men crazy, and this gold will bring you sadness."

Claire thought, *First the dolphins say this and now this wise old man. He may be right.* "Tell him I understand his wisdom. I must use this gold to take these boys to their father."

Kataga and Gani spoke. "My grandfather said we will help you."

Claire smiled and so did Gani.

In the morning, the boys hauled the gold to the top of the hill and buried it near the grotto. Just above the grotto, at the place they called Spyglass Rock, the boys scratched their names in the stone. James scratched Ada's name on the rock as well. Everyone spent the rest of the day gathering coconuts, dried fish, and casks of water for the voyage. Gani worked on his dugout.

That evening Claire walked alone. *We've been too long on this island.*

We'll be with you, Nami said. *Our family and friends are already swimming out to sea in every direction. They will tell us of any ships that might come near you that could be dangerous.*

Gani, Kataga, and Ada have agreed to come with us.

We will be along to guide you.

Chapter 18

Calico Jack

They sailed at first light. James and Ada rode with Gani. Edward and Kataga sat in the bow of the longboat. Claire sat at the tiller of the longboat with Phillip next to her.

"I think I'll actually miss our island," Phillip said.

"You'll be with your father soon."

"Yes, it's been a long time. I can't wait to see him."

That night they stopped on a small barrier cay and slept on the beach. In the morning, the two boats sailed north, side by side. Kataga sat at the helm of the longboat. Gani yelled something and then waved and pointed. "My grandfather said the dolphins always stay near us," Kataga explained. "He says they swim toward Nassau. He says it is powerful magic."

"It is that," Edward said, looking at Claire. "Magic, and I think much more."

Claire smiled at Edward.

On the third day, they decided to sail on through the night, hoping to reach New Providence Island and Nassau under the cover of darkness. Claire sat across from Edward during the night. She handed him a small canvas pouch. "Here, you take half the gold. If something happens to me, or we become separated, your half of the gold should buy passage for you and your brothers to Jamaica. Wear it around your neck."

"Just make sure nothing happens to you," Edward said, as he looped the string over his head and dropped the pouch under his shirt.

The moon rose, silvering the rippling waves. Gani sailed close to the longboat, talking to Kataga.

"My grandfather says we will see the land in the moonlight. We should land before we reach Nassau, hide the boats, and walk along the beach to the town."

What will you do if there's a pirate ship in Nassau? Nami asked.

I think we should hide on the island until we see a friendly ship approach. A ship with no cannons on her will be a merchant ship, and I'll try to buy our passage on her.

The most evil of the ships carry no cannons, Nami said.

What do you mean? Claire asked.

The slave ships.

Well, I might be able to pay one of them to take the boys and me to Jamaica.

No, never get on one of them.

Sanjay broke in. *From the bellies of those ships come sounds of horrible suffering. The sharks always follow the slave ships.*

You would be in danger on a slave ship, and we might not be able to help you, Nami said.

Help me find the right ship.

You know we will.

Kataga sat at the helm. Gani, in the dugout, sailed close by. Claire dozed. She couldn't stop thinking of the challenges ahead and the promise she had made to Elizabeth.

———

Nami and Bolo skimmed over the water as they speed-swam into Nassau harbor. They slowed at the dock on the far side of the harbor.

Are you awake?

Yes.

Bolo and I swam here from Claire. She is on her way to Nassau with the boys and the islanders.

I heard from some of the others.

They need our help. We can't let a pirate ship slip up on them.

They say you took her to the gold.

Yes, she was determined to take the boys off the island and on to Jamaica. We thought the gold might help them. While she has been on that island her thoughts have been troubled. The gold might give her some peace of mind.

It might very well do that.

That ship over there, on the other side of the harbor, it has cannons. Is it a pirate ship?

I'm not sure I'd call the men who sail her pirates, but they're not honorable men—that I can tell you for sure.

We may need your help. Nami and Bolo turned. *Tomorrow they'll be here.*

Declan Flynn leaned against a piling on the small dock near his cottage. He watched the dim, flickering lights across the harbor in Nassau town.

———

Claire took her shift at the tiller. Gani called out and pointed ahead. A gray wrinkle of land distorted the edge of the moonlit sea. Kataga sat close by. "We'll be there before the light comes."

Sanjay's mind reached out to Claire. *Nami and my son went to Nassau harbor in the night. They should be back with news. If you reach the island before they return, stay near the beach. Your mind's power grows, but if you go too far inland, we might not be able to reach you.*

I understand.

The land loomed ahead; soon the white beach became visible. Gani came close to the longboat and quietly gave directions as the boats moved parallel to the beach. "My grandfather says we will sail toward Nassau harbor, land, and hide the boats at first light."

As the sky grew lighter, they nosed into the beach. By daybreak, the boats sat covered under piles of branches and palm fronds.

The band trudged along the beach toward Nassau, loaded down with all the muskets, pistols, and bows they could carry.

Nami called out, *We bring news from Nassau harbor. There is a large ship docked there. It carries cannons; you should be wary.*

I'll be careful.

Gani walked ahead of the others, climbing a low hill just off the beach. He turned, waving his arms over his head, and the rest ran to the summit. There, before them, sat the town of Nassau, which consisted of a few rows of low, whitewashed cottages and huts, with several more bunched together on a hill behind the docks and the pier. In the harbor, a lone ship hugged the pier running out from the main street.

Claire opened her spyglass. "I can make out a few people walking around, and some men working on a building. The ship is a good-sized sloop with twelve cannons on her deck. I don't see anyone on her."

"Is it a pirate ship?" Phillip asked.

"She flies no flag."

They walked back down the hill and sat in the sand. "We cannot go into Nassau with you," Kataga said.

"Why?" Claire asked.

"Gani believes the white men will put us in chains."

"Come to Jamaica with us," Edward said. "Our father will reward you for helping us."

"We should keep to our island home."

Claire stood. "Edward, you come with me. James, you and Phillip remain here. Kataga, stay with the boys, and when we set sail for Jamaica, you can take the longboat and go back."

She put her hand on Kataga's shoulder. "I hope I will see you again."

She handed James the spyglass. "Watch from the hill. When you see me board the sloop, I will walk to the bow wearing my hat. If I don't appear, or if I'm not wearing the hat, you will know something is wrong. Kataga, promise me, if we encounter a problem, you'll take James and Phillip with you. Do not try to come for me. You'll be outnumbered." Claire patted Phillip on the shoulder. "Be brave now. Ada, I shall see you soon. Edward, give James the pouch. It would be better if we separated the gold."

Gani stepped close to Claire. He took off his necklace of shells and shark's teeth and draped it around Claire's neck. He put his hands on her shoulders and spoke to her.

"My grandfather says the dolphins know of your kindness and that is why they love you. He says your power and magic come from your heart, and the magic of the heart is greater than any other."

Claire nodded at Gani and patted him on the shoulder. "Strange that I should come to this place to find a great philosopher." She and Edward walked down the beach toward the town of Nassau.

"Now remember, Edward, you're Allen Smith and I'm Mary Bell. Speak as little as possible."

Edward carried two pistols and a musket. A pistol stuck out of Claire's belt. She did not feel the least bit secure as they walked down the cobblestone path in front of a row of rough, white structures. Shutters of blue, green, and red covered some of the windows. Men and women stood in the doorways, watching them. No one spoke. A dozen longboats and skiffs lay tilted, half-in and half-out of the water. The buildings sat close to each other, and narrow alleyways curved and twisted behind some of the buildings. From the open doorways came smells of rum and smoky, spicy cooking.

Claire and Edward walked out onto the pier toward the sloop. A wiry little man, his greasy, black hair pulled back in a ponytail, sat on a large barrel blocking their way. He stopped carving on the piece of wood he held in his lap and watched them without expression.

"A good day to you, sir," Claire said.

The man jumped off the barrel. He wore a stained, beige fustian shirt knotted in front, and baggy pants falling to his calves. "And who might you be?"

"My name is Mary Bell. I would like to speak to the master of this ship."

"The captain will be at the Green Shutter Inn." He pointed with his very large, thick-bladed knife.

Claire turned to see the gray stone building with green shutters about halfway up a small hill. "What is his name?"

"Captain Rackham." The little man sat back on the barrel and continued to look at the two, obviously puzzled.

As Claire and Edward walked up the hill, two men smoking pipes came toward them.

"Good day to you, miss," one of them said.

"A good day to you, sirs," Claire said. "Is Captain Rackham about?"

"Well, miss, he'll be right up there and through that green door."

"Thank you, sir." Claire and Edward continued to walk toward the Green Shutter Inn. Glancing over her shoulder, Claire noticed that the two men had turned and were following them. She murmured to Edward, "Keep walking."

"What do you think we should do?"

"It's too late to do anything else now." Claire took a deep breath and pushed open the door. The room, filled with loud talking and laughter, fell silent.

The dark tavern smelled of cooking fish, rum, pipe smoke, and unwashed bodies. She and Edward surveyed the shabby group and walked toward the center of the tavern as every pair of eyes followed them through a haze of smoke.

Claire took another deep breath. "I am looking for Captain Rackham."

"Over here, miss." A voice came from the far corner of the room.

The man who spoke sat with his back to the wall, flanked by two grimy-faced men. One sported a yellow bandana around his head; the other wore a slouched hat that hid his eyes in the dark room.

"Captain John Rackham at your service, miss," he said with a grin.

Between the wall and the back of Rackham's chair stood a young black girl performing a peculiar task. The small girl was working Rackham's hair into many tightly woven braids.

His long, dirty blond hair, partly hanging down and partly in a half-dozen braids, gave Rackham a playful, almost comical look. An ominous feeling tugged at Claire. Rackham's stubbled face, with its broken and bent nose, was not the face of a gentleman. He wore an unbuttoned blue navy tunic with gold swirls on the sleeves. A thick gold chain with a gold medallion sat against his tanned chest.

"I'm Mary Bell and this is Allen Smith. We seek passage to Jamaica." Claire mustered a faint smile.

"To Jamaica, you say?" The captain pulled his head away. "Enough; get away from here, girl." The little girl disappeared. "You two swabs move your arses and give the chairs to these fine people." The two men jumped up and went over to the bar. "Sit here, Miss Mary. Allen, have a seat. So tell me, how did you two find your way to Nassau town?"

"We were on our way to Jamaica. Our ship sank in a ferocious storm, and we washed up on an island. Some natives found us and brought us here," Claire said.

"And you, young Allen, did you swim ashore with those pistols and musket?"

"No, sir." Edward bristled at the question. "I traded the Indians for them."

"And what did you trade them to get the natives to part with such a fine brace of pistols?"

Claire pulled the pouch from under her shirt and pulled out a coin. "The same thing we will use to pay you to take us to Jamaica." She dropped the coin. It clinked on the table.

The men at the bar turned in unison toward the shining piece of gold lying in the middle of the table. The captain fingered the gold piece, his eyes gleaming. "Well now, miss, where did you get this?"

"My father gave them to me for safekeeping. He drowned in the storm."

"I wonder how he came to be the owner of Spanish gold."

"How much will you need to take us to Jamaica?" Claire asked.

"I'm sure whatever you have in that there pouch will be more than enough."

"Then you'll take us?"

"Yes, miss, I surely will."

"Good. When can we leave?"

"First thing in the morning."

"You'll get half the gold when we set sail and the other half when we reach Jamaica."

Rackham grinned, his eyes sparkled with avarice. "That'll be a fine arrangement, miss."

Claire reached over and plucked the gold piece from the captain's fingers.

He stood. "Billy, go and roust out the crew. Tell them we sail for Jamaica in the morning."

"Aye, Captain," a voice came from across the room.

The captain strolled over to the bar, whispering to the two men who had been sitting at the table with him earlier.

"Claire, what do you think? We should—"

"Quiet. Not now." Claire raised her voice. "Captain, we would like to see the ship and inspect our quarters."

"Of course, miss." The captain turned to the man with the yellow bandana. "Go down and make sure the captain's cabin is presentable. If you and the lad have no lodging for the night, you can stay on the *Wanderer*." His smile sharpened Claire's distrust.

"The *Wanderer*, a wonderful name."

"She's a fine and seaworthy ship, miss."

"We would like to stay on board tonight."

"Walk down with me then; you can take a good gander at her."

They walked out of the tavern and down the hill. Two more men followed them.

———

James lay on the ground, peering through the spyglass. "I see them walking with some men toward the ship."

"Does she have her hat on?" Kataga asked.

"Yes."

"We should go down to the ship," Phillip said.

"No," James said. "Claire said she would come to the bow of the ship. We should watch for her signal."

Gani spoke. Kataga listened thoughtfully. "My grandfather said these may not be good men, and we should be careful."

James kept looking through the spyglass as Claire, Edward, and the men stood on the deck of the sloop.

———

"Let me show you to your quarters." Captain Rackham swept his hand back toward the stern of the ship. Claire glanced at Edward and took off her hat. Edward rested his hand on one of his pistols.

"The cabin at the bottom of the ladder is mine, but it'll be yours for the voyage to Jamaica," the captain continued.

"Thank you, Captain," Claire said. She walked down the ladder with Edward behind her. The captain and a few other men followed, making her more nervous.

Claire opened the door. Rackham shoved Edward hard, and the two sprawled on the floor. Edward rolled over pulling a pistol from his belt. The hammers of pistols clicked and four gun barrels pointed at Edward's face. The steel blade of a huge knife came to Claire's throat. The little thin man who had been sitting on the barrel earlier gritted what was left of his rotten teeth. "Easy, miss."

Claire dropped the dagger she had pulled from her boot. The five men pulled Claire and Edward off the floor. Rackham took the big knife, pulled the pouch out from under Claire's shirt, and cut the cord. He spilled the coins out on a table and threw one to each of the men. "We'll be finding plenty more of this."

He turned and held the knife under Edward's chin, pressing the blade against his flesh. Edward winced as he stood on his toes. "I'm sure this lad will tell us where the gold came from."

"Leave him alone," Claire said. "He doesn't know anything."

"We'll see about that, Miss Bell—or is it Miss Radstone?" The captain smirked. "Chain them together and keep a close eye on them. I think Bouchet will pay us handsomely for these two. Bouchet said there was five of you. I wonder where the rest of your family might be."

"They're dead," Claire said. "Lost at sea. My mother died on an island to the south of here."

"Yes, well now you'll be my guests for a while. Since we'll be shipmates you can call me Calico Jack." He smirked and walked out. Two seamen stood guard at the door,

———

Kataga held the spyglass. "Claire and Edward did not come on deck. Some of the men are on the deck talking. There is something wrong."

Ada pointed down. "Dolphins."

From their vantage point, they could see eight of the gray forms moving in the clear blue water out in the middle of the harbor.

"We should go down there," Phillip said.

"No," Kataga said. "We should keep watching and wait until nightfall. Then we will sneak down to the ship."

———

Claire called out with her mind, *Nami, Sanjay, can you hear me?*

Yes, we're in the harbor, Nami said.

We're chained below on this ship.

We will try to help you.

No. Help the others. They'll be watching from the hill just to the west of the town. Help them to get away if you can.

We can't force them to get in their boats and leave. If they get out on the water we'll swim in front of them. The old man might think to follow us.

Try, try to help them.

Declan Flynn stood on the end of the pier leading from his cottage. *Where are the others?*

We think they are on the high ground to the west, watching and waiting, but we're not sure, Sanjay said. *They may be trying to get back to their boats. They hid them far down the beach to the west.*

I'll find them, Declan said. He walked off his pier toward the open-air blacksmith's shed near his house. A whiff of smoke curled from the red-hot hearth. A rhythmic tapping and clanking filled the air as a hammer slammed down on the glowing steel. Sparks flew.

The smith filled the shed; he stood six-and-a-half feet tall, a glistening obsidian statue. A pink-and-white shell hung from his neck, outlined by his black, muscled chest. He wore black pants cinched with a piece of rope. Sweat poured off his bald head as he worked the steel bar.

"Nangwayago," Declan yelled. As he approached, the clanging stopped. "We've got a dangerous job to do."

Nangwayago put down the iron and his hammer. "What you need, boss?"

"Put every weapon we own in the skiff. I don't think we'll be coming back."

Nangwayago packed the little boat, and the two rowed across the harbor to the town, paying careful attention to the helter-skelter activity around the *Wanderer*.

The skiff pulled to the shore in front of town, and Nangwayago jumped out. He pushed the boat back out as Declan raised the sail.

"Be quick and cautious," Declan said. "They'll be skittish."

"I'll make noise when I get near them."

"Hurry. I'll see you around the point." Declan hoisted the sail on his little boat and moved out of the harbor.

Nangwayago walked through the town, then broke into a run.

James watched through the glass. "The big black man got out of the boat and walked into town. I can't see him now. The other man is sailing out of the harbor."

"What about Claire and Edward?" Phillip asked.

"I don't see them. The crew is loading a goodly amount of provisions. It looks like they're going to set sail soon."

He pulled the spyglass away from his eye. They knew they could not leave without Claire and Edward. They knew they would disobey Claire's order.

"It will be dark soon," Kataga said.

"How will we get on the ship?" James asked.

Gani spoke.

"My grandfather and I will go in the dark," Kataga said. "We will swim to the ship. We can be very quiet. If we do not return, you, Phillip, and Ada take the longboat and go."

"No, Phillip and I should go with you," James said.

"You cannot leave me behind," Ada said. "I am as quiet as a mouse, and I can help."

James turned back with the spyglass trained on the sloop.

Gani heard him first and spun on the ground. In one quick move, he drew his bow back with an arrow ready to fly. James dropped the spyglass and drew a pistol, as did the rest.

Nangwayago stopped behind them, his chest heaving from the run up the hill. He held his hands up, palms out. "I am a friend. I am the friend of a friend." He pointed down at the sea. "Declan Flynn."

"Declan Flynn? Did you say Declan Flynn?" James said in utter disbelief.

Nangwayago pointed again. "There."

James touched the shaft of the arrow Gani held trained on Nangwayago. Gani lowered it. James reached for the spyglass, peering down at the skiff as it turned toward the shore below them. "By God, it *is* Mr. Flynn," he said, snapping the spyglass shut.

"Who is he?" Kataga asked.

"A good friend," James said. "Come on."

They ran down the hill. Gani followed at a distance behind Nangwayago. He kept the arrow in his bow, ready to draw.

Declan nosed the skiff onto the shore and stepped out. James and Phillip ran to him with the rest behind. "Mr. Flynn," James said. "It's good to see you. How did you come to be here?"

"It's a long story. I'll be telling you another time. I'm the blacksmith and carpenter for Nassau. Everyone in Nassau knows me as James Sullivan, and I live on the little island across from the town. I heard that a young woman and young man appeared in Nassau town without a boat. From the description, I knew it could be no one else. My great friend here and I came to find you—this is Nangwayago. Just call him Nango." Nangwayago made no expression.

"Claire and Edward went aboard that ship down there. We haven't seen them for hours, and we believe they've met with some treachery," James said.

"You can be sure of that," Declan said. "The story of you boys and Claire came to Nassau long ago. I can tell you there isn't an honorable man living anywhere near this town, and Calico Jack Rackham, the master of that ship, is the worst of the lot." Declan looked around at them with piercing eyes. "I think tonight we'll take Claire and Edward back from Calico Jack."

Everyone drew together. The seven of them sat on the beach, and a plan took shape as darkness fell. Gani and the boys retrieved their boats and readied every weapon they had.

Leaving the bulky longboat on the beach, the group drifted in the two smaller boats just outside the harbor. They hunkered down and waited. They waited for the darkest part of the night. When the sounds from the taverns waned, they rowed the skiff and Gani's native craft toward the *Wanderer*. Only the garbled singing of a rum-induced, off-key ditty echoed across the harbor in the still night. Nango, Kataga, and James pulled the skiff alongside the *Wanderer*. James held the boat fast as Nango and Kataga crept up the side and waited. Phillip, Ada, and Gani swung the dugout around to the far end of the pier. Gani motioned for Phillip and

Ada to stay in the boat as he crept onto the end of the pier. Gani stood against a piling and watched.

From the landside, Declan jauntily walked onto the pier. The little man with the big knife sat on his barrel, continuing to block the pier.

"Look alive there," the little man alerted a sailor standing watch on the deck of the sloop.

"Sullivan, what do you want?" the little man said.

"The captain told me to come and make a few repairs before he sets sail in the morning, is all."

The little man stood. "What are you talking about? At this time of night? You take yourself up to the Green Shutter and get Capt'n Jack or you ain't getting on this ship."

"All right, but you're wasting my time. Why don't you go get him while I get me tools up on the deck?"

"Where the hell are your tools?"

"Nango is on his way with them. He'll be here in a few minutes."

"I ain't moving an inch from this here spot."

Kataga and Nango eased over the railing. Nango bounded across the deck and grabbed the sailor watching Declan and the little man. The little man heard a grunt and turned to see arms and legs flailing up on the deck. He pulled his knife, turning back toward Declan. Declan stepped back, pulling a dagger from his belt.

The little man didn't see or hear the cat-quiet Gani at the end of the pier. Gani stood in the shadow, drew back, and let loose. The arrow zipped into the little man; he threw his shoulders back, dropped the knife, and contorted as he tried to reach the arrow buried deep between his shoulder blades. The next arrow drilled into him just below the first. He gasped, and the air gurgled back out of his gaping mouth. Wide-eyed, he dropped to his knees and fell face-down in front of Declan.

Nango released the sailor, who fell to the deck, his neck broken. Two men from below ran to the top of the ladder, cutlasses drawn. Kataga's arrow hit the first one in the chest. The second man darted to the left and dove off the ship before Kataga could get off another shot. A dolphin shot toward the swimming sailor. The huge dolphin's blunt nose rammed into the man with bone-crushing force. Another dolphin hit him from below. The man rose out of the water. He splashed back, face-down and motionless. Frozen for a moment by the amazing sight, Kataga slackened his drawn bow.

The boys and Ada loosened the lines as they ran aboard. Declan ran up the gangplank, and they slid it aboard. Nango jumped in the skiff, tied a heavy rope to the bow of the sloop, and knotted the other end around his body at his chest. He furiously pulled at the oars, straining every muscle in his massive body. Nango leaned back against the tightened rope and slowly began to pull the *Wanderer* out into the harbor.

Declan found the boat hooks and poles. He gathered everyone together. "Nango has us moving, but only by inches. Quickly now, take these poles and push. Push with everything that's in you. Push us away from the pier."

They all pushed against the pier with the polls, and as Nango continued his mighty rowing, the *Wanderer* crept out into the harbor and far enough away so that a man standing on the pier could not jump over to her. Declan watched as two men stumbled out of a doorway into the street. Even in their drunken state, they realized the sloop was moving away from the dock. A shot rang out and the two men ran, yelling. Men poured out of the buildings and down to the pier.

Gani shot an arrow and a man fell into the water. Another arrow hit home, and another. Unable to match the accuracy of Gani and Kataga, the not-so-sober pirates sent their bullets whizzing over the escaping thieves' heads or splintering into the side of the *Wanderer*. Declan and the boys pulled at the ropes, struggling to hoist the sail. The sloop inched away at an agonizingly slow pace.

Calico Jack gathered enough of his crew to launch a longboat. He stood in the bow, screaming, "Pull, men, pull. Cut her off before she gets out of the harbor. Pull, you dogs, pull."

Nango climbed back aboard the *Wanderer* and joined Declan and the boys on the lines hoisting the main sail. With his extraordinary strength added, the sail rose up the mast and unfurled. Meanwhile, with eight men rowing, the longboat gained on the sloop. Gani and Kataga waited, their bows ready.

The longboat was now only a few boat-lengths behind the sloop. Calico Jack fired a shot. "Come on, lads. They'll not take our ship. We've got her."

Gani drew his bow. The back of the first man rowing was an easy target. Seawater exploded skyward as a gray mass arched up and slammed into Calico Jack with a thud. He screamed as the huge dolphin catapulted him out of the boat and the two tumbled into the water. Astonished, the men stopped rowing. Calico Jack slapped and splashed in the water, and then hung onto the oars. "Help me, damn it."

Gani and Kataga lowered their bows and looked at each other. Gani stood there for a time, looking down into the water. The shouts of the men in the longboat faded.

Chapter 19

The *Wanderer*

The triangular sail of the *Wanderer* caught a brisk evening wind. Declan took the wheel, sailing the sloop west out of Nassau harbor, and then he turned the ship to the east and out into the Atlantic.

Carrying a lantern, Ada got to Claire and Edward first. "Are you hurt?"

"No. What's happened?" Claire asked.

"We took the ship with the help of two men. One of them comes from your village. His name is Declan."

"Declan? Declan Flynn?" Edward said.

"Yes, he helped us."

"How did he get here?" Edward asked.

"I don't know."

"And the boys?" Claire asked.

"They're on deck. They're sailing the ship."

Nangwayago's body filled the doorway.

"This is Nango," Ada said.

He walked over and tugged at the chains holding Claire and Edward. "I will break these." Nangwayago left the room. He returned with a hammer and chisel.

Nango hammered away; Claire closed her eyes and turned her head away. The clasps sprang open. Claire and Edward ran onto the deck as the colors of predawn pushed against the shadows covering the sea.

As Claire stepped on the deck, she saw him. "Mr. Flynn—Declan," she called out.

"Good morning to you, Claire," he called back.

Claire walked to him and gave him a big hug. "I'm so happy you're alive. And even happier to see you here. How did you come to be here?"

"The answer to that question will be quite a story for another day. Let's just say that when Bouchet got back aboard the *Brilliant*, he had little interest in me. He did want you back in the worst way. It's a fine thing he never caught up with you."

"Now, that's a story for another day, as well. This is the second time you've saved us. I don't know what to say."

"Think nothing of it, lass. Fate has brought us together again. Don't you know Saint Patrick sent me to watch over you and the boys? They told me about their mother, and that's sad news, indeed. It's all behind you now. You're standing on the deck of a fine ship, carrying us north and east, out into the ocean. We have plans to make."

Spirits soared as they gathered around Declan, talking of their escape, their time on the island, their plans, Jamaica, Lord Radstone—and the dolphins.

"Did they get your gold?" James asked.

"Yes—but, then, we did get their ship," Claire said.

"How much gold did they take?" Declan asked.

James reached under his shirt. "About the same as is in here."

"Then you made a fine purchase, and the kindness of Calico Jack knows no bounds. He saw to it that you sailed with the best of provisions on board," Declan said. "You paid for this ship with gold—and almost your life. I believe that makes you, Miss Riley, the master of the *Wanderer*."

"Captain Claire," said James.

Claire pointed to the rigging. "It will be difficult for nine of us to sail this ship."

"It won't be easy, but we can keep her going in mild weather," Declan said.

"We can do it. I believe Nango here," James slapped him on the back, "can raise and lower the mainsail by himself."

"Gani took the wheel for me for a while in the night. He'll make an excellent helmsman," Declan said. "But we'll need to learn how to fire these guns."

The boys' eyes got wide.

The *Wanderer* sailed to the east for the day. Claire sat in the bow as eight dolphins broke the surface in unison off to starboard.

I'm happy you're safe, Nami said.

We're all safe. I heard what you did to the man in the longboat. It must have been Calico Jack.

That was Stark.

Stark, you could have been injured or killed.

The sound of laughter filled Claire's mind. *I'm Stark, the strongest and fastest dolphin in all the oceans. Those men could never hurt me.*

I wonder what Calico Jack thought just as you came out of the dark water and slammed into him? Claire chuckled.

Gani stood next to Claire. He put his hand on her shoulder, watching the dolphins for a moment. He turned to her, looked into her eyes, and said a single word, "Good."

Claire stood at the rail. The dolphins had moved away and the apricot sun dipped toward the sea and painted the blue sky and white clouds with shades of pinks and grays. They had escaped the clutches of Calico Jack. The boys were on their way to Jamaica, and the beauty of the moment could be no more spectacular. Claire should have been happy. She was not. She could not overcome her sadness. Tears dropped from her eyes.

Edward walked up next to her. "A beautiful evening."

"Yes, so very beautiful." Claire did not face Edward but kept looking at the sun.

"We were lucky in Nassau. I only hope I can be as brave as you some day."

Claire looked at Edward. "I'm not so brave; I just hide my fear. You and your brothers are stalwart young men, and I am proud of you."

"What's the matter?"

"Nothing, it's just the girl coming out in me. I'm happy to be here is all."

The two of them stood in silence and watched the sun set.

The next morning, the *Wanderer* kept to her easterly course with Gani at the helm. Declan gathered the others at a gun. "Today, ladies and gentlemen, we'll learn how to load and fire these guns. I watched the men on the *Brilliant* do this, and I'm sure we can master it. Remember, we will be able to fire all the guns in a broadside once. After the first firing, we must reload as many as we can."

Everyone worked through the day, firing the cannon a number of times. They toiled together, hauling the powder from the magazine far below, where it was kept so that there would be no danger of the powder being accidentally ignited. They loaded the cannon, and then grunted and heaved as they worked the ropes and pulleys used to move the guns into firing position. The cannonballs sat in a rack next to the cannon but were not used in practice.

"All well and good, but we're not sure if we can hit anything."

"True, Edward," Declan said. "We have plenty of powder, but we must conserve the shot in case we need it. Don't ever think we can fire these guns as the British navy does. Still, if we keep our heads, we might be able to scare off an adversary."

"I would like to do more than just scare Bouchet," James said.

Declan put his hand on James's shoulder. "So would I, but for now, if we encounter Bouchet, it would be best to run."

"And so, my friends, let's not forget our other task," Claire said. "We must be as good as we can be at sailing this ship."

Claire and Declan leaned over the chart covering a small table in the cabin. "I think you purchased some very good charts from Captain Rackham."

Claire grinned. "I hope so. He did get a pretty penny for all this."

Declan smiled back at her. "This is our fifth day on this easterly tack. The sextant is a good one, and yesterday I reckoned us to be about here. We're far enough out in the Atlantic. If we turn south, we shouldn't run into any trouble. I think we should sail down here, turn west between the islands, and head to Jamaica from the south."

"It sounds like a fine plan, Declan."

The *Wanderer* turned south, and Claire told the boys of their course and destination. The boys talked about sailing into the harbor at Port Royal.

"We should fire cannon in salute when we enter the harbor, like the navy does," Phillip said.

"Let's do it," Phillip said. "Father will be impressed."

"I wish we had a Union Jack to fly," James said.

"We should think of a way to fashion one," Edward said.

"I am not English," Nango said. "Gani, Kataga, and Ada are not English. Declan and Claire come from Ireland. We must make our own flag."

The boys looked at each other and nodded.

"Nango," Edward asked, "what does the word *oshe* mean?"

"*Oshe?* Where did you hear that word?"

"From a boy chained in the hold of a pirate ship."

"In Africa, there are many languages. In western Africa, for most people, *oshe* means thank you."

Edward nodded and thought about the boy on the other side of the hole.

The *Wanderer* ran with no lanterns lit, lazing her way to the south in a warm, gentle wind. Claire stood alone at the rail, wrapped in blackness. She thought about God throwing more handfuls of sparkling diamonds across the sky tonight than ever before.

Do you think any ships will sail near us any time soon? she asked.

We have a hundred of our friends and family scattered across the sea, Nami said. *If a ship comes toward you, we will tell you.*

I must get these boys to Jamaica and to their father. Then maybe I can persuade Lord Radstone to hunt down Bouchet and avenge the death of my mother and his wife.

We'll help you find him when the time is right, Sanjay said.

The world would be a better place without men such as Bouchet, Claire said.

Yes, Nami said, *we don't understand why humans can be so hateful and evil to other humans. The sounds coming from the bellies of the slave ships fill the sea with sorrow.*

Slave ships? Are there many of them?

They come from the east, sailing to the islands and western lands.

James and Edward joined her at the railing. "The stars are beautiful tonight," Edward said. "How long before we reach Jamaica?"

"A week or two, depending on the weather," Claire said. "We must make sure we don't run afoul of the likes of Bouchet."

"This is a fast ship with fine cannons," James said.

"True," Claire said. "But, with only nine of us, we could never outgun a ship like the *Brilliant*."

James looked at the billowing sails. "But we can outrun her."

"I am certain of one thing." Edward's eyes darted back and forth. "I never want to be chained again."

The morning came, bringing a rolling sea. The boys, Nango, and Declan sat on the deck eating a breakfast of biscuits and fruit.

Phillip pointed at Declan. "Mr. Flynn, why do you have those curious lumps on the sides of your hands?"

Nango looked at Declan, then at the boys, and then back at Declan.

"I was born this way. Mother Nature provided me with the little deformities. Never bothered me much at all. The way I look at it, it's far better than having a camel's hump on me back or a unicorn's horn growing out of the middle of me forehead."

The boys laughed.

Nango picked up another biscuit. "The ship sails good."

Ada hung from a rope high on the mainmast. Claire stood with Kataga at the wheel. "Your sister climbs like a monkey."

"She is happy to be with you, and I know she is happy to be near him."

Claire arched her back, looking up. James hung near Ada, high in the rigging. He waved. Claire waved back. She looked at Kataga, who stared at the pair. Claire made a mental note to keep an eye on Ada and James. She wondered why she hadn't seen this complication coming.

Nami's mind came to Claire. *One member of our family has just returned from out at sea. There is a ship to the south and east. It is coming toward you.*

Pirates?

No, it is a slave ship. We can hear the sorrowful sounds coming from the ship's belly.

Claire walked to the larboard side and stared out at the eastern horizon for a while. The words "sorrowful sounds" nagged at her.

"Sails! Sails to the east!" Ada called down, pointing to the horizon.

"Where?" Kataga yelled.

"Far to the south and to the east," she pointed.

Kataga snapped open the spyglass, gave the wheel to Claire, and searched the sea. "There she is."

Everyone ran to the rail. A speck of white peeked over the edge of the sea.

"We should turn to the west," Edward said.

"What if it is a British warship?" James said.

"Or a pirate ship," Edward said.

Claire gave the wheel to Gani and called to Ada. "Come down and get the spyglass to take back with you."

"Stow away what is left of the morning meal," Declan said, "and then we will load the guns. We'll load both sides. We might need to turn and fire, so we must be prepared."

They worked and watched as the two ships converged. Ada came down from above and handed the spyglass to Claire. "I cannot see any gun ports."

Claire, using the glass, said, "And she flies a Dutch flag."

"She has to be a merchant ship," James said.

"Or a slave ship," Edward said.

Nango put his hand on Edward's shoulder. "As a small boy I came to the islands on a ship like that one. We were all crammed together in the hold of the ship. My mother and brother died, chained to me. Many from my village died in the darkness of the ship."

"Claire," Edward said, "let's find out if that's a slave ship. If it is, we must stop her."

"And how would you propose we do that?"

"We've got cannons and they probably don't," Edward said. "We might be able to fire on them. The thought of the boy chained below on the pirate ship has never left my mind. If Mum were here, she would want us to help them. They chained us for only a few hours. Think of the poor souls on that ship; chained below for a month."

"Edward, your mother would want you safe."

"If it is a slave ship," Phillip said, "freeing the people would be a good thing."

"How about you, Declan?" Edward persisted. "If it is a slave ship, do you think we should stop her?"

"It would be far too dangerous a day's work."

"We have faced our share of danger in the last year or so," James said.

"What do you say, Nango?" Edward asked.

"I am with you."

"I say we put it to a vote," James said.

"There will be no voting." Claire raised her voice, glaring at Nango, then at the boys. "I don't even want to sail close enough to that ship to get a good look at her."

James turned to Kataga. "Ask your grandfather what he thinks we should do."

"Enough of this," said Claire.

Kataga looked at Claire, then back at James, and then at Claire again. He turned and spoke to his grandfather.

Gani, standing at the wheel, said nothing for a moment. When he spoke, he fixed on Claire. Claire could not comprehend his words. She understood the intensity exuding from his face, and she could not draw her eyes from his.

Kataga nodded. "My grandfather says you have been given your freedom two times. He believes God has done this so one day you could give freedom to others. If there are people chained below on that ship, you must free them. It is God's will."

Everyone nodded, but remained silent.

Claire broke the silence. "Have a closer look at her if you must. If she carries cannons, or looks too strong, we'll turn away, and I don't want to hear a word out of any of you."

She walked away from them, gazing out at the sea and the ship. *The boys are too young for this. I promised Elizabeth. What am I doing?*

The black-hulled brig turned more to the north. The heavily laden ship was slower than the sloop and the *Wanderer* drew closer to her. The *Wanderer* soon sailed on a parallel course to the fat ship.

Declan stood next to Claire, using his spyglass. Claire looked through her glass.

"Do you see those slots running along the hull about six feet below the railing?"

"Yes." Claire kept looking.

"Those openings let a little air into the hold so the people below can breathe. She's a slaver, all right. Shall we?" Declan asked.

Claire gripped Declan's forearm. "We can't do this. If we get on board and there are too many of them, we could be captured or worse."

Declan patted her hand and said, "Well, she is on the smallish side for a slaver, and her master is probably a tightfisted Dutchman who has the fewest crew he could manage with. We've got these twelve cannons, and they know we could stand off and tear her to pieces. But you're right; the problem might come once we get on board."

Claire frowned at him.

"Don't be worrying yourself. Nango's good for ten men in a fight," Declan said.

"Not if someone puts a ball in his head."

"Well now, if that happens, it'll put him in one hell of a bad mood."

Claire didn't smile as the *Wanderer* closed in on the bigger and slower ship.

"All right now," Declan said. "We'll fire one or two shots at her, then reload. Ada, you stay on board at the wheel. When we hook up to her, leave the wheel, and be ready at the cannon amidships. If I give you the order, fire into the slaver's hull. Phillip, you man the swivel gun. We'll try to get the crew to move toward the rail where they'll see you pointing the gun at them. It may give them pause, if they're thinking of resisting."

Phillip nodded, looking serious.

"James, you and Gani get on their quarterdeck. We will be outnumbered, so carry as many pistols as you can, but remember, we must try to avoid a fight."

Kataga explained everything to his grandfather.

"This is madness," Claire said. "They will be watching us through their glasses."

What are you doing? Nami asked.

We are going to stop this ship and free those people.

This will be a glorious day for all, Nami said. *Be careful. These men do not put much value on life.*

Let us hope they are concerned for their own lives, Claire said.

James and Declan worked the gun. Ada held a smoking wick at the end of a wooden rod as long as her arm.

"A little more elevation," Declan said. "We don't want to damage the ship, just scare them. Ready, Ada? Fire."

The cannon recoiled as gray-and-white smoke belched from the muzzle. The shot howled over the black ship, tearing through the mainsail. Claire watched through the spyglass. "That got them scurrying about."

"Nango, you and the boys reload that one," Declan said. "Fire again."

Ada touched the glowing wick to the next cannon. The shot flew over the ship and ripped another hole in its sail.

The *Wanderer* came even closer and Declan yelled through a speaking trumpet. "Ahoy, what is your cargo, and where are you bound?"

Someone using a speaking trumpet came back. "We carry slaves, and we sail for the port of Savannah!"

"Lower your sails, or we will fire on you!"

A few long moments passed. Men climbed up, and the sails began to come down. The two ships gently bumped together as Nango and Kataga lowered the *Wanderer's* sail. Grappling hooks latched on to the slaver. James and Gani swung over to the quarterdeck of the slave ship. A man stood at the wheel with a mate next to him. They both drew knives. An arrow flew between them, sticking in the hub of the wheel. They flinched; Gani drew another arrow and stood ready to fire.

James, a pistol in each hand, jerked his head toward the ladder. "Move down to the main deck."

The men backed down the ladder. Sailors came up from below and down from the rigging. The entire ship's complement, twenty-two in all, faced the intruders. "I am Captain Fredrick Paulus, master of this ship. Why do you board us? Why did you fire?"

"How many slaves do you have aboard?" Declan asked.

"We carry no gold or goods."

"How many?"

"The slaves are bought and paid for. I have the names of the plantation owners in America." The captain sounded baffled.

The man standing next to him, holding a cutlass, was not baffled. "These are nothing but boys, women, and savages. We are twice their number. Come on, men, we can best them." He raised the cutlass and took a step forward. Everyone tensed; Claire's eyes bulged, and she gripped her cutlass and pistol even tighter. An arrow hit the man in the back, then another. The man writhed and crumpled. The next arrow whizzed past the captain's ear and thudded in the deck. The captain turned back to see Gani at the quarterdeck rail with his bow pulled taut and another arrow pointed at him. No one else on the slaver crew moved.

James held his pistols at his waist. "He dips his arrows in poison. If you are even scratched by one, you will most certainly die."

The captain turned, looked at the man with the arrows sticking out of him, and laid his sword and pistol on the deck. The rest of the men dropped their weapons. Nangwayago motioned them back toward the starboard rail, where Phillip pointed the swivel gun at their backs. Nango gathered the weapons, and now James, Edward, Kataga, Declan, and Gani leveled their weapons at the unarmed crew.

"These slaves carry the marks of their owners. You will not be able to sell them," the captain said.

"Marks, you say. Nango, open the hatch," Claire said.

The ladder led down into darkness. Even from the top step, the fetid stink of urine, feces, sweat, and putrid flesh gripped her. She felt sick. Bodies squirmed at the foot of the ladder. Claire moved down slowly. A single plank ran the length of the hold, disappearing into darkness. She paused a second, then forced herself to move along the narrow walkway, using a bandana to cover her face. The bodies lay packed together in such a way that they seemed to be one great living thing. This thing moved, twisted, and struggled, moaning and seething with the moist body heat of hundreds rising up. Hands reached out to her, held back by the chains. The gasping, crying, and inhuman howling mixed together with the clanking and rattling of the chains to form the most sorrowful of sounds. More horrible than the sounds was the stench. Claire turned, stumbling back to the ladder and out of the hold. She ran to the railing, gasping, and hung over the edge, fighting the sickened feeling in her belly.

Nango came up from below, his eyes filled with tears. He drew his huge knife, and, screaming in his African tongue, ran at the crew of the ship. Declan stepped in front of him. "No, Nango, no." Nango pushed him aside. The crew cowered as the huge, knife-wielding black man rushed toward them.

Declan yelled, "Nango, will you kill just a few or slaughter the whole lot?"

Nango stopped. He stood there for a moment, then turned and walked away. Declan put a hand on the big man's shoulder. Looking into his friend's face, he saw something he had never seen before. Tears were rolling down Nango's cheeks. Nango walked toward the captain of the slave ship with the knife still in his hand. The crew stepped away from their captain. He put his knife back in his belt, reached down and took the ring of keys hanging from the captain's belt.

"You can't unchain those slaves."

Nango glared at the captain, then reached out and pulled him by the hair until they were nose to nose. "Speak again and your blood will run. I will hold you in the water, and we will wait together for the sharks to come for you."

Wide-eyed, the captain gasped and shuddered.

Nango went down and started unlocking the chains around the slaves. The first of them crept up the ladder, a thin woman with a small piece of dirty cloth wrapped around her waist. She carried a small child in her arms. The rest of those still alive came crawling out of the hold one at a time, stumbling, flinching from the sun, some too weak to stand. They shielded their eyes from the brightness. Nango spoke to them in a West African tongue. Most of them understood, and they limped to the bow of the ship, their muscles little-used over the last month. Nango offered weapons to a few of the young men, who took them and stood guard over the crew.

Edward, Ada, and Claire dipped water from a barrel at the mast and handed the ladles to eager, outstretched hands. The freed men and women gulped the water. They gently poured some into the mouths of those too feeble to hold a cup. Soon the deck filled with dark bodies, and some of the more able climbed over to the

Wanderer. There were a few dead still below. Nango forced the crew of the slave ship to bring up the bodies and throw them overboard.

"Nango," Declan said, "get some of these men to lower the longboat."

Claire addressed the crew, disgust plain in her voice. "You can either face the wrath of these people or try your luck in the longboat. I suggest you sail to the northwest."

The seamen of the slave ship climbed down into the boat. "But we sail with no provisions," the captain called.

Nango and James lowered a keg of water and a bag of biscuits. "It's far more than you provided to these people," Claire said. "Now be away before we change our minds."

The longboat pushed off. Nango climbed the rigging and leaned out between the two boats. He called out to the Africans. The freed slaves on both ships hushed as he spoke. One voice rose in a high-pitched, lilting chant. Another voice joined in, then another. The freed slaves sang and swayed.

It's a beautiful sound, Nami said.

Yes, it is.

The two ships stayed tied together for the day. Claire, Declan, and Nango leaned over the charts in the cabin on the *Wanderer* and talked about where to take these newly freed people.

"It should be a place where they can live and sustain themselves, a place where they can live free," Claire said.

James walked in. "Everyone is fed. We used the porridge on the slave ship and the biscuits we brought along. We won't be able to sustain this many people for long. I can't believe how they were packed down below." James leaned over the table, looking exhausted and ill. "The hold of that ship has got to be the most filthy and horrible place on this earth. They chained the people on two levels of racks, one above the other. The piss and everything else from those above fell on those below. How could anyone do that? The smell is unbearable. We dropped eleven bodies into the sea; some of them had been dead for a while." His eyes were troubled, shining with unshed tears. "Four of the dead were babies. One young woman would not let go of her child. She wanted to jump in the sea clutching her dead baby. Those around her pulled the little body away from her, turned her away, and threw it overboard." He paused, swallowing hard, and held his emotion in check. "We did the right and honorable thing by stopping this ship."

Claire, eyes wide, fought back tears as well. "What I saw down there shook me to my bones, to my very soul. I had no idea. You're right. We surely did the right thing."

They all stood for a moment, contemplating the horror of what they had witnessed, and the depths to which humans could sink.

. "James," Claire said. "I have been meaning to ask you something. Poison-tipped arrows?"

James shrugged; a mischievous look came over his face. "Well, at the moment, it seemed like the thing to say." He grinned.

"Ha, it was the perfect thing to say, lad," Declan said with a laugh. "The perfect thing, to be sure."

James smiled and walked out.

Declan returned to the chart and pointed. "I think I know where we can take these people. I've been along this coast at the western end of Hispaniola. It is called Saint-Dominque. Here is Tortuga, a pirate stronghold, and on this northwest part of the main island are many French plantations. Across this great gulf to the south is this southern peninsula. It is part of Saint-Dominque, but I am told it is almost uninhabited. I believe these Africans can build a life along here in peace and freedom."

"That sounds perfect," Claire said. "Let's set sail to the west. We'll put these people ashore right there. Come, Nango, let's tell them our plan."

Claire and Nango climbed in the rigging and spoke to the people on both ships. The Africans cheered and began to chant again.

Claire, Nango, Gani, and Edward crewed the *Wanderer*. Declan, Phillip, Ada, Kataga, and James sailed the black-hulled ship. With fresh air, food, and water, the Africans began to recover their strength, and they eagerly helped with the work on both ships.

The two ships separated, hoisted their sails, and set off to the southwest.

Where will you take these people? asked Nami.

Through the Leeward Islands to a place called Hispaniola.

We'll keep watching for ships, Sanjay said. *We'll not let a ship come near you without you knowing.*

"The dolphins always stay close to us," Edward said as he walked with Claire. "I wonder if they are the same ones who swam with us on the island."

"I think some of them are."

"How do you know?"

"The different shapes of the fins on their backs. See that one? There is a notch along the edge of the fin, and that one is rounded at the top."

Edward nodded. "I remember that one when we were hiding on our island. It seems they have adopted us."

Dolphins swam and leaped next to the ships, and the Africans pointed, laughed, and sang into the night.

Chapter 20

Sailing on the *Freedom*

The two ships sailed between the Leeward Islands and into the Caribbean Sea. A brisk wind blowing from the east served them well, and the *Wanderer* crashed through the swells, spraying water along the deck. Most of the freed slaves had recovered their health, although some were still very ill and were being nursed by their family members, Claire, and Gani. Some of the children and a few adults leaned over the side and let the ocean foam splash them. The sounds of laughter and shrieks of joy filled the ship. "When we drop off these people, we'll be close to Jamaica," Declan said.

"How long to Jamaica from Hispaniola?" Claire asked.

"I'm not sure. Depending on the wind, I would think a few days."

"That's wonderful. The boys will be thrilled. Their father will be so happy to see his sons."

"That'll be a grand day, indeed," Declan said.

———

They swung around the point of land and headed back to the east, inside the gulf along the southern coast of Saint-Dominque. Claire stood at the rail looking at the majestic verdant mountains of the peninsula. She thought of Ireland. On the larboard side Declan stood alone looking at the sea. Claire thought about the fact that when she talked to the dolphins she always looked at the sea. She stood there and watched Declan for a time.

The two ships anchored off a sandy beach, and by midday everyone was ashore. Ada and Kataga told Nango and Nango told the Africans where to find tropical fruits and other foods. Men hunted in the jungle and climbed up into the mountains while women and children gathered fruits, roots, and berries. Within a few days, shelters were constructed and life began to settle down. Singing and laughter filled the air, along with the smells of wild game cooking on spits. Claire spent much of her time walking alone on the beach.

These have been good days, Sanjay said.

Yes, the people from Africa are very happy. You all played a big part in freeing them.

We dolphins have long been troubled by their suffering, but we were unable to help them, Nami said. *Now you have come and brought these people here.*

We have done this together, Claire said.

Many more slave ships come from the east, Nami said. *Sad, woeful sounds follow them across the sea. So many bodies fall from these ships that the sharks can't eat all of them.*

Claire walked away from the water's edge and steadied herself against a palm tree. Her eyes watered as the haunting image of the sharks ripping at her mother came to her. She thought of the black baby being thrown to the waiting jaws. Claire took a deep breath and began to walk again. *We must do more. We must go back out to sea, stop more of these ships, and free the people. We can bring them here.*

All the dolphins will help you, Sanjay said.

The young dolphins of our pod swim very fast, Bolo said. *We can find these ships and tell you of them, long before you would see them or they would see you.*

Excited at the thought, Claire walked back toward the flickering fires at a quickened pace. Declan, Kataga, Nango, and the rest of the band sat around one of the blazing fires.

"I want to talk to all of you." They gathered around her.

"What is it?" asked James.

"We have brought freedom and happiness to these people. The babies and the children will grow up here in peace, never knowing bondage. But more slave ships come toward the Americas every day. I know I will be forever haunted by the thought of so many more innocent souls being chained in the holds of such ships. We may not be able to stop this evil, but we must do more."

No one spoke for a moment. "It'll be dangerous," Declan said. "The luck of the Irish helped us, and there was no fight in those men."

Claire nodded at James. "And the poisoned arrows won us the day."

Edward slapped James on the back, and they both chuckled a little.

"But now," Claire said, "some of these freed men are strong enough to sail with us. With enough men to work the sails and the guns, we'll have a fine fighting ship."

Kataga spoke with his grandfather and then turned to Claire. "Grandfather says God sent you to these people, and we will help you."

"First, to Jamaica," Claire said. "And then we'll be about the business of stopping as many of these slavers as we can."

A look of incredulity came across James's face as he looked at his brothers and then back at Claire. "And leave us out of it. You can't do that. We're staying with you."

"I'm not missing this, either," Edward said.

"I want to help, too," Phillip said.

"Phillip, I promised your mother before she died. I must get you to your father. Jamaica lies a few days to the west. It is time."

James raised his voice. "No. Gani is right. My brothers and I can help you. We fought together to free these people, and we want to continue the fight."

"Remember my promise to your mother. We'll talk more of this in the morning."

"But we—"

"Not now, James—in the morning." Claire turned and walked to a skiff. Two men rowed her out to the *Wanderer*.

Nango walked among the freed people, talking into the night.

———

A cool breeze blew through the open windows as the sun brightened the cabin. Claire realized she had slept far longer than was her custom. She woke, got out of bed, and put on the baggy blue pants that she wore almost every day. The blousy white shirt draped over her shoulders. She liked the light, cool cotton. Since their own clothes were so worn, they had been lucky to find some other clothes on the ship. She stepped out on the deck and wrinkled her brow.

Declan, Nango, the three boys, Ada, Kataga, and Gani sat in a circle, and now stood and faced her. Fifty ragged African men gathered behind them. All looked at Claire.

"What is it?" she asked.

Nango stepped forward. "These men will go with you to free people. They will fight to do this."

"We will all go," James announced in a firm voice. "We cannot go to Jamaica now. If Ada is old enough to join you in this mission, then so are we."

Claire stepped in front of the Radstone boys. "I put you in harm's way once; I can't do it again."

"Harm's way?" Edward motioned behind him. "These men will be with us. We have an army about us, and we're older than many of them."

"You might be older than some of them, but you're the sons of Lord Radstone. I can't believe you don't want to get to Jamaica and see your father. I know he thinks about you every day."

"We spoke with these men last night. Nango talked to them with us," said Edward. "They want us to be with them; they expect us to be part of the crew. For God's sake, Claire, we can't be shirkers. We'll see Father soon enough."

"What these men think of you is not my concern. Your safety has been part of my responsibility since we left Bantry. I ask you, lads; what would your father think of me if I could have brought you to Jamaica and did not do so? Answer me that."

"Please listen to us, Claire." James stepped closer to her. "Your mother and our mother will not have died in vain if we succeed. We must take part in this. Here and now, we release you from any responsibility."

"You and your brothers, James Radstone, do not have the authority to release me from my responsibility."

"We've been together through all of this, and now you intend to carry on without us?"

"Yes, I do."

"Then, if you intend to take us to Jamaica, you'll have to shackle us below. I dare say none of these men will help you chain us to anything. So I am not so sure it is within your power to take us to Jamaica."

Claire glared at James and then at Declan and Nango. Nango looked away.

Phillip nudged James. "Please, Claire, let us help you for the honor and the memory of our mother and yours."

Claire turned to Declan, who shrugged. She walked past the boys and into the throng of Africans, who stepped aside as she moved past them.

Claire walked to the bow and sat. The men sat or squatted, murmuring; no one approached her.

Nami bobbed just below the bow. *I understand what you are saying, but are they not old enough to decide for themselves?*

I promised their mother before she died that I would get them to their father. It is the right thing to do.

The three young ones have seen evil in the world and I think they believe the right thing is for them to fight against that evil.

Claire sat and thought. After a time, she rose and joined the assembled group. "All right, let us work to prepare the ship. We'll hunt for more slavers in the South Atlantic, and we will take these three fledgling pirates with us."

Nango translated the words, and a cheer erupted.

———

Three days of gathering food and working made the ship ready. The women fashioned a bright new flag. The material for the patchwork flag came from garments and cloth found in the crew's cabins aboard the slave ship. It had blue and green stripes with the yellow letters

F R E E D O M emblazoned across it. Declan found paint in the stores of the slave ship. He painted over the name *Wanderer* and, with an artistic flair, gave the ship its new name. Declan carried a bottle of rum forward and smashed it against the bowsprit, rechristening the ship as the *Freedom*. Nango explained all this to the amused Africans as they watched the ceremony.

The next morning the crew chanted as they winched the anchor. A skiff rowed out toward the ship with a little man standing in the bow, yelling and waving. The crew yelled back and motioned for him to hurry. Claire and Nango stood at the rail.

"Who's that?" Claire asked.

"Lambala. He has been in the jungle gathering since the day we landed."

"Gathering what?"

"Leaves, plants, things to make potions and powders. He is a powerful medicine man."

"You mean he's a doctor, a witch doctor?"

"Medicine man is better."

Claire watched as the crew helped the little man on board and brought on a good number of satchels and baskets for him. She made a mental note of the little man's popularity with the crew.

A light morning wind blew from the east, filling her sails, and the *Freedom* began to move away. People on shore waved and called out. Nango saw to the men and their duties, while Phillip stood next to Gani at the wheel. Ada and James hung high in the rigging. Declan strolled over to where Claire leaned against the aft railing.

"I love it. A beautiful flag," said Claire.

"It is that, and the most unusual pirate flag to ever fly."

"Pirate flag? Do you think people will consider us pirates?"

"Some people will. I do believe most of the world will be thinking we're quite a noble lot."

"The boys should not be with us."

"They've grown up since they first stepped on the deck of the *Brilliant*. You didn't have a choice in the matter. I'll do what I can to protect them." With that, Declan walked down the deck to inspect the guns.

Chapter 21

A Costly Battle

The *Freedom* sailed around and past Hispaniola, through the Leeward Islands, and eastward out into the Atlantic. The dolphins always showed Claire the way. Declan accepted her directions without question.

Claire lay in her bunk. She watched the moon cast its silvery glow on the black sea.

Claire?

Yes, Nami, what is it?

We bring news. Two of Bolo's friends have just returned. A large slave ship sails north-northwest. They said they could hear the moaning and cries from far away.

Claire jumped out of bed and walked out on the deck, where Edward stood at the wheel. "Edward. How's everything?"

"We're sailing due south on a gentle evening breeze."

"I think I'd like you to turn back to the north."

"Why?"

"Just a feeling. If we sail northward, we may find what we are looking for."

Edward looked at her for a moment, then smiled and turned the wheel. "Aye, Captain, due north." Claire stood at the wheel with Edward until daybreak.

As the sky lightened, a few men moved around the ship, performing their morning tasks. The cooking fire came to life in the galley. Ada walked across the deck, bidding a good morning to all. She took a spyglass, tucked it in her belt, and then climbed the mainmast to her lookout post. She also had traded her dress for loose cotton pants and a shirt.

"A lovely girl," Claire said.

"James seems to think so," Edward said. They both chuckled.

The morning wore on as the now-skillful crew went about the day's work.

"Sail ho!" The cry came from Ada. "Sail to the east!"

Many of the men ran to the starboard side. Claire snapped open her spyglass and caught the speck of white appearing on the horizon.

"That girl has the eyes of a falcon."

Edward stared right at Claire. "What made you want to turn north last night?"

"Intuition."

"Intuition?"

Claire looked at him, her face deadpan. "Actually, Edward, the dolphins told me to turn north."

Edward mustered an impassive look of his own, highlighted by cocked eyebrows. "You know, Claire, I believe you."

Claire turned and walked away from the wheel.

With Gani at the wheel, the *Freedom* closed on the much larger and slower ship. The three-masted ship had a red stripe around her dark blue hull just above the waterline. "She stands tall at the quarterdeck and foc's'le, and she's a lot larger than the first one," Declan said.

Claire lowered her spyglass. "I can't make out any gun ports. Do you think she carries slaves?"

"No way of knowing until we get a little closer."

Claire wished she could do away with this charade.

Declan kept looking. "There is your answer—look."

Claire pulled open her spyglass. "What is it?"

"Look at the mainmast."

"My God, poor devil." A naked black man hung by the neck, swinging as the ship rolled on the sea. "Get the men ready."

Declan rushed off to organize the crew.

Claire gathered the boys together. "You promised to wear those doublets. Get them on."

"They're hot and heavy," Edward complained.

"I don't have time to argue. You need them for protection. Get them on now."

Declan stood behind the first gun; James, Edward, Kataga, and Claire each commanded a cannon. The gun crews knelt next to their black tubes, ready to fire and reload.

Declan crouched behind his cannon, sighting along the barrel, then stepped to one side. He fired and nothing happened. The shot sailed over the slave ship.

James cocked his head. "It's a big ship—you missed."

Declan gave a disgusted nod. James sighted down the barrel of his cannon one more time. He lit the wick, the cannon recoiled, and the shot tore through the mainsail. He smiled at Declan.

"Bring her closer," Claire yelled.

Declan called through the speaking trumpet, "Heave to! Heave to, or we will fire on you!"

Six muskets fired from the slave ship; a swivel gun shot at them. The side of their ship splintered, and bullets whizzed over their heads.

"Well now," Declan said. "I don't think they intend for us to board her." Declan stepped to Edward's gun. "Let's give them something to think about. Try to hit her high on the hull near the quarterdeck. We don't want to hurt those people shackled below."

Edward squinted down the barrel and adjusted his gun's elevation. Declan checked it and stood away. Edward fired. The cannonball slammed into the ship. Timbers and splinters blasted out from the point of impact. The men of the *Freedom* cheered.

A moment passed and then the slave ship's crew began climbing in the rigging. The slave ship's sails furled, and its sailors returned to the deck. Declan called out to the big ship, "Stand away from your larboard side." The crew of the slaver was nowhere in sight.

The men of the *Freedom* threw their grappling hooks, leaped at the hull of the ship, and clambered up the side. Others swung from the rigging and dropped down on the deck.

Gani, Kataga, and three men dropped onto an empty quarterdeck. The boarding party stood in the middle of the slave ship in an eerie quiet. Puzzled, Claire said nothing. She pulled back the hammers on the two pistols tied to the baldric hanging around her neck. The body of the slave gently swung from a spar at the main mast.

Frenzied screams and shouts came from under the quarterdeck and the fo'c'sle. The entire crew of the slave ship charged from both ends, brandishing pikes, cutlasses, and guns. Their first volley crashed into the boarders and a dozen men fell. A sailor charged Claire with a pike. Claire fired and the man crumpled. Behind him, a sailor with an ax and a knife came at Claire. She pulled the trigger on her other pistol. Its hammer snapped; the gun did not fire. She tried to draw her sword, but it was too late. The man, with an evil sneer, raised the ax and swung. Declan jumped in front of Claire and grabbed the ax handle as it came down. He caught the man's knife hand as it thrust forward, and for a few seconds the two men stood facing each other in a deadly dance. A crushing blow from an African's club split the slaver's head open, and he fell from Declan's grip.

The crew of the *Freedom* found themselves surrounded. In close hand-to-hand combat, the Africans had no equals. The knowledge of what the bowels of the ship held, and the sight of the naked body hanging on the mast, fueled the Africans' determination and a vicious anger. They charged back in both directions, fighting the slavers with unmatched agility and ferocity. The warriors of the *Freedom* sprang on their enemies like lions on their prey. The slave ship's crew withered under the onslaught of swords, guns, knives, spears, fists, and teeth.

Splattered with blood, Claire stood in the middle of the ship; her spent pistols hung around her neck and she leaned on her cutlass, gasping for air. Declan stood next to her. The battle waned as the slaver crew gradually dropped their weapons and gave up. They fell to their knees, begging for mercy. The Africans were not inclined to give any quarter; Claire had to scream and grab at them to keep her crew from cutting the throats of the surrendered men.

During the fight, no one heard the swivel gun on the *Freedom* fire. A dozen of the slave ship's crew had brought the fight to the *Freedom*. The few of the crew that remained on her deck fought the slavers valiantly but were outnumbered, and the slavers closed in on Gani, Ada, and Phillip.

Kataga gasped at the sight on the *Freedom's* deck. Two men from the slaver crew stood near the aft. One held a knife to Ada's throat; Phillip lay on his back while the other man held a pike to the boy's chest.

Nango had jumped back over to the bow of the *Freedom*, and, with two others, moved toward the two slavers. Kataga swung over on a rope from the slave ship and dropped down on the deck behind them. He aimed his pistol at the man holding Ada. Kataga gently touched the muzzle to the back of the man's head and clicked the hammer back. "If you cut her, you die. Drop the knife and you live."

The man held the knife against Ada's throat and did not move. Nango raised his spear to his ear and cocked his arm back. His massive arm and shoulder muscles rippled with tension. The man threatening Phillip looked at Nango. Phillip instantly grabbed the pike just above the steel tip and pushed it away. The slaver thrust the pike down with all his weight, driving it into the deck an inch from Phillip's ribs. Phillip rolled to his left. Nango's arm snapped forward, and the spear thumped into the sailor's chest. He gasped, fell to his knees, and sprawled on top of Phillip.

Phillip squirmed out from under the corpse in a panic. Nango rolled the impaled sailor over, put his foot on the lifeless torso, and wrenched the spear out. Phillip took short, gasping breaths as he stepped back, his gray doublet soaked with the dead man's blood.

"You hurt?" Nango asked.

Phillip, breathing heavily, managed to reply, "No."

The sailor holding the knife at Ada's throat witnessed the fate of his shipmate. The knife slowly moved away; Ada stepped out of the man's grip. Nango took the knife and prodded the man back aboard the slave ship. Kataga surveyed the scene. Men lay everywhere, pierced by arrows, attesting to Gani's accuracy. Then Kataga saw him.

Gani's lifeless eyes stared up at the sun. The knife, plunged to the hilt in the old man's chest, must have belonged to the sailor lying next to Gani. Gani's knife stuck out of the slaver's chest. It looked as though the two men had simultaneously stabbed each other. Ada stood next to Kataga; she reached down and closed Gani's eyelids. "After he fired his last arrow, he dropped his bow and ran at them with his knife."

Kataga knelt next to his grandfather. "We have lost a great man."

Ada touched his straggly gray hair. A tear dropped on his forehead.

The crew of the *Freedom* began bringing up the people from the stinking hold of the slave ship. The wretchedness of their condition caused the men of the *Freedom* to transform from vicious warriors to gentle shepherds, although some of the *Freedom's* crew screamed in their African tongue at what was left of the slave ship's crew. Nango stood in front of the captured crew and persuaded his angry shipmates not to slaughter them.

James ran up the ladder to the quarterdeck. Emotions of anger, disgust, and horror swirled together, distorting his face. "It is as bad as the first one, if not worse. Look at that group over there." A dozen people lay together almost in a pile. "Look at them. They are living skeletons, nothing but skin and bones. They are too weak to stand. Some of the others told us that many of them were trying to commit suicide by refusing to eat. What kind of treatment would cause a human being to do that?"

Claire put her hand on James's shoulder and tried to calm him. "Go and help them. Make them understand that their ordeal is over."

James took a deep breath. He turned and walked down the ladder. As he passed the crew of the slave ship, now under guard at the starboard rail, he stopped and faced the captain. James slapped him in the face as hard as he could and walked away. The captain reeled from the blow. He said nothing.

They forced the surviving crew of the slave ship, along with their few wounded, into a longboat. The freed slaves helped dispose of the dead and washed the blood from the decks. Claire stood on the quarterdeck of the slave ship watching the mass of humanity squatting and sprawling on the deck below her. Their faces turned upward toward the blue brightness, and Claire saw relief and gratitude in their faces. Kataga and James took half of the *Freedom's* crew and prepared to sail the slave ship. The two ships separated and sailed to the west.

Declan stood next to her. "Half of the slaver crew died, and they carried away four wounded. The fighting spirit in these African lads has a wild fierceness about it."

"Do you blame them?"

"They're not interested in taking any of these slavers prisoners or just wounding them."

Claire looked at Declan with saddened eyes. "Awhile ago, when Nango was standing in front of those filthy dogs, I thought about going down there and having him help me cut all their throats. God forgive me."

"Don't worry yourself; I know you wouldn't do it. Twelve of our men died and eighteen are wounded. I have tended to them as best I can. A few more may die, but most should survive. Lambala is tending to them. He's an amazing fellow."

"Twelve and eighteen—over half of our ship's company," Claire said. "Was it worth it?"

"They died to free their countrymen from the horrors of this ship."

"And Gani—Gani is gone," she said. Her shoulders slumped.

"He saw something in you, Claire, something powerful, brave, and mystical. He died for you."

"Declan, don't ever say anything like that to me again. I don't want anyone dying for me. My mother died because I wanted adventure. Lady Radstone died a painful death, and I was powerless to help her.

"Well alright then, these men didn't die for you, but they did fight and die for the idea and the hope you have given them; the idea that we can stop these slavers and the hope that the people of Africa will someday be able to live without the fear of being enslaved. Look at them, Claire. They know we freed them and they know you're the leader of this band of warriors. The captain's cabin on this ship is a comfortable one, and we've readied it for you." Declan put his hand on her shoulder. "Go and rest."

Claire went down onto the main deck. The freed slaves stepped apart. She walked under the quarterdeck to the cabin. Dozens of candles gave the room a warm glow. Rich curtains of burgundy velvet hung on the walls. A round table, a writing desk, and a large four-poster bed filled the room. Claire looked at the ledger on the writing desk. It listed the cargo, and how many slaves had been lost during the voyage. She shook her head in disbelief and then began to cry. She slid off the chair and crawled under the desk, crying and sobbing. An hour passed and then another. Claire was weak from the emotion of the battle and the grief that always haunted her. She finally got up and steadied herself by taking some deep breaths at the window. She thought that she must always hide her feelings. She thought that if anyone saw her sobbing they might consider it a sign of weakness. Claire knew it was a time to lead.

Two elegant armoires stood against the wall, along with three oversized trunks. Claire opened the first armoire to find the captain's dress uniforms and a plumed hat, which she tried on. The second closet held more clothes.

The captain dressed well, she thought.

The three trunks, each large enough for a man to sleep in, begged to be investigated. Claire opened the first one, finding bolts of silk, cotton, and wool cloth, boxes of sewing needles, spools of thread, and dozens of pairs of scissors of various sizes. A piece of paper sat on top of the goods, listing, in Dutch and English, the items in the trunk along with prices these goods were sure to bring in the colonies. Claire thought the women back on Hispaniola would put this bonanza to good use.

Claire opened the second trunk and stepped back. The radiant greens, blues, yellows, and whites of luxurious silk gowns jumped out. The third trunk held more of the same. When Claire dug down, she found undergarments and delicate lace camisoles. She held a pale-blue gown with white lace against her body and sighed at the image in the full-length mirror inside the door of the armoire. She thought about Lieutenant Garrison, and wondered what had happened to him after he reached Port Royal. Would he like to see her in one of these? Claire decided to reward herself for her piracy with a few of the gowns. She thought she would keep them until she had a reason to wear one. She hoped the reason was still somewhere in the Caribbean, and was thinking of her. She sighed.

A smaller trunk sat next to the writing table. She opened it and, smiling, began pulling out the books. She read the spines, stacking the books on the floor. She found a book on the flora and fauna of the New World and books written in English, French, Spanish, and Italian. For Claire, the treasure in this trunk equaled the gold doubloons of the cave. She sat on the floor among the books, reading passages. She wondered what kind of a man would peddle sewing materials, bring beautiful women's clothing to market in the colonies, collect scholarly books, and, at the same time, sell human beings into slavery.

Claire couldn't concentrate. She closed the book she was browsing through, and concluded that the captain and the entire crew must have convinced themselves that these African people were nothing more than farm animals. A tear fell on the book.

Claire, how do you feel? Nami asked. *We can sense that your mind is troubled.*

Claire sat at the window. *I'm sick—so many good men lost their lives.*

The sea ran red around the ship, a dolphin said.

Hundreds of sharks came, another dolphin said. *We had to move away. The sharks become frenzied when there is so much blood.*

Men died, Claire, but you saved many more. Some of our pod had been following this ship for some time, and every day bodies fell into the sea as it sailed to the west. You and your men did a great deed this day.

A great deed? Many men died today. I killed today.

Get some sleep.

I may never sleep again.

You should sleep knowing that you saved many lives.

The next morning Claire stepped out of the cabin to the sounds of children playing. The crowd of Africans receded as they bowed to her.

"Please, no." She gestured for them to stand.

Claire climbed to the quarterdeck, where Edward and James stood at the wheel with Declan next to them.

"She sails very well," Edward said.

Declan pointed. "Except for the large hole Edward put in her, she is in fine shape. I'll begin repairing the damage today."

"What do you think about keeping her and moving the cannons over from the sloop?" James asked.

Declan nodded. "I could begin fashioning gun ports. We'll place the guns on the main deck."

"She carries plenty of sail," Edward said. "She might not be as fast as the *Freedom*, but I am sure she can close in on any one of the slavers we might encounter."

"We'll be able to carry hundreds more men," James said.

"They'll be eager to join us," Declan said.

Claire was not listening. "How are the wounded?"

"Everyone is coming along. Lambala is tending to them," Declan said. "How are you feeling?"

Claire smiled and nodded.

On the voyage back to Hispaniola, Claire moved about the ship, helping to care for the new passengers with the scant medical supplies she had found on the ship. A little band of children followed her wherever she went. When Claire was not working on the ship, she was in her quarters, where she scattered her newfound treasures to every corner of the cabin. She had not read a book for a year or more, and she dug into the volumes voraciously. The reading helped her fight off the depression that continued to haunt her.

Chapter 22

Skeletons of Ships

Claire watched from the quarterdeck of the *Freedom* as people waved and shouted from the shore. Longboats and skiffs carried the weakest people, while the more fit and energetic men and women dove or jumped into the crystalline water and swam to shore. To the surprise of some, dolphins came under the swimmers and nudged them. The swimmers splashed in panic until one man held on to a dolphin's dorsal fin, and the dolphin pulled him. The man laughed and shouted as the dolphin spun, leaving him standing in shallow water. After that, the dolphins spent hours pulling people ashore and giving rides to the children. Other dolphins leaped and spun in the air to the cheers of the people on the beach and the ships. Claire recognized Stark as he flew into the air and flipped end over end.

James, Edward, and Phillip watched, smiled, and remembered. James and Phillip watched the dolphins; Edward watched Claire. He noted that every time the dolphins were about, a strange and distant look came across her face. It was as if she would put herself into a sort of trance as she stared at the water.

"Ahoy, Claire," Declan shouted, as he and Nango came alongside, rowing a skiff. Claire waved to them. They climbed aboard. "A great feast in your honor will begin before dusk," Declan announced. "The people are calling you the Queen of the Dolphins."

"Well, that's silly. I'm not the queen of anything."

"All the same, you might as well enjoy the evening, lass," Declan said.

Smoke rose from dozens of cooking fires along the beach. "It does look as if there will be a fantastic feast. Excuse me while I get ready for the festivities."

Declan and Nango bowed. "Your majesty," Declan said. "We await your command."

Claire laughed, and then wrinkled her brow in mock sternness. "Enough now, and don't you dare do any bowing when we get ashore."

Nango grinned a toothy grin. "Yes, my queen."

Claire opened the trunk and took out the three gowns she had decided would fit her. She stood in front of the mirror, holding each up. She thought about which one Charles would like the best. Claire stepped into the bright yellow one. She realized it would be impossible for her to fasten the myriad of buttons, hooks, and ribbons on the back of the bodice. She thought about seeking out some female help but decided against it, and she certainly did not want to ask Declan or Nango to come to her aid. Claire stepped out of the dress and began rummaging through the clothes in the armoires.

Barefoot, Claire padded across the deck to where Declan and Nango waited. She tipped her cocked hat. "Gentlemen."

"That is a grand uniform," Declan said.

"An admiral and a queen," Nango said.

"Would you gentlemen care to row me to shore and accompany me to the festivities?" she said in a light, airy manner.

"It'll be our honor," Declan said.

Claire stood in the bow as the two men rowed the skiff. She wore an oversized blue coat, with two rows of brass buttons and gold epaulettes, over a white blouse. She had rolled up the sleeves, which hung past her hands, and the red silk lining made lovely cuffs. A too-long black belt held up the baggy white silk breeches.

As Claire approached the beach, hundreds came to greet her. She jumped off the skiff and waded ashore. The throng separated, and people reached out to touch her as she walked toward them.

Further down the beach, people milled about among woven mats piled high with coconuts, fruits, roots, and berries. James, Edward, and Phillip stood by a huge fire where two young boys turned a massive spit. The fire sizzled and smoked as fat from the wild boar dripped down.

The three Radstones ran to Claire. "A smashing outfit," James said.

"I must have a coat like that," Edward said.

"Where did you get those things?" Phillip asked.

"One of the armoires in the captain's cabin is full of uniforms. Tomorrow, go out and take some things for yourselves. I am sure a few of the women can sew them to fit."

Claire sat down with a square wooden plate on her lap. She ate wild boar, smoked fish, and fruit. Ada, Kataga, and the rest were nearby, talking about their adventures and their plans. They remembered Gani with smiles and tears, telling stories of his feats and kindnesses. They talked about his wisdom. Everyone remembered a time when the little man had awed them with an arrow flying from his bow.

———

Crews of fifty men each took turns with the block and tackle to hoist the cannon from the sloop to the large blue ship. More men swarmed over the ship, repairing and refitting under Declan's watchful eye. They removed the chains. Nango helped some of the men set up smith's fires, and they began pounding the iron into much friendlier and more useful things, such as tools, hoes, shovels, hammers, nails, and hinges for doors. A hundred women and older children cleaned and scrubbed the lower decks for a week. They hauled up bucket after bucket of foul bilge and succeeded in washing away the filth and putrid stench of slavery from the holds.

With the new blue ship renamed *Freedom,* the men loaded her with provisions and readied her for the sea and another hunt. Claire stood at the railing on the quarterdeck with Declan. The first slave ship sat near the beach. The exposed ribs of the hull pointed skyward, resembling the skeleton of a giant sea animal rotting in the tropical sun.

"They wasted no time in taking her apart," Claire said.

Declan nodded. "They will dismantle her to the waterline and then pull what is left onto the beach. Nango told them to do the same with the sloop. We have taken everything we might need off of her."

"I'll miss her. She served us well," Claire said. She turned to see Kataga, Edward, and Phillip standing there in their newly tailored officers' uniforms. Kataga wore a blue coat over his native garb. A large knife stuck out of his belt where the unbuttoned coat flapped open. Edward's jacket had one gold epaulette and another of silver threads. Phillip's coat engulfed him, and he wore it with a pair of peach-colored satin breeches. The three of them remained barefoot.

She smiled. "Gentlemen, you look very…well, very official—sort of."

"What do you mean, sort of?" Edward said.

"One would not call this," Claire touched the lapel of Edward's jacket, "a proper English navy uniform."

"I dare say one would not call this band of ours the proper English navy."

Claire stepped back and inspected them. "How true, Edward, how very true."

James strolled over, head held high in a display of feigned superiority, his blue tunic buttoned and the white breeches buckled below the knee. White stockings covered his calves, and he sported a pair of shiny black pumps.

"Good God, James," Claire pointed. "Shoes."

James pointed one of his feet, touching his toes to the deck as if performing a delicate dance step. "What do you think?"

"Well, I don't know what to say," Claire said.

"I like them." James gestured to his three companions. "These swabs simply don't understand; if you're going to be an officer on this ship, you should look the part."

They laughed.

Nango said, "We begin now."

The group walked to the quarterdeck rail and gazed down upon the ship's company gathered on the deck. Some hung from the rigging in order to see. Claire spoke out as Nango translated. "We are a ship with a purpose like no other. We sail to make men free!"

The men cheered. Claire held her hands up for quiet. "I thank you for being part of this crew, and I pledge to you that I will do my best to captain her well. We sail on a ship called *Freedom;* we sail three hundred strong, and we will not fail!"

Cheers erupted, and men began to move about the ship. Ada jumped into the rigging and climbed to the crow's nest on the mainmast. The men sang as they weighed anchor and unfurled the sails. Every person left ashore gathered on the beach, waving and singing. As the newest *Freedom* moved away, Claire found Declan beside her. "The thought nags at me that the boys should not be with us," she said.

"You didn't have a choice in the matter at all. Having them along is the right thing to do."

"I doubt Lord Radstone would agree."

Declan shrugged.

The *Freedom* sailed west out of the great bay, rounded Cape Dame Marie at the southwest corner of Saint-Dominque, and headed east. The ship tacked into the prevailing trade winds as she passed the Leeward Islands and moved out into the Atlantic. The sailing proved challenging at first, but the crew understood the purpose of the voyage and soon improved as sailors.

Claire directed the ship with great skill and accuracy. The crew talked about Claire's mystical ability to find and intercept slavers sailing on the vast Atlantic. They believed no slave ships coming from Africa could elude the *Freedom*. The crew also noticed the dolphins always swimming near the ship.

———

With its white female captain and ferocious black crew, the *Freedom* became legendary. At the sight of the now-famous blue, green, and yellow flag, many ships would furl their sails and surrender without a fight. Some fought, but none withstood the onslaught from the crew of the *Freedom*.

As the months passed, the *Freedom* took ships flying the flags of France, the Netherlands, Portugal, Spain, and even Great Britain. The population on the southern peninsula of Saint-Dominque flourished. The people continued to dismantle the captured ships, using the lumber to build communities of small cottages along the coastline. Many of the buildings featured nautical touches such as spars, pieces of masts, and railings. Hammocks fashioned from canvas sailcloth hung everywhere.

Chapter 23

The Spaniard

For a week the *Freedom* had languished in the Atlantic, waiting for the next slaver to pass by. In the evenings Claire sat in her candlelit cabin, relishing her quiet time to read and, of course, to talk to her friends.

We're proud to help you find the slave ships. Helping humans is something we want to do, Nami said. *Our teachers want us to do this.*

If your teachers love humanity so much, why don't they reveal themselves? Why don't they join us?

It's their law, Sanjay said. *Their law tells them that they must not interfere with the world. It's why we help anytime we can. It's why we'll always be here for—*

A ship. A large ship. A male dolphin's voice broke in.

Where? Sanjay asked.

Claire stood at the window, though she could see no dolphins in the black sea.

The ship is sailing directly south and is behind us. It's moving much faster than this ship and should be in sight by daybreak.

Is it a slave ship? Claire asked.

No, I don't think so, the dolphin said. *This ship has many cannons.*

Probably a man-of-war. I wonder if she's looking for us?

Claire hurried up to the quarterdeck. "Good evening, gentlemen."

"Good evening," Edward and James said.

"What is our condition and course?" Claire asked. Her stomach began to churn a little.

"Just cruising." Edward tapped at the glass covering the compass. "Our course is due south."

James sat on a cask next to his brother. "While we were waiting, we thought we would use only a few sails."

"That's fine," Claire said. "I think we should turn a little to the west."

Edward looked at her.

"Let's try our luck to the west."

"South-southwest it is," Edward said.

James walked to the railing of the quarterdeck; a few men on the night watch sat below. "Do you want more sail?" he asked.

"No, not yet. The crew should sleep awhile longer." Claire stood at the aft rail and stared back into the darkness. *I can't tell them there could be danger lurking out there. How would I tell them I knew of such a ship behind us? There may be nothing to it.*

Claire did not go back to her cabin. She rested her hand on Edward's shoulder. "Turn toward the west a bit more."

Edward nodded.

The night wore on. Claire paced around the quarterdeck.

"Is something bothering you, Claire?" Edward asked.

"No, I'm just a little restless." Claire always had the feeling that Edward could tell what she was thinking.

James peered out into the night with his spyglass. "Claire, what do you think of that?"

"What?"

"There." He pointed and handed her the spyglass. "There, behind us and a bit to larboard, do you see the light?"

Claire pulled the glass away from her eye. "James, darken the ship. Douse every lantern and torch—now."

"What's the matter?"

"If we can see them, they can see us."

Edward looked over his shoulder. "It could be a slave ship."

"Coming from the north?"

James gave the orders.

"Edward," Claire stood next to him. "As soon as they get rid of the lights, I want you to turn hard to the west."

Edward wrinkled his brow, and his eyes narrowed. Claire patted him on the back. "Let's not take any undue chances."

With the lights doused, the *Freedom* turned even more to the west. Like a cat fixated on a strange twinkling object, Claire moved back and forth across the quarterdeck, watching the light in the distance. She saw a glimmer of light on the water just below her and looked over the rail. She spun around. "Edward, I left a lantern lit in my cabin."

"James," Edward yelled, "Claire's cabin, a lantern!"

Claire woke Declan and Nango and showed them the light. They, in turn, rousted out the crew, and before long, every stitch of sail the *Freedom's* masts could hold snapped taut, catching the wind. The light of daybreak bounced off the sails of the ship behind the *Freedom*. Three masts sprang up from the mystery ship. James snapped his spyglass closed. "She has as much sail aloft as she can muster. I believe she intends to overtake us."

"I should have put up more sail sooner," Claire said.

"Stop fretting about it. You didn't know what that ship was all about last night," James said.

Claire looked at him. *But I did know. How could I have been so stupid?*

Declan and the others gathered on the quarterdeck. She turned to them. "After we doused the lights, we turned smartly to the west. Our pursuers anticipated that we would run west and followed us—or they caught the glow of that last lantern."

"Don't worry yourself about it at all," Declan said as he held up his spyglass. The sails and the hull of the ship were now visible. "She is a ship of the line, and she has a fat bow."

The sailors of the Caribbean knew that a thinner, more streamlined bow meant the ship was a British or French vessel. A fatter, more rounded bow indicated a ship of Spanish or Dutch origin.

"She is most likely in the employ of King Philip of Spain; those men are probably not very happy about our doings here on their main."

"*Their* main?" Edward said.

"Philip has proclaimed it so," Declan said. Phillip gave Declan a puzzled look. Declan smiled. "You do have the same name, but you're far more of a gentleman, I'll tell you. Think of it, lads—half French pig, half Spanish donkey, a foul-smelling and ignorant combination, don't you think?"

The boys all laughed.

Claire did not laugh. She turned to Nango. "Rig more sail if you can."

The ship behind the *Freedom* continued to come closer.

"You're right, Declan; she flies the Spanish flag," James announced as he looked through his glass.

At noon, the warship fired her two forward-facing cannon. The shots fell far short of the *Freedom*. As the afternoon wore on, the Spanish ship fired from time to time. The crew remained quiet as they went about their tasks, but, to a man, their faces reflected the seriousness of the situation.

"That last shot came closer. Those gunners will soon have us in range," Claire said. "I don't believe we will make it to nightfall without being hit."

"You're right," Declan said.

"What if we turned and fired at her? Maybe we could sting her a little."

Everyone on the quarterdeck looked at Claire.

"If we do, we must be very fast and turn back away. The Spaniard will fire a broadside back at us—a deadly proposition," Declan said.

They gathered at the wheel and made their plan. "Nango, get the men ready to make the turn. Edward, you and Phillip man the wheel. James, you and Kataga command the guns. Remember, you will only get one shot, so aim well," Claire said.

Shots from the Spaniard howled overhead and tore through the *Freedom*'s sails. Rigging and a snapped spar fell to the deck. With the starboard guns ready, Claire nodded to Declan.

"All right, men, move sharply now. Turn her, lads," he said to Edward and Phillip. "Due north and keep her turning. After we fire, turn her back to the west as quickly as you can."

James and Kataga moved behind the guns, adjusting their aim. The wheel spun, and the *Freedom* turned to the north. The Spanish ship reacted, turning to the north as well. The *Freedom* got into position first, and Declan yelled, "Fire!"

The six cannon roared. Shots ripped through the rigging of the Spaniard. One shot hit her amidships, and another ball blew a hole in her bow at the waterline. The Spaniard kept turning to starboard as the *Freedom* started to turn away and sail back toward the west.

A broadside from the warship boomed out. Plumes of water erupted around the *Freedom*. Shots whizzed overhead; more rope and tackle rained down on the crew. A cannonball ripped into the aft. Another shot struck the third gun position, tossing the cannon across the ship. Men and timbers flew in every direction.

James lay sprawled on the deck, moaning, with his left arm torn apart. Blood poured from the tattered sleeve of his naval jacket.

Ada rushed to him, tied a leather strap around his upper arm, and cinched it tight. "Help. Help us," Ada cried. She held his head and talked to him, as his face twisted in pain.

Men ran to help the wounded. Ada and three men carried James below.

The warship followed. Its two forward-facing guns continued to fire, but to no avail. The maneuver had gained the *Freedom* a little more distance from her pursuer.

Nango took the wheel and shouted orders along with Claire. Below deck, Edward and Phillip held their brother; Ada stood next to him. The moans and cries of the wounded filled the lower deck. Declan walked over, wiping blood from his hands. He cut the sleeve of the coat away and inspected the mangled arm. He poked, probed, and studied James's arm. From the elbow to the wrist, strings of sinew held together smashed red muscles and splintered bones. "I'm sorry, lad, I'll not be able to repair this. I'm going to have to cut it away."

"No," James cried. "Please, no." James grabbed at Phillip, staring with wild eyes. "God, it hurts. The pain, damn it, the pain."

Phillip held his brother tight around the head and right arm. "You'll be all right. Hang on, James, hang on."

"The pain, damn it—please, make it stop."

"Edward," Declan yelled, "fetch me the surgeon's instruments, and find another bottle of rum." Declan gently wiped the sweat from James's face with a bloodstained rag. "When he comes back, I want you to drink down as much of the rum as you can."

The boys and Ada held James. Edward poured rum into his brother's mouth. James sputtered and coughed, but drank it down. Edward held up his brother's head and poured more into him. The little man named Lambala moved around the room with a tray of his potions, powders, and ointments. Everyone knew Lambala to be a medicine man of wondrous ability. The ointments he made staved off infection and healed most cuts and scrapes in days. He had the men chew a bitter-tasting leaf to control nausea, and in rough seas, no member of the *Freedom*'s crew ever got seasick. Lambala inspected the mangled arm and gave James a small sip of an elixir. He looked at Declan, nodded, and then moved away to help some of the others.

Claire jumped down the ladder as Declan prepared to cut away the arm. She froze at the sight of James. "Declan. What are you doing? Stop, you could kill him."

"He'll bleed to death if I don't do this."

"We'll get him to Jamaica."

"He doesn't have that much time."

"Please, Declan, don't. The shock could kill him."

Phillip and Edward looked at Claire. Declan spun and grabbed Claire's shoulders. "You go and make sure those Spaniards don't catch us. I'll take care of James and these other men. If she overtakes us, we're all lost. Go and command your ship."

He turned back and told the boys and Ada to hold James tight. Declan had James bite down on a leather strap, and he poured rum on his knife and the elbow. He began to cut.

Claire watched and felt sick. She turned and climbed the ladder. Nango and Kataga stood at the wheel.

"Do we have every yard aloft?" Claire asked.

"All she can hold, and they have not been able to reach us with their cannons," Kataga reported.

Claire put her spyglass to her eye. "That hole in her bow may slow her down a bit."

"They will fix the hole," Nango said.

Claire nodded. "Keep us on course for the Leeward Islands. Maybe we can elude them in the dark."

"How is James?" Kataga asked.

"He lost his left arm," Claire said as she walked to the aft rail, tears streaming down her face.

Are you safe? Nami called out.

Yes. James lost an arm.

Will he live? Bolo asked.

I hope so. He's still in danger. He has lost a lot of blood.

Many dolphins live with one flipper and swim as well as any of us, Sanjay said. *He's young and strong. He'll recover.*

I pray you're right. I'll never forgive myself if he dies. I knew the Spanish ship was coming, and I didn't move away soon enough. Last night I acted stupidly. I can't let that ship, or any like it, ever come near us again.

After a few hours, Declan came up from below. The blood smeared on his clothes attested to the grim work he had been doing. "James will live. We took off his left arm at the elbow and bound the stump well to stop the bleeding. Four other wounded men will survive as well. Three men died. Ada is staying with James. He's a brave young man."

"Is he conscious?" Claire asked.

"He's sleeping in fits. I put a good amount of rum in him to help with the pain, and Lambala gave him something. I think he will sleep for some time. What of the Spaniard?"

Claire walked to the aft rail. "She doesn't seem to be gaining on us. The hole in her bow has slowed her. I had hoped to lose her in the dark, but there'll be a full moon and no clouds. I don't think the Spaniard is inclined to let go of us."

"We might need to turn and fire at her again," Declan said.

"Let me think on that."

Declan walked the deck, instructing the men who hammered and sawed, repairing the damaged areas of the ship. Claire went down to check on James and the others. She came back up and wandered the quarterdeck, absorbed in her thoughts.

The *Freedom* sailed into the setting sun as hues of yellow, red, pink, and blue spread over the sky above the tropical sea. Later, the night sky sparkled and the moonlight glowed on the gentle waves. The sails of the warship behind the *Freedom* took on a ghostly pallor. Both ships ran without lights.

Claire watched the Spanish ship, thinking of ways to gain the advantage. No idea came to her.

Nami's mind broke into her thoughts. *Two of our family just returned from the islands ahead. We think we have found a way for you to escape from this ship.*

Claire leaned on the rail. *What can we do?*

Two small islands lie ahead with a reef of jagged coral between them. A deep channel winds through the reef. We'll take you there and guide you through the channel. The channel is very deep, but we scrape our bellies when we try to swim over the reef on either side of it. If the warship does not follow your exact path, it will run aground.

Be precise in your sailing, Sanjay said. *Follow us exactly. The channel is not wide.*

We can do that, Claire said. *This may be our only chance.*

Come to the bow and make sure you can see us.

Claire ran to the bow. Six dolphins broke the surface of the phosphorescent sea. Claire ran back to the wheel. "Declan, stay at the wheel tonight. There may be a way to escape. I'll stand in the bow and guide you. Make sure you can see me."

"What'll we do?" he asked.

"I'll tell you as we get closer."

Declan smiled, nodded, and asked no other questions. The *Freedom* sailed toward the islands and shifted to the south. The Spaniard followed. The islands came into view on the moonlit horizon, and Claire explained her plan.

Declan woke the crew before first light. He relayed the plan to Nango, and then to the others as dawn broke, silhouetting the Spanish ship. Claire stood on the fo'c'sle at the bowsprit.

Our family and friends are ahead of us in the channel. I will swim near you and tell you when to make the turn, Sanjay told her.

We are ready, Claire answered.

Edward and Phillip came up behind Claire. "How is James?" she asked.

"He's sleeping," Edward said. "He has looked at his arm, and I think he's starting to come to terms with it. Lambala is tending to him. He's put herbs and ointments on the wound. Nango says it will help. Lambala has been sitting with James in his arms for hours, rocking him and chanting. When James wakes, Lambala has him chew some leaves and drink some sweet-smelling tea, and he goes back to sleep."

Phillip shook his head in disbelief. "James is sleeping like a babe and seems to be feeling better. My brother and a witch doctor—now that will be a story to tell."

"Why did you pick this channel?" Edward asked Claire. "These islands are close to each other. This could be a dangerous place."

"We might be able to elude this Spaniard by sailing through here."

"You're not answering my question."

Claire knew that, but, as she had done so many times before, she just gave Edward an expressionless look and said nothing.

Phillip shouted, "Look, dolphins! A good number of them to starboard and up ahead."

"The dolphins," said Edward. "Will the dolphins show us the way between these islands?"

"Maybe they will swim in the deeper water," Claire said, "and maybe we will follow them."

Edward raised an eyebrow. "Yes, maybe, but how did you decide to do this? You don't know these waters."

Claire turned to Edward. "I'll guide this ship, and if each of you does what is expected of you, we will get through this. Go and help Declan, Nango, and Kataga. Phillip, go to your post."

Edward paused; his eyes pierced the façade of calm authority that Claire assumed. He turned away to help the others. The *Freedom* began sailing in the narrow channel separating the two islands. Claire looked up at the sails and cursed. The hills of the island diverted some of the wind. The cannon on the warship fired; two shots whizzed overhead.

We have slowed, and the Spaniard has us in range. How much longer? Claire asked.

Can you see the dolphin in front of you? Sanjay said.

A dolphin jumped repeatedly, landing in the same spot.

Yes, I see him.

Turn quickly to the north before you come to him. Just past him the coral is hard, sharp, and dangerous.

Claire yelled down, "Phillip, run back and tell Declan to be ready to turn hard to starboard on my signal." Phillip ran; when he reached the wheel, Declan waved at Claire in acknowledgment.

Their pursuer fired again, and two spouts of water erupted on either side of the *Freedom*, amidships. The *Freedom* ran close to the leaping dolphin.

Now, Claire, now. Turn to the north now, Sanjay said.

Claire waved her arms and pointed to starboard. Declan spun the wheel, and the *Freedom* responded.

Good. Straighten her out, Sanjay said.

Claire waved and pointed back the other way. *How long on this course?*

Not long. There will be another dolphin marking the last turn. You'll swing around the edge of the reef, and then you can run out to sea.

The *Freedom* cut behind the northern island, losing sight of the Spaniard for a few moments.

There, Claire. There is the place, Sanjay said.

Claire saw a dolphin leaping. "Ada, go tell Declan to be ready to turn hard to larboard."

Ada darted between the men as she scampered aft. Claire watched her jump on the quarterdeck and talk to Declan.

"To larboard!" Claire yelled and pointed. "Hard to larboard!" The *Freedom* turned back to the west and the Spaniard came into view.

Claire ran back to the quarterdeck. "We've done all we can do. Now pray he comes straight at us."

White and gray smoke billowed from the bow of the warship, followed by booming reports. Two shots tore through the sails of the *Freedom*. The men knew the next shots would be on the mark.

The man-of-war closed on the *Freedom*. It sailed straight between the islands and never made a turn. Claire and Declan watched through their spyglasses. The bow of the Spanish ship rose out of the water as the coral smashed through the hull. The mortally wounded ship heeled to her larboard side. Her masts rocked, and rigging fell to her deck.

"Ha," Declan said. "It worked. She's run hard aground." He slapped Claire on the back. "It's the luck of the Irish. Do you think those dolphins are from Ireland?"

Claire's eyes quickly cut toward Declan and then back. Men patted Claire on the back, shook her hand, and a few bowed.

We heard the ship's hull tear open, a dolphin said.

We could hear the water rushing into her, Bolo added. *The reef will hold that ship forever.*

Alongside the *Freedom*, twenty dolphins leaped in perfect unison, arched over, and splashed back in at the same time. The men cheered and laughed.

Claire could hear the cheers of the dolphins. One of the dolphins jumped and spun, while another flipped end over end. Claire recognized Stark.

The crew watched the dolphins—and Claire—until the dolphins quieted their celebration.

Nango took the wheel. Ada, Kataga, Declan, Edward, and Phillip gathered on the quarterdeck.

"What course?" Nango asked.

Claire put her arm around Phillip's shoulder and looked at Edward. "It is time, lads. Time to sail to Port Royal." The boys said nothing. "Due west, Nango. Take us to Jamaica."

"Then Jamaica and Port Royal it is," Declan said. "I'll get the charts and set the course."

Claire walked below to visit the wounded men. When she came to James, she knelt beside him. "James, how do you feel?"

He lifted his head. "The pain is not too bad. Declan and Lambala saved my life." James managed a slight smile, fighting back a tear. "I'm right-handed, so maybe I shan't miss it much. I heard what you did, Claire. You're a great captain."

Claire touched his hair. "We're bound for Jamaica and your father."

"No. Don't do it on my account. I'll be up and around in a few days."

"It isn't because of you, James. There will be other warships."

"The men say you can do anything. They believe you possess powerful magic. We can defeat other warships."

"Not without more cannons and shot."

"My father will give us what we need."

"Well then, we are off to Port Royal, where we shall ask him for a bit of powder and shot. Maybe your father will give us one of His Majesty's ships of the line," said Claire with mock seriousness.

James smiled.

"Get some sleep now."

The *Freedom* sailed toward Jamaica. Claire strolled on the quarterdeck, and she began to relax. She had not experienced a calm day in a very long time. Edward sat on a keg in the corner of the deck, watching her.

Chapter 24

The Pink House

The *Freedom* drifted off the coast of Jamaica, waiting for the dawn. With most of her sails furled, she made no wake as she crept past a few small cays toward the harbor of Port Royal. The ship's green, blue, and yellow flag fluttered in the light morning wind. Claire and Declan stood at the starboard rail, looking through their spyglasses.

Claire lowered her spyglass. "I've been thinking. You know we've broken a few of His Majesty's laws, and a number of those slave ships were bound for Jamaica. These people might not be too happy to see us. Maybe we should just drop the boys off and sail away."

"Jaysus, what are you talking about? You've been wanting to bring these boys back to their father for years, and now you're about to do it. You might as well bid the man a good day. I'm sure he'll think you're a hero. Do you think Lord Radstone will be arresting his own sons?"

"What if Lord Radstone is no longer the governor?"

Declan paused for a long moment and then smiled. "Well now that is something to consider. I surely wouldn't want us to have to fight our way out of here. Ah, but don't worry yourself. Remember, these lads are English nobility. The governor will surely show a little respect. I do think I'll have the men reload the guns after the salute."

Claire looked at him with a furrowed brow.

A few people moved about the town, and men walked on the red brick battlements of Fort Charles. As the *Freedom* sailed around the point of land where the town of Port Royal stood, three black-hulled British warships came into view. Their masts and spars rose up as if tangled together, like a grove of barren, closely planted trees.

Claire watched Fort Charles through her spyglass. Declan nodded and the larboard guns fired a broadside salute. Men began scurrying on the walls of Fort Charles. Everyone in Port Royal would now know that the *Freedom* had arrived. The men furled the sails and dropped the anchor out in the middle of the bay.

James, Edward, and Phillip gathered on the deck, resplendent in their quasi-naval officers' uniforms. Ada had repaired, folded, and pinned up the lower part of James's sleeve. James himself looked wan. Claire thought he had begun his recovery nicely. The potions from Lambala had helped his healing and given him back a little of his energy. Claire, wearing her blue admiral's waistcoat and white breeches, joined them. "Well, gentlemen—are we ready to go ashore?"

They all looked both excited and apprehensive.

"Do you think father will be there to greet us?" Phillip asked, pointing out at the pier, which was filling with people.

"If he's on this island, I can assure you he will be on that pier."

"Should we be wearing shoes?" Edward asked.

"Why start now?" Claire said.

James said nothing as he sat watching the dock and the gathering crowd. Claire looked at him. "Your father will be so very proud of you, James. Don't worry." James looked back at Claire, a slight, crooked smile appearing on his face.

Ada, her brother, Nango, and Declan gathered with Claire and the boys. "The longboat is almost ready," Nango reported.

"Will you come ashore with us on the first boat?" Claire asked.

"No," Declan said. "You take the lads in—that is the most important thing. We'll be along later. These men have never seen a place like Port Royal. I believe Nango and I will take them ashore in small groups and be with them as they wander about. I want to make sure there are no confrontations between these men and the plantation owners."

Claire nodded. "Good thought."

The boys climbed down into the longboat. James refused any help and performed the task nimbly with one hand. The men rowed toward the town.

Good luck to you, Claire. This is a happy day. Don't be nervous.

You know I'm nervous?

We can feel your mind.

You know my feelings?

Sometimes, when the feelings are strong. The dolphin turned away from the longboat and swam out toward the sea.

You have done so much for us. So much that no one will ever know.

We'll be outside the harbor in the open sea. Call us if you need us. Your mind has become powerful, and we will hear you.

Phillip sat close to Claire and gestured toward the dolphin. "When you're near the sea, you'll never be alone."

Claire nodded. "So it seems."

A crowd of men, some in blue coats and some in red, filled the pier as the longboat nudged against it.

A tall, lean man wearing the uniform of a naval captain called down, "Are you Miss Claire Riley?"

"Yes, sir, I am, and these three gentlemen are James, Edward, and Phillip Radstone."

"Well then, this is a very special day."

"Yes, sir, it is that," Claire said.

The boys climbed onto the pier; Claire followed. The naval officer touched his cocked hat. "I am Captain Samuel Watson, at your service."

"So, Captain, how did you know my name?"

"Your ship flies a blue, green, and yellow flag. It had to be you. You are the most talked-about person in this part of the world and, I dare say, the entire British Empire."

"Is Lord Radstone—?"

Lord Radstone almost pushed the captain off the pier as he rushed forward. "Where are my boys? Boys! Boys!"

Phillip and Edward jumped at their father and gripped him. "Father."

He looked down at them as tears rolled down his cheeks. "My God, boy, look at how you've grown." Lord Radstone lifted his eyes and looked at his oldest son's apprehensive face as James stood behind his brothers. Lord Radstone smiled, reached out, and pulled him in. He scanned the dock over the heads of his boys and called, "Elizabeth!" The boys stiffened. The three sad faces told their father what he did not want to hear.

James shook his head. "Mother is gone."

Lord Radstone composed himself. "We'll talk of it later." He stepped past the boys toward Claire, who stood by herself at the end of the pier. She did not want to curtsy with breeches on, so she gave a slight bow. "My lord." Her head bumped into his chest as he enveloped her in a bear hug.

"God bless you, Claire. You brought my boys to me. God bless you."

"I am so sorry, my lord. Lady Radstone saved my life. She told those pirates I was her daughter, and they never touched me. I was powerless to save her life."

Tears continued to fall from Lord Radstone's face. "You have brought my boys back to me." He hugged his boys again, and they clung to their father. "I heard about your mother's death. We have both lost women we loved."

"After we escaped from the pirates, we found ourselves on an island and—"

Lord Radstone gripped her shoulder. "Claire, I want to hear the whole story in great detail. Let's wait until we get you settled. You brought my sons back to me. It is a gift greater than I could have imagined. A bit later than I had expected, but you performed your duty, and so much more. I will always be grateful to you. Come, King's House is not far."

As James climbed into the waiting carriage, Lord Radstone could not help asking, "James, tell me, what happened?"

James sat across from his father. "We tangled with a Spanish man-of-war. The guns I commanded fired first; we hit the Spaniard at the waterline. A terrible broadside came back at us. You know, Father, the Spaniard probably carried sixty guns. A ball hit the cannon where I stood. Three of my men died, and the planking slammed into me. When I came around, Phillip was holding me. Ada had cinched the arm with a leather strap." James shrugged.

A wide-eyed look of surprise came over Lord Radstone's face. "The guns you commanded? Your men? Who is Ada?" Claire, Edward, and Phillip smiled. "Well, there is much to talk about, but we will do that later. Today I am grateful to God for what he has returned to me." Lord Radstone called out, "Captain Watson."

The captain stood next to the open carriage. "Yes, my lord?"

"Summon Doctor Macgregor to King's House immediately."

"Right away, sir."

"I'm fine, Father,"

"I'm sure of it, my son. Doctor Macgregor is one of the finest young surgeons I have ever known, and I would just like him to take a look at your arm."

The carriage clopped down the cobblestone street. People lined the street, bowing and curtsying. Some clapped and cheered.

The oddest sensation came over Claire. She realized the people were not doing this for the governor, but rather cheering for her and the boys.

Lord Radstone noticed the expression of disbelief on Claire's face. "Everyone here knows of your exploits; many of these people consider you to be a great hero. Opposition to slavery is growing in England, and many think it should be outlawed in the entire British Empire, and I believe it is the right thing to do." He paused for a moment. "You should be aware, however, that here in Jamaica there are a number of wealthy plantation owners who each own hundreds of slaves. They think of you as just another pirate scourge."

"People are calling us pirates?" Phillip asked with a twinkle and a half smile.

His father chuckled. "I don't think there will be anyone on this island calling you a pirate, my boy—at least, not in front of me. At any rate, once I heard of your exploits I issued a letter of marque to Captain Claire Riley and the good ship *Freedom*. So you see, you are legally not pirates. You are in fact privateers in the employ of our good King George."

"I'm not sure I understand, my lord," said Claire.

"I'll explain it to all of you over dinner."

Flower-laden bushes and shrubs lined the graveled path leading to the magnificent mansion with white Grecian columns. Thousands of aromatic flowers in pink, red, and lavender overwhelmed the eyes. The sweet smells made Claire want to breathe in deeper and deeper, as if she could not draw enough air through her nostrils.

Six black servants stood on the porch of the mansion as the carriage pulled up. The three male servants wore white jackets, beige breeches, and buckled shoes. The three females wore spotless white dresses with white scarves wrapped around their heads.

"So, what do you think of it? It is the official residence of the governor of Jamaica. It was rebuilt after the earthquake in 1692."

"It's beautiful, my lord," Claire said.

"Boys, go in, bathe, and rest. Tonight we will dine privately, and I want to hear everything you've done since the last time I saw you."

The boys walked into the mansion, followed by the attendants.

"Claire, please come with me." Lord Radstone motioned and they walked along a grassy path that meandered through an orchard of coconut palms. Ahead, Claire could see a wall of pale pink peeking through the trunks of the palms. As they walked out of the grove, Claire paused in front of the beautiful pink cottage with pale-green shutters. More flowering bushes and trees surrounded the house. The palms towered and twisted above.

"I've kept it ready for you these past years. The house sits on the grounds of King's House. I have deeded this parcel to you, my dear."

Claire's eyes glistened. "My mother should—"

"Your mother and Elizabeth would be so very proud of what you have done. Stay here and enjoy this place. Go in, rest, and then come for dinner tonight at seven."

Claire walked up the steps. A small, wrinkled black woman opened the door. She wore the same style of white dress as the others, but without the headscarf. Her silvery-gray hair exploded in short bunches of tangles. "Good day to you, Queen Claire. I'm called Mamma Hattie."

"Why would you call me 'Queen Claire'?"

"It's what the island people call you. They call you the Queen of the Dolphins."

Claire touched Mamma Hattie's hand and smiled. "Thank you, Mamma Hattie, but I'm not a queen." Claire turned in the middle of the room and breathed in the sweet tropical scents. The browns of the teak, pine, and mahogany floors, walls, and furniture served to enhance Mother Nature's most vivid colors. White gardenias floated in a crystal bowl of water. Sprigs of red, purple, and pink bougainvillea twisted out from vases around the room. On the pedestal table in the middle of the room, a woven basket overflowed with magenta hibiscus blossoms, their yellow pistils pointed in every direction.

"Do you like it?"

"Oh yes, Mamma Hattie. It's the most beautiful place I've ever seen. I only wish my mother were here."

"Well, child, she ain't here, but she can see it. Lord Radstone told me all about her, and I just know she's watching from heaven and smiling along with you. I'll draw you the bath. I want you to soak yourself and relax."

"A bath, I can't think of anything more delightful," said Claire with a huge smile. Soon she was relaxing in hot, sudsy water in a deep white porcelain tub that rested on polished brass feet. Double doors opened onto the porch, and gauzy white curtains moved in the doorway. She sighed in contentment as the water soothed her aching muscles. "This is my first hot bath, in a real bathtub, since

Radstone manor." Mamma Hattie poured more jasmine-scented hot water into the tub. "This is wonderful, Mamma. I had forgotten how lovely a hot bath could be, and to be sure I've never had a bath with flowers floating in it."

The two women talked through the afternoon about the islands, the island people, and Claire's adventures. Claire learned that Mamma Hattie worked for Lord Radstone and, along with the rest of the staff at King's House, received an honest wage.

"You know, Mamma Hattie, I would like my friend to come and enjoy a bath, as well."

"Tell her to come tomorrow in the morning."

"I doubt she has ever taken a bath before. She's a native island girl."

"There ain't too many of them around these days," Mamma said.

"She is more than my friend—she's like a sister."

Mamma Hattie smiled a big, toothy smile. "I'll be sure to make it a very special bath."

Claire walked to King's House wearing a pale-blue cotton dress. Mamma Hattie had insisted on pinning a big red flower on it, just below the shoulder. As she entered the mansion, wonderful smells assaulted her. The aroma of roasting beef and freshly baked bread made her mouth water, transporting her back to the kitchen in the manor house in Bantry.

Lord Radstone stood next to an overstuffed, dark-blue velvet chair in an ornate sitting room. Portraits of various English nobles covered the walls. Claire recognized the painting of a young Elizabeth Radstone that had once hung in the library at Radstone Manor. The painting commanded Claire's attention as Lord Radstone walked up to her. "It is good to have this memory. Come, Claire, come join us and have a glass of wine. The boys tell me they rather prefer a bit of rum. Ha. Did you hear that? Rum."

Claire took her glass. "Well, my lord, along with liberating a large number of slaves, we also liberated a good quantity of rum."

James bowed to Claire. "And a few very lovely dresses."

Claire spun around in an uncharacteristically girlish manner. "It was in the stores of the second ship we took. I kept a few of them, hoping I might be able to use them someday. Today is the first 'someday'."

Lord Radstone held up his glass. "To Claire Riley, a great woman, a great sea captain, and, I am told, a queen."

"Hear, hear," the three boys repeated.

Lively conversations, stories, and laughter accompanied the meal. There were so many stories to tell.

Lord Radstone sat back. "Dr. Macgregor told me your Declan Flynn performed one of the most skillful surgeries he has ever seen. And I understand this Lambala, this witch doctor, applied ointments and gave James medicines that, according to Macgregor, have had a miraculous healing effect."

"We prefer 'medicine man' to 'witch doctor,'" Edward said.

"Well then, medicine man it is. I intend to have both of them here to King's House. I shall personally honor and thank them. Dr. Macgregor intends to invite Mr. Flynn and this Lambala over for tea in a day or so. He wants to question the African. I suppose they will need an interpreter. He thinks there is much he can learn. Can you imagine the look on Mrs. Macgregor's face as she pours the Africans a cup of tea and they pick up a cake? Ha, I'd love to be there to see it."

Everyone smiled politely.

James began to chuckle. He said to the table, "Do you think Nango will be along to be the interpreter?" Everyone broke out laughing.

"What is this merriment?" Lord Radstone asked.

"Nango is the largest man you will ever see," Edward said. "He stands as tall as a draft horse and may be as strong as one."

James touched his father's arm. "You must meet him. Phillip, tell father about that pike pointed at your chest."

Lord Radstone, eyes wide, quickly looked back and forth as the group told the story. "Make sure this Nango comes to King's House in the morning."

At evening's end, Lord Radstone walked Claire back to the pink house. "You know, my lord," she said as they strolled, "I tried to keep your sons out of this. They insisted on being a part of it. On the first slaver we took, the boys witnessed the wretched conditions in the hold of the ship. They saw the evil of the slave traders. The boys' anger swelled, and there was no holding them back."

"I know; they told me. Edward said he and his brothers had witnessed firsthand—how did he say it?—'the most fiendish examples of cruelty and inhumanity one could ever imagine'. A remarkable comment to come from a lad of just over sixteen, don't you think?"

"Yes, my lord. You know I would have given one of my own arms to spare James the loss of his."

"Claire, I am sure you did all anyone could, and so much more. When I received Bouchet's ransom letter, I was heartbroken. When no one came to collect the gold, I was sure you were all dead. Then came the reports of your exploits and I knew we would be reunited some day. I left boys in Bantry over three years ago and you returned to me three fine, stalwart young men. I could ask for nothing more. Your mother, Lady Radstone, and I are very proud of you." Lord Radstone bowed deeply. "Good night, Claire Riley."

Claire watched Lord Radstone walk into the darkness.

Claire got into a clean nightgown and lay down in the luxurious, fluffy four-poster bed, sighing with contentment. Gossamer netting, gathered at the ceiling, hung all around the bed. A night breeze carried the smell of jasmine through the open doors. A feeling of comfort and well-being, such as she had not felt for years, enveloped her. She pulled a light cotton sheet over her and thought about Ireland. She thought about how she had pushed her mother to leave Bantry, and now the only two women she had ever loved were dead. Claire's mind drifted toward the death and unbelievable depravity she had witnessed. She also saw the smiling faces of those people on the deck of the *Freedom*. The word freedom kept swirling through her mind, and she again recalled the words of Patrick Keenan. Claire smiled; now, she thought about the fact that when she returned to Bantry she would return with gold, a lot of gold. For the first time in a very long time Claire fell into a deep sleep.

In the quiet of the early morning, Ada and James walked on High Street. They ambled along the tree-lined road leading away from Port Royal on the spit of land that connected the town to the rest of the island. Two young men galloped past, a little too close for James's liking. The riders stopped down the road, and after a moment trotted back.

"Good morning," James said.

The two men glared down from their tall horses. "What would a fine Englishman like you be doing with that dark native thing?" one of them said. "I wonder if we might have an interest in her," the other said. "Why don't you come over here, little brown girl?" The two men dismounted. "You're from that pirate ship, aren't you? Some of those Africans probably belong to us. Maybe this girl belongs to us."

James moved back closer to a large oak and motioned for Ada to stand behind him. Ada was not inclined to do that. These two were older and James knew the odds were against him. He also knew he could not back down. The unmistakable sound of James drawing his sword from its scabbard broke the silence. The two men drew their swords and began to inch toward James and Ada. An arrow whistled past the faces of the two men and thudded into the oak. Everyone looked toward the road. Kataga stood in his blue tunic, a knife in his belt; two pistols hung from a baldrick around his neck, and his bow was drawn taut. The second arrow was ready to fly as Kataga moved closer.

James said, "That first arrow was a warning. The next one, I can assure you, will be on the mark. You should know he dips his arrows in poison; if you're just scratched by one you will most surely die." Ada looked at James with a furrowed brow.

Kataga walked toward them, his face twisted in a palpably devilish rage. The hand and arm holding back the bowstring quivered. The two men dropped their swords and stepped back. Ada picked up the swords

Kataga loosened his bow, dropped it, and pulled out his broad-bladed knife. James stepped forward and put the tip of his sword at the throat of one of the men.

Kataga hissed, "Take off your clothes."

"What?"

"Take off your clothes."

The two men took off their waistcoats and shirts. "Take off everything," Kataga said.

"Are you out of you mind? Do you know who we are?"

Kataga's grim face was an inch from one of the young men. He gently touched the huge knife to just below his ear, and pressed the point aginst the sensitive skin of his neck. He spoke through a clenched jaw, "Yes, I know who you are. You are one of the men who threatened my sister."

The young man's eyes grew wide with fear, and his chest heaved with deep, panicky breaths. He didn't move a muscle.

"Take off all your clothes and do it now," Kataga said.

Soon the two men stood there completely naked, holding their hands over their crotches. "They are very white," Ada whispered in James's ear with a bit of a giggle.

Kataga gathered everything, tied the clothes into bundles, and then knotted them to the saddle pommels. With his bow, he smacked the first horse hard on the rump, and it bolted. Kataga whacked the second horse, and it followed the first at a full gallop toward Port Royal.

James tapped the two men on their lily-white butts with the flat side of his sword. "I believe you two should be on your way back to Port Royal. Those are a fine pair of steeds. I'm sure you'll find them at the watering trough at the corner of High Street and Lime Street. Now, on your way."

The two silently turned and walked off down the road.

The three stood under the oak for a while, watching the white-bottomed young men stumble down the rocky road. "Why did you follow us?" Ada asked.

"Some people are not friendly here. It is good to be watchful."

Ada and James nodded.

"So tell me, Kataga, have you ever dipped your arrows in poison?"

"No, it would ruin the kill. I only hunted for food with arrows. I have fired more arrows at men since I met you than in my whole life."

"I'm sorry for that. You're the best friend a man could have. We'd better go tell my father about this. I'm sure he'll want to know."

That evening, James, Edward, Phillip, and their father sat with Claire, Ada, and Kataga near the kitchen. James, who had been a little concerned about his father's reaction to humiliating the two men, was relieved when Lord Radstone laughed heavily and heartily as Ada described the two men stepping down the road with their white cheeks glistening in the sun. "I only wish I had seen it. Those two Chapman boys walking into town naked had to be quite a sight. They walked right down High Street and past King's House. They walked down the main street of Port Royal looking for help; I'm told no one offered either of the arrogant pair a cloak until they were well past New Street. Considering their actions, I'd say they deserved what they got. I have an audience with Lord Chapman tomorrow at ten. It should be a rousing affair. I think all of you should be there. Edward and Phillip, to support your brother. Claire, you are the captain of the *Freedom* and may be required to speak for your crew members."

Lord Radstone looked around the room. "I want there to be no challenges, duels, or confrontations. I know you lads have seen and done much, but those Chapman boys are a dangerous pair. Remember, we have the law on our side, and until King George replaces me, I am still the governor of Jamaica."

"One arm is all a good swordsman needs."

"James, I said there will be none of that."

"They insulted me and Ada. If I hadn't been there and Kataga had not been watching, they might have harmed her. And why? Because she is not English? Because her skin is a darker shade of brown than their own?"

"Well, my son, changing the attitudes of men toward those they deem to be different or inferior may be an impossible task. You will certainly never do it with the point of a sword, or, for that matter, with the power of law."

Claire changed the subject back to a much more pleasant topic. "And so, my lord, the gold hidden near Spyglass Rock should be sufficient to give your boys a wonderful start in life. It is a seaman's pay for a job well done."

"I should say." Lord Radstone sipped his wine. "And what of this harbor where you believe these pirates hide?"

"I'm sure I can find it," Claire said.

"A new frigate will be joining us soon. When it arrives, we will resupply our four ships, sail along the coast of Cuba, and mete out the justice these men have avoided for so long," announced Lord Radstone.

Claire stood and bade all a good night.

"By the way, Claire," said Lord Radstone. She turned to catch a slight twinkle in his expression. "That frigate is commanded by Captain Garrison. He has often spoken of you."

Claire broke into an uncontrollable smile. "I would like to see Captain Garrison again, my lord." She turned and walked toward the pink house. *He spoke of me. I wonder what he said about me. Lord Radstone said he spoke of me often. How often? And in a friendly way? Or a more special way? It has been more than three years—that's a long time. Perhaps by now he has a lady in his life—he's a very attractive man, and an officer. He must have plenty of young women interested in him. And what will he think of what I've been doing? Will he come to visit me? What will I say? What should I wear?*

———

Everyone gathered in the audience chamber at King's House. Three oak tables formed a "U" shape in the middle of the room. Lord Chapman and his sons sat at one table. Across from them sat the three Radstone boys, Claire, Kataga, and Ada. Lord Radstone sat at the third table, flanked by two soldiers and a scribe.

Lord Radstone began, "James Radstone's two brothers are here in his support. Claire Riley, as the captain of the *Freedom*, requested to be present. Since all of these people served under her command, I saw no reason to exclude her. Here we have Lord Roger Chapman and his two sons, Reginald and Arthur. I expect us all to remain calm and civil, and I expect the truth to be heard this morning. I have already heard the story from this side of the room. I would now like to hear what the Chapmans have to say."

Lord Chapman began. "Lord Radstone, this proceeding is repugnant to me and my—"

"I'm sorry, my lord, I believe I would like to hear from one of the young Chapmans. You will, of course, have your chance to make any comments you wish at a later time." Lord Radstone motioned to the two young men. "One of you, please begin."

"We rode past those two and then turned and came back to bid them a good day," one of the young men began.

"It is my understanding that you galloped past them and then came back and dismounted," Lord Radstone said.

"That is true, my lord."

"Why did you not remain astride your horses and bid them a good day?"

"We thought it more polite to dismount, my lord."

"And then what happened?"

"He," the young Chapman pointed at James, "drew his sword."

"And why do you think he would do that?"

"That savage came out of hiding from somewhere and fired a poisoned arrow at us. I could only think they intended to rob us."

A look of incredulity came across Lord Radstone's face. "Are you telling me you think the son of the governor of Jamaica intended to become a highwayman?"

The other young Chapman smirked. "Who knows what influence the brown-skinned wench might have over him?"

James bolted out of his chair and flung it back across the room, and his fist slammed against the table. He looked at the Chapmans with the gaze of a hungry hawk.

"Sit down, James," Lord Radstone commanded. A soldier brought the chair back.

James was asked to recount his side of the story for the Chapmans to hear. Ada and Kataga sat and said nothing. Kataga never took his eyes off the Chapmans.

Lord Radstone questioned the Chapmans again. "Witnesses have told me that when you found your horses and clothes, you retrieved your swords and all of your valuables. Is that true?"

The young Chapmans looked at each other. "Yes, my lord, that is true."

"Well then, if they intended to rob you, why did they send all of your belongings back to Port Royal on your horses?"

The two young men said nothing, glancing at their father, who sat stone-faced.

Lord Radstone looked down and paused for a moment. He looked up and pointed to the two young Chapmans. "Lord Chapman, I want you to keep those two on your plantation. They are not to set foot in Port Royal for a fortnight. At the end of that time, I expect you to present yourselves here at King's House. I will then consider any further banishment."

Enraged, Lord Chapman bellowed, "You are going to allow those savages to humiliate two Englishmen of noble lineage? This is an outrage. The heathens should be hanged today."

"It is my understanding," Lord Radstone said, "that your boys threatened the young woman called Ada. I'm quite surprised that her brother, the young man sitting at the end of the table there, did not cut their throats. This seems to have been a matter of honor."

"Honor? Indians such as those have no honor. Are you going to believe those godless savages and not my boys?"

"May I speak, my lord?" Claire said.

"Yes, of course."

"Kataga and Ada have served with me for years. I have never known them to utter a falsehood. They have performed their duties with the utmost skill. The entire crew respects them, and they have always acted as any English lady or gentleman would."

Lord Chapman scoffed. "This is ridiculous, Lord Radstone. First you listen to savages and then to the opinion of an Irish pirate?"

Lord Radstone turned to him and said, "Be careful what you say, my lord."

Lord Chapman shot back, "Most importantly, *you* cannot be the judge in a proceeding in which your son is involved."

"It seems I have just done exactly that."

"I intend to inform King George of this outrage and this mockery of justice."

"When you send your dispatch to the king, please remember to mention to him that your taxes have not been paid."

Lord Radstone stood. "These proceedings are concluded."

As the Chapmans walked out of the room, Lord Radstone called out, "My lord, before you quit this room, remember, if I find out that those two have set foot in Port Royal without my permission, I will slap them *and you* in irons, and throw you all into the darkest hole at Fort Charles."

James, Ada, and Kataga smiled at each other in satisfaction. Claire patted Ada on the back.

"Well done, Father," said Edward.

"I am the governor."

"When did you decide on your course of action?" Claire asked.

"Interesting question, my dear. I did something I normally never do. I made my decision early on in the testimony."

"And why was that?" James asked.

"One of those Chapmans said they came back and dismounted because it was the 'polite' thing to do. There isn't one drop of polite blood in either of those mongrels." Lord Radstone smiled and motioned. "Shall we have a cup of tea in the parlor?"

———

His Majesty's frigate *Tempest* sailed into Port Royal harbor a week later. Claire wanted to be at the pier when Charles came ashore but decided it would be better if he chose to see her. Claire waited, and laughed at herself for being nervous. Several times the next day, Claire looked out her window, and then she decided to sit on the porch and read or pretend to read. He didn't come. The morning of the third day Claire stood in the doorway of her house, looking out intently. A swarm of butterflies fluttered in her stomach. Captain Charles Garrison walked up the path through the coconut palms, dressed in his finest naval officer's uniform.

She broke into a smile and wanted to run down the stairs. She stopped herself on the porch, her heart pounding. *Maybe he's just here to make a polite call.* Charles gave her a big smile as he approached, then took off his hat and tucked it under his arm as he reached the stairs. "Claire, it is so good to see you."

"I am glad you are well, Charles—and a captain, no less," she said.

"Well, there are plenty of captains in the British navy. I dare say none are as famous as Captain Claire Riley." Charles went up a step, took her hand, and gently kissed it. A shock ran through her entire body, and the butterflies now pounded in her stomach so hard she thought they would soon pour out of her. Holding both her hands in his, he continued, "I have thought about you every day since we last saw each other on the *Brilliant*. I wondered often if you thought of me."

Claire felt herself blushing a bright red. *He thought about me every day.* She smiled at him. "Yes, I thought of you, Charles, and our wonderful conversations on the ship. I prayed you were well. Do come in. We have so many things to talk about; I don't know where to begin."

They talked the day away and into the night. One story led to another, and it seemed they never finished any of them. They just kept talking, and laughing, and smiling at each other. Mamma Hattie brought fruit and tea, and they walked among the palms and the flowers.

"I must get back to my ship." They faced each other. Claire turned her head, ready for a slight, gentle touch of the lips against the cheek—the gesture genteel people performed when greeting or departing from a friend. Charles's hand gently touched her cheek and slowly turned her head back. He leaned down and pressed his lips against hers. Her eyes shot wide open. His eyes were closed, so she closed hers too, hoping it would last for a very long time. It didn't, but she didn't care. It had happened.

"Good night, Claire. I'll call on you tomorrow."

"Thank you, Charles. Thank you for a most wonderful night." She watched him walk away, and, as she curled up in bed, she relived their evening and the kiss. She thought of the kiss over and over again. Claire told herself that the next time, and she was sure there would be a next time, she would put her arms around him and hold him tight. She would make sure it lasted much longer.

Over the next week, Charles tended to the resupplying of his ship and spent every other moment with Claire.

The plan for the attack on the pirates' lair solidified after a series of meetings. Claire and Declan impressed the captains with their knowledge of tactics, seamanship, and the charts of the Caribbean.

While studying the charts, the British officers realized that their maps and charts were probably in error. With thousands of islands in the Caribbean, the pirates' hidden harbor, as Claire described it, could have very easily not been noted on the charts of the Royal Navy.

Claire convinced everyone that she could take them to the place.

Claire dined with Lord Radstone and his three young men.

"Are you sure this is what you want?" asked Lord Radstone.

"We wish you would stay," said Phillip.

"You will soon be in England in school," Claire said.

The boys agreed.

"No, lads, it is time for us to part. I know I must return to Ireland and to Bantry. Ada, Kataga, Nango, and the crew all want to see Ireland. They want to see where I'm from. Declan and the others agreed to take me home, and then sail the *Freedom* back to the Caribbean."

"What of the ship?" asked Edward.

"Declan will have her. I did not think you three would have any use for her."

"Rightly so." Lord Radstone rapped on the table. "I would not think it advisable for my sons to continue their pirating ways."

Everyone laughed.

"After the navy brings justice to those filthy animals, I will take the *Freedom* to Ireland. On the way, I will stop to retrieve the gold and send it back to you with Declan."

Lord Radstone nodded. "It is comforting to know my boys will be wealthier than I am—thanks to you, Claire. Will there be enough to sustain you?"

"Yes, my lord. It is a great treasure and there is enough for all of us."

———

The next day, Lord Radstone and Claire walked through the gardens. "Upon my suggestion, the commander of our flotilla agreed to assign Captain Garrison to escort you." Claire kept walking, smiling in her heart as Lord Radstone continued. "After we dispatch these pirates, he will transfer over to your ship with a contingent of marines and sail back to Ireland with you." He stopped and turned to Claire. "For the purpose of providing you with some additional…safety."

Claire met his twinkling eyes with her own. "Yes, my lord." Claire tried to return his bland look with some difficulty. "I believe I would welcome the additional…safety…that the marines and Captain Garrison will provide. Thank you, my lord."

"It's the least I could do for you, Claire."

Chapter 25

Grand Affairs

Before the five ships sailed, Lord Radstone organized a festival that culminated in a grand ball.

A week before the ball, Claire decided that Ada should have a beautiful gown. The words "brown-skinned wench" still rang in her ear, and Claire was determined to prove everyone wrong about this strong, proud, and gorgeous girl.

The two women walked down High Street and stood in front of a shop. The sign hanging above the door read LONDON FASHIONS—MRS. R. BARNSWORTH, PROPRIETOR. A small bell tinkled as Claire pulled open the door. Gowns and dresses hung from pegs on one wall. Hats and bonnets of every color and style imaginable covered another wall. A woman dressed in a plain cotton dress with a white apron over it appeared from a back room. "Please have your servant wait outside," she said.

Ada paid no attention as she touched a burgundy silk gown.

"Please don't touch that," the woman said.

"This is my sister, and she needs a gown for the ball," Claire said.

"Your sister," the woman said with a raised eyebrow. "Well, if you had the same mother, then your mum certainly had an exotic taste for men."

Claire bristled at the affront. She walked up to the woman, who stood her ground, arms folded in front of her, with a haughty expression on her face.

"My mother died while tending to wounded English seamen during a battle on the high seas. Her memory is very dear to me."

The woman's expression did not change. "I am so sorry about your mother. I simply cannot sell the savage a gown."

Claire opened the small purse she carried. "Madam, we do not have much time, and you do have some lovely gowns. There are four things I would like you to remember." Claire put a doubloon on the table. "First, Lord Radstone has invited this young lady to the ball, and we would like to have the loveliest gown in this shop." Claire placed a second doubloon on the table. "Second, although we have different parents, she is my sister, and I will do anything for her." Another doubloon dropped to the table. "Third, I shall expect you to tend to my sister in the most gracious manner." A fourth gold coin clinked on top of the others. "Lastly, if you fail to sell us a gown, or if it is not the most beautiful gown in all of Jamaica, you will make me and most of my crew very, very angry."

The woman, eyes wide and mouth open, picked up the gold coins and took them to the back. She returned in a minute with an angelic smile, startling Claire. "Come with me, young lady," she said to Ada. "I believe I have a few wonderful gowns that will be just perfect for you and will highlight your lovely, smooth skin."

In the afternoon before the grand ball, the crews of the five ships gathered around the north docks near Fort James to eat, drink, and celebrate. African chants and the rhythmic beating of dozens of drums attracted a crowd of Port Royal's citizens. The men of the *Freedom* danced and performed athletic leaps to the amazement of almost everyone. Not everyone was enamored with the antics of the crew of the *Freedom*. A few plantation owners gathered, grumbled, and made a few loud comments about the invasion of

Port Royal by free black men. The Africans ignored them, and the celebration went on into the night.

Charles Garrison walked up the steps of the pink house. Mamma Hattie, in her always-perfect white dress, greeted him. "I have come to escort Miss Riley to the ball."

"Yes, Captain, Please come in. Miss Claire will be with you in a moment. Mister James already came calling for Miss Ada. Should of seen her. The loveliest thing on this earth. Well, except for Miss Claire, of course."

The captain walked into the parlor as Claire came from the other room. She wore a pale-pink silk dress with a white lace overlay. The low-cut bodice made her a little nervous. Claire clasped her hands together to keep herself from tugging at her neckline. She wore a necklace of shells and sharks' teeth.

"You look exceptionally lovely this evening, Claire, and your necklace is fantastic. Where did you get it?"

"It was given to me by a wonderful and wise friend. He died during a battle with a slave ship. I know it doesn't exactly go with this dress. I wear it in his honor."

"Everyone at the ball will be talking about it, and it is worn by a queen."

"Please, Charles, don't call me that."

"But you are a queen in the eyes of so many. You know, you've changed in the most remarkable ways since we first met."

"I have had a few interesting experiences of late, but I'm the same person you met back on the *Brilliant*."

"Claire, there is not much of you that is the same. Today you are surrounded by a glow of confidence and beauty."

Charles bent his arm and offered it to Claire. "May I escort you to the ball, Miss Riley?"

Claire took his arm. Mamma Hattie followed them out on the porch. Claire lifted a fold of pink silk and glided down the porch stairs.

"Be merry, and dance into the night," Mamma Hattie called.

Claire turned back. "We will, and thank you for everything."

As they walked toward King's House, Claire stopped. "Charles, look how beautiful this is."

Hundreds of lanterns hung from the palms, tree branches, and the poles lining the paths. The candlelight glowed yellow, flickering within the foliage and among fronds and flowers.

"It's as if the fairies of Ireland herded thousands of fireflies together and descended upon this place. I will never forget this moment." Claire kissed Charles on the cheek. "Thank you for being my friend."

Charles stepped in front of Claire and held her shoulders. He kissed her on the lips, and the kiss lingered for a long time. She put her arms around his waist and held him close. He drew back. "I hope and pray, Claire Riley, that I am much more to you than just a friend." He kissed her again.

She said nothing for a moment as they resumed walking. "You *are* so much more to me than just a friend. I often prayed for your safety and dreamed about us meeting again." She held his arm tighter, and pulled herself closer to him as they walked. Claire was sure he could hear her heart beating.

The din of social gossip, polite laughter, and the enchanting strain of a dozen violins playing a minuet greeted them.

A butler stood at the entrance to the ballroom. "Please wait here for a moment." He turned and walked into the crowded room.

Claire looked at the colors swirling before her. She thought that this ball was as grand an event as anything she had ever witnessed at the Radstone manor back in Bantry. It struck her that tonight, for the first time, she was not serving; she was attending the ball, and it was a ball given in her honor. Claire thought of her mother. The orchestra stopped, and the governor's voice boomed across the room. "Ladies and gentlemen, tonight we honor an extraordinary woman; a woman who is an accomplished sea captain, a woman who, with bravery and guile, has returned my three sons to me—and a woman, I am told by the island people, who is a queen! Ladies and gentlemen, it is my pleasure to present Miss Claire Riley!"

Charles motioned. "This way, my queen."

They walked into the room as people on both sides bowed and curtsied.

Declan, Nango, James, Edward, Phillip, and Kataga stood together, wearing their versions of naval uniforms. Nango's size always elicited stares of amazement and awe. Tonight his dress caused even more intense stares. He wore white silk breeches, but remained barefoot and wore a gold ring on one of his big toes. Red piping trimmed the dark-blue tunic that fell to the middle of his thigh. Gold braid swirled on the sleeves, and two rows of gold buttons angled down the front of the jacket. His muscled, bare black chest made a sharp contrast with the gold doubloon hanging from his neck on a gold chain. Loops of gold, almost large enough to put one's hand through, hung from his ears.

Claire stopped in front of them. "You all look wonderful this evening, especially you, Nango."

"A woman in the town made it for me. With you being a queen, I must be an admiral."

"And a fabulous admiral you are," Charles said. "I will be honored to serve under your command."

"Ha." Nango slapped him hard on the shoulder.

Kataga walked up to Claire. "Your necklace is beautiful."

"I wear it in honor of Gani. Where is Ada?"

Edward motioned over his shoulder. "She is here somewhere. I believe she has been surrounded by the British navy."

Claire and Charles exchanged pleasantries with Lord Radstone. The orchestra began again, and the crowd danced and mingled.

Claire found Ada. Her yellow dress accented her olive skin, long black hair, and dark brown eyes. The attendees talked about Ada, using the words "mysterious," "exotic," and "enchanting." Ada loved every minute of being surrounded by four young naval officers, but she was pleased when James reclaimed her and escorted her through the blockade and to the dance floor.

After years of roughing it, Claire was happy to be able to dress up in the most beautiful dress she'd ever worn, and was thoroughly enjoying her special evening with her handsome escort. They savored the food and danced the night away, getting a little closer with each dance. Claire and Ada had been practicing the minuet with James and Edward, and Charles led so well that Claire didn't feel self-conscious at all—just happy and exhilarated as he led her around the dance floor. James had figured out a way to dance with Ada with one arm, and they looked like they were having a wonderful time.

At the end of the evening, Charles and Claire walked back to the pink house, stopping a few times along the way.

"Tomorrow we sail," Charles said. "Are you sure you can find this harbor?"

"Yes, I'm sure I'll recognize the coastline."

"Until tomorrow, then."

"Tomorrow." He kissed her, and they held each other for a moment, then he turned and walked down the path.

That night, Claire stared up at the gauzy netting surrounding her bed, reminiscing about the evening they'd had. She thought about Charles and what would come next. She thought about how fate, luck, and tenacity had brought her to this place. She fell asleep, only to dream of dolphins. They always swam through her dreams.

Chapter 26

Revenge

As the sun rose, the crews swarmed to their tasks. Anchors rose; sails snapped as they caught the wind. The *Freedom* sailed from Port Royal, followed by the four British ships.

Claire stood at the window of her cabin with the flotilla behind her.

A few of our family swam ahead to see if the pirate ships rest at anchor in their home harbor, Sanjay said. *Bolo will be back in a day or two. He swims faster than most of us.*

How long will it take us? Claire asked.

Four or five days, Nami said. *The wind blows against you now. When you turn back to the west, you will move a little faster.*

We will tell you when you are getting close to the harbor, Sanjay said.

When Bolo returned with news of two ships in the pirates' lair, Claire's pulse quickened. She drove the men to sail as hard as they could. Claire walked the quarterdeck with Declan and Nango on the night of the fifth day out. The dolphins kept her informed with a steady stream of chatter about the two ships as they closed in on the harbor. Claire peered through her spyglass into the night.

You should be able to see the fires from the village any moment now, Nami said.

Claire called out, "Declan, Nango, look!"

Flickering bits of light came from the dark coastline. "This is the place," Claire said.

"Are you sure? Those lights could be from any little village on the coast," Nango said.

"I am sure. This is where Bouchet brought us when he held us for ransom. When we escaped, we sailed right out of that harbor. I remember it perfectly. Furl the sails and signal the other ships."

Before morning, the four warships sat anchored in a line blocking the harbor entrance. Marines began landing at sunrise. Two cannon, mounted on hills outside the harbor, fired on the ships, announcing that there would be no surrender.

A fusillade of cannon fire erupted from the warships, and the land-based cannon soon fell silent. Claire and the crew watched from behind the English ships. Lord Radstone had insisted that Claire and her men keep out of harm's way, and Claire had agreed.

Claire watched men on the two ships, one of which was the *Brilliant*, in the harbor scurrying about. The pirate ships fired. They were no match for the larger fleet before them. Within the hour, the *Brilliant* was heavily damaged, and the other pirate ship was partially sunk in the shallow harbor. Red-coated marines swarmed through the town as the crack and clatter of musket fire rattled over the water.

Two English ships moved into the harbor, and by midmorning the noise of battle had subsided. The soldiers torched the pirate village, and smoke billowed from dozens of fires.

A longboat came alongside the *Freedom*, and a young officer climbed aboard. After introducing himself to Claire and the others, he said, "The pirate leader, Bouchet, died on one of the ships. The marines encircled most of the remaining pirates near the beach and shot them down. We have taken some prisoners and have put the town to the torch. We will take *HMS Brilliant* back to Port Royal and burn what is left of the other pirate ship."

"Thank you, Lieutenant," Claire said. "I hope there were not too many of our men injured."

"We sustained a small number of casualties," he said. "Lord Radstone requested you remain at anchor. He and Captain Garrison wish to come aboard in the morning."

"Please tell them I will be anxious to see them then."

Inwardly giddy, Claire could not wait to set sail for home with Charles. She sipped a little rum with Kataga, Ada, Declan, and Nango, as flames from the burning pirate ship leaped skyward. The fire burned through the night, lighting the entire harbor and the surrounding jungle.

When morning came, the pirate ship was still smoldering. A few charred planks remained above water. Pockets of grayish-white smoke hung in the harbor, waiting for the morning breeze to whisk them away.

Claire stood in the bow of her ship. Six dolphins bobbed below.

Will today be the day? Nami asked.

Yes, today we sail north.

We'll take you to your island, Sanjay said. *Maybe the gold will do some good in your hands.*

It will.

Longboats are coming, another dolphin said.

Claire turned, opening her spyglass. Four longboats came toward her. One held a contingent of marines; another, Lord Radstone and his sons, who had come along to watch the battle and to say good-bye to Claire. The third longboat held Charles Garrison and three other naval and marine officers, and the fourth was piled high with chests, kegs, and boxes. Claire assembled her men to help those coming aboard.

Greetings and hugs abounded. The gathering settled on the quarterdeck around the usual table fashioned from planks and kegs, talking and drinking tea.

"Will you visit us?" Edward asked Claire.

"Where? You mean when you get to school in England in a few months?"

"Yes, visit us at Oxford," Phillip said.

"That's a grand idea."

"We'll write to you. We should meet in Jamaica for a reunion someday. You know, a gathering of pirate shipmates," Edward said.

"Privateers," said Claire.

James sat close to Ada as they talked in whispers. When the gathering broke up, those leaving started to climb down to the longboats. James faced Claire, his eyes sorrowful. "I will miss you desperately."

"As much as you will miss her?"

James looked at Ada, who stood away from the group, then back at Claire. "Well, I think so—in a different way."

Claire patted the top part of James's left arm. James smiled a little. "I've come to terms with it. Now I wear my sleeve pinned up as a badge of honor. We've done dangerous things and accomplished important deeds. Think of the stories I'll be able to tell. I dare say no one at Oxford has ever had a whale breathe in his face, or been thrust into the air balanced on the nose of a dolphin. I'm sure none of my school chums ever fought to free a slave. Recounting those tales will be a glorious time."

Claire put her hand on his shoulder. "I love you, my brother." She turned and spoke to Edward and Phillip, hugging them both.

Laughter and fond farewells blended as the *Freedom* prepared to set sail with the morning breeze. Lord Radstone remained on board, almost the last to climb down to the longboats. "There is nothing I can ever do to repay you for bringing me my sons. I wish you would stay in Jamaica."

"I swore to a most uncommon fisherman in Bantry that I would return, and I intend to do so. But it is not just that, my lord. I left Bantry seeking a different life. I thought nothing in Bantry would ever change. Now I am sure I can change the lives of so many people in that little village, and maybe far beyond it. I must go home." Claire looked at Lord Radstone with a whimsical smile and raised eyebrows. "I hope Captain Garrison will decide to stay with me."

"Well now." Lord Radstone put his arm around Claire's shoulders. "You needn't worry about that, my girl. The good captain glows when he speaks of you, and you are practically the only thing he speaks of."

"I hope you're right, my lord."

"I *am* the governor. Would you like me to order him?"

Claire smiled. "I will send your boys their gold. They will be wealthy men."

"God bless you, Claire. I wish you a happy and wonderful life." Lord Radstone began climbing down to the longboat. "James, it's time to be off, lad."

James looked at his father, turned back to Ada, and kissed her. He ran to the side and, glancing back at her, climbed down to the waiting boat. Ada paused. Then her face broke into a wonderful smile. She ran to the railing and waved.

Claire leaned over the side. "My lord, thank you again for arranging for Captain Garrison to accompany me. The additional safety will be welcome."

Lord Radstone twisted his head up to look at her. "I am quite sure you will have a safe and pleasant voyage. Good luck."

Claire waved as the longboats rowed away. Phillip stood, yelling back, "Goodbye, Queen Claire!" He held a fist over his head. "Freedom for all, pirates forever!"

Edward stood next to his brother. "Tell the dolphins we said thank you and farewell!"

Claire watched as they rowed away. Her eyes glistened. Nango stood next to her. "Are you ready? I want to see this place called Ireland."

"Yes, Nango. Get us underway."

Chapter 27

Treasure

The *Freedom's* sails unfurled and the ship began to move away. "Don't be sad," Charles said.

"Sad? I think it's more of a feeling of emptiness. I've been with those boys every day for most of my life."

"They are no longer boys."

"Watching over them has consumed me these last few years. We cried and laughed together. We witnessed the good and evil men are capable of. Until today, I never knew how it would all turn out."

"Now, I hope, something else will be an important part of your life," Charles said, as he took her hand and smiled. "You know I intend to stay by your side forever—that is, if you'll have me."

She looked at him blankly for a moment. *He asked me to marry him. He said forever. My God, he wants to marry me.* Claire leaned up and kissed him.

"Yes, Charles, I will have you. It has been my fondest dream."

They dined alone on the quarterdeck and continued their habit of never finishing a subject. They laughed and smiled until their faces hurt.

The next morning, the wind chilled Claire as she stood on the bowsprit, holding on to a rope as the ship sailed toward a purple-blue horizon.

You should stay on this northeasterly course for a day more, Sanjay said, *and then we will tell you when to turn more to the north.*

Amazing. I have often wondered how you find your way in the vast ocean with no charts and no means of navigation.

The earth guides us. We see the stars and we feel the currents. We can never be lost at sea.

It is a gift men will never understand, Claire said.

Charles walked up next to her. A dozen dolphins swam in front of the ship. "They swam near you when we sailed from Bantry, and they still swim near you now, years later. The legend is true. The special connection between you and the dolphins is very real."

Claire just smiled.

"The people of the islands think you have a powerful magic," Charles said. "The boys believe you can actually communicate with the dolphins. Is it possible you comprehend their language?"

Claire's pulse quickened; she fought to conceal her inner feelings. With a bland expression, and not really looking at Charles, Claire said, "The only way I think I can explain it is that, for some reason, the dolphins and I have a kind of affinity for each other. It is a special and mysterious relationship, which I can't explain, but I do cherish it. You might think of it as the same kind of relationship a shepherd has with a sheepdog."

"A sheepdog, you say? From what the Radstone boys told me, this is far more than just a shepherd and his dog."

Claire put her arm through his. "Let me ask you something, Captain Garrison. Do you want to spend this lovely morning talking about dolphins? Perhaps we could talk about something more interesting—like you and me."

They walked the ship arm in arm. She wondered if she would ever be able to tell him the whole story. She hoped so.

———

Claire recognized the shapes of the hills, and the *Freedom* anchored off the island in deep water.

"I don't understand why we cannot accompany you," Charles said.

"I would rather do this alone," Claire said, "with just Declan and the others."

"Everyone knows of the rumors. They understand why we have anchored at this place. These men are all trustworthy. There is no reason why they should not help you."

"Please, Charles, let me do this my way."

Charles said nothing as Claire climbed down to the skiff alongside the longboat. The two boats sailed out of sight around the island with Declan and Nango in one and Ada, Claire, and Kataga in the other. They landed the boats and gathered on the beach near the rocks.

"Before we leave, we'll climb to Spyglass Rock and retrieve the gold we hid up there." Claire turned and pointed. "But now I want you to look across the channel. Do you see it over there; the white shell wedged in the rocks on the ledge? Just below that white marker is the underwater entrance to a cave. The treasure is there."

Ada's face showed her puzzlement. "An underwater cave—how could you have found an underwater cave?"

"I was diving for the giant sea snails over there against those rocks, and I saw the entrance and went in."

"Why didn't you tell us of this when you found it?" Kataga said.

"I thought it better if no one else knew at the time. If we were recaptured, I would be the only one who would know the secret."

Dolphins swam into the channel, and Claire decided to cut off this inquisition. "Come on, Ada," Claire said, slapping the water as she walked in up to her waist. "Let's ride over."

"Come on, Nango," Ada said.

Puzzled, Nango walked into the water.

A dolphin nudged Ada. "Come on, Nango. You'll see."

"Declan, bring the skiff over to those rocks," Claire called, as the two women held on and rode toward the hidden entrance. Stark swam next to Nango. Nango hesitated and then held his dorsal fin.

Whoa. This fellow is a big one, Stark said.

Is he too heavy for you? Bolo said.

Of course not. He's just the biggest man I've ever seen.

The dolphins, with their passengers, submerged, and then popped up in the cave and swam to the ledge.

Nango crawled up on the sandy ledge. "There is much gold and silver here. I could buy the freedom of many people with this gold."

Claire touched his muscled arm. "And you shall have a goodly amount of it, my friend."

Kataga came up in the cave and swam over to the ledge. "You swam in here alone and found this?"

"Yes, and, as you can see, there is plenty of air."

"And plenty of gold." Nango offered his hand to Kataga and pulled him out of the water.

They worked through the day, filling leather bags and transferring the gold, first to the skiff and then to the chests, boxes, and kegs they had brought and set up on the beach across the channel. With all the containers filled and loaded back on the two skiffs, they sat on the beach and rested for a few minutes.

Kataga sat next to Claire and pointed across the channel. "No one would have gone into that hole for fear of being trapped. You did not know where the passage would lead."

Declan sat on the other side of Claire. "You know, we Irish have a knack for finding gold. There is a pot of it at the end of every rainbow, and I'm sure there's been many a rainbow ending right on top of those rocks. And that's all there is to it." Declan jumped up. "Let's be getting back to the ship. After all this, I could use a bit of rum."

Kataga tilted his head to one side and looked at Declan as a dog might when it pretends to understand what its master is saying.

Everyone joined Declan in pushing the boats out. Ada stepped into one of the skiffs with Claire and Nango. "The dolphins took you to the gold, didn't they?" Ada asked.

Claire controlled her face, which betrayed only the trace of a smile. Nango pulled at the oars.

By late afternoon the heavy bags and chests were back aboard and stowed in Claire's cabin.

The *Freedom* weighed anchor and sailed to the north. Charles stood next to Claire as she watched the island fade away. "I wonder if I will ever see that place again," Claire said.

"Do you want to?"

"I don't know. I experienced great sadness and great happiness there. After dinner I will show you what we brought aboard."

Claire and Charles dined at a small table on the quarterdeck. After dinner, Claire asked Kataga, Ada, Nango, and Declan to gather in her cabin. She opened the largest of the chests. Gold and silver glittered inside. Charles reached down and dug his hand in. "My God, King George himself would not have this much treasure."

"I intend to give some of this to the crew and to all of you. You must take three sacks back to James, Edward, and Phillip. Whatever I keep, I will use for myself and to help the people of Bantry."

"You are a remarkable woman, Claire," Charles said as he leaned over and kissed her cheek. They spent the evening talking about their plans.

The next morning Nango carried a large chest out onto the deck and distributed its contents to the crew. The men cheered and celebrated.

In a few days, Nami's mind came to Claire. *It is time for us to leave you. We must begin swimming back to the islands.*

I shall miss you all very much.

Some of your other friends have come to bid you farewell.

Ada, perched high above, called down, "Whales off to starboard!"

The crew saw spouts of white, steamy water off to the east as whales swam parallel to the ship. Countless dolphins rolled along between the whales and the ship. Some of them jumped from one wave to the next. Voices shouted out: *Good-bye. We love you. Farewell.*

A whale's deep, booming message came to Claire. *May the seas be calm and kind to you.* The whales turned away from the ship, toward the east, and the dolphins followed them. Then everything in Claire's mind grew quiet. They were gone.

After a moment, Sanjay's lone voice called out to her. *Claire.*

Yes, Sanjay?

To the north of the Bahamas and out toward Bermuda, evil lurks. Sail far to the east of Bermuda as you head for home.

Why? What evil?

Sail out into the ocean far to the east.

No other sounds came to Claire's mind.

Chapter 28

Black Wooden Slates

The voyage to Ireland proved to be beautiful sailing. Claire and Charles spent every spare moment with each other. Claire thought about the dolphins of the Caribbean and wondered about the dolphins of Bantry Bay. She knew she would never tell Charles the truth about the dolphins. They would be married and the secret would always be with her. A great secret in the middle of their marriage might not be a good thing; but then it might not be a bad thing either.

A cold North Sea wind blew into the cabin as Claire sat at the window reading her favorite Shakespearean sonnets.

It is you. It could only be you. A voice came to her mind. Claire twitched upright, closed her book, and leaned out the window.

Meara?

It is none other.

Other voices called out.

We could feel your presence and hear the poetry.

We missed the poetry most of all.

It's wonderful to hear you, Claire said. She looked out. In the distance, a large pod of dolphins swam toward her.

Welcome home, Bannon said. *We've heard many tales, but we must hear them from you.*

You shall, my friends, Claire said.

Claire met Clairin, who asked her question after question. The image of Clairin's tail coming out of his mother came back to Claire in the most vivid fashion. Claire talked to the dolphins from time to time throughout the day as the ship moved up Bantry Bay. In the early evening, the *Freedom* tied up at the town of Bantry.

Claire waited until morning to go ashore. By then, every citizen of Bantry—and many of the people from all over County Cork—had gathered to greet her. She stood at the top of the gangway with Charles. "You know, Claire, it just occurred to me that the last time you stood here, you were leaving Bantry as a tutor in Lord Radstone's employ. Today you return as a hero, a legend, and, I dare say, the wealthiest woman in Ireland, a remarkable feat. Congratulations, my love."

Claire smiled and winked at Charles, then stepped down the gangway to shouts and cheers. She paused halfway down, her face alight with joy. There they stood, in almost the same place they had stood on the day she left. They stood in a row, holding black pieces of wood with the letters W-E-L-C-O-M-E H-O-M-E. Patrick Keenan stood next to them. The big fisherman's eyes met Claire's. He pulled his slouch hat off his head and gave a slight bow.

Lord Radstone's steward and cousin, Lord Henry Smythe, stood before the crowd.

"Welcome home, Miss Riley."

"Thank you, my lord; it is good to be back in Bantry."

"The navy brought us Lord Radstone's dispatches every few months. They told a remarkable story. I posted them in the village square for all to read. You're a hero, and we are very glad you have come home."

Claire walked through the crowd. Eileen stepped in front of her with a babe in her arms and a three-year-old girl at her side.

"Eileen?"

"Kevin and I got married." Kevin stood behind Eileen and nodded. "This is Patrick and this," Eileen looked down, "is Claire."

Claire looked at Eileen, astonished. "My God, Eileen." Claire knelt down and the little girl pulled behind her mother's dress and shied away. Claire stood up, smiling.

"Well," Kevin said. "She told everyone that you were the only family she ever had. She would stand in the square and tell anyone who would listen that you were not only the smartest but also the bravest person to have ever lived it Bantry. I told her, that if it was a girl, she had to name the child Claire."

Claire gave Eileen a gentle hug, encircling the baby as well. "We'll have plenty of time to talk."

Claire walked in front of her class. "Your letters have improved."

"We worked on without you; we helped each other," one of the women said.

Claire came to the big fisherman. "A good day to you Pat Keenan."

He grabbed her shoulders. "You kept your word. I knew you would." He surrounded her in a hug.

"We'll begin again soon," Claire said.

Claire decided to stay aboard the *Freedom* with the crew, savoring every moment before they left. They would sail back to the Caribbean all too soon.

Over the next week, there were parties, teas, dinners, and the spinning of wonderful tales in the pubs of Bantry. Lord Smythe hosted an elegant banquet on the night before the *Freedom's* departure. Toward the end of the meal, Captain Garrison rose to propose a toast. "As you know, Claire Riley has become known as a great sea captain, a champion of freedom, and, to the people in the Caribbean, a queen. I am so pleased to tell you that she has consented to take one more title—that of Mrs. Charles Garrison. A toast then—to Mrs. Charles Garrison."

Everyone stood. "To Mrs. Garrison."

"Hear, hear!"

"Cheers!"

Claire beamed at Charles.

When the morning came, Claire walked among the crew. She hugged Ada and Kataga with tears in her eyes. She held onto Declan, and then buried her head in Nango's chest.

Nango held her by the shoulders. "This Ireland is a cold place. Be warm and live happy, my queen."

Claire hugged the big man as hard as she could. She walked down the gangplank, where Charles waited to say good-bye. "Please hurry back. I love you and I'll miss you terribly."

"I'll deliver the gold, resign my commission, and be back as soon as I can. I love you." He kissed her, turned, and bounded up the gangplank to the cheers of the men.

The *Freedom* moved away from the dock, her bow pointed seaward. Declan stood at the aft railing and called down to Claire, "I'll make sure to tell the dolphins you will see them again." He waved and turned away.

As Claire stood on the dock, a peculiar feeling about Declan came over her. A feeling that had nagged at her before. She had dismissed the ideas she had had about Declan. He seemed to be so much more than just a carpender. The dolphins told her that she was the only one who could communicate with them. She wondered if that was the truth. She watched the men unfurl more sails, and the *Freedom* sailed away. An African chant rose from the ship, echoing across the bay. The people of Bantry would talk about those exotic sounds for many years.

Epilogue

Lord Radstone's fleet captured or drove away the remaining pirates in the Caribbean. Calico Jack died battling the British navy and Nassau became a thriving port of call.

Kataga and Ada purchased vast amounts of land in the Caribbean, becoming successful plantation owners. They employed the island people, paying them fair and honest wages. Kataga and Ada, however, did not stay together as business partners for very long.

Nango used his part of the treasure to buy and free as many slaves as he could. He took them to the same peninsula in the southern part of the French colony of Saint-Dominque. Eventually Saint-Dominque would become the country of Haiti. Nango later returned to Africa, where he became his people's most famous chief. He fought against slave traders for the rest of his life.

The Radstone boys returned to England and completed their educations. At school, they excelled in their studies, and also in pistol shooting and fencing. Edward and Phillip displayed an uncanny ability at archery. The target records they set in competition endured throughout their lifetimes. They told their opponents that their archery teacher could hit a fish almost without looking and regularly shot birds from the sky. Edward and Phillip doubted that anyone ever believed any of this.

The three young men invested well and married happily. They spent evenings regaling family and friends with exciting stories of dolphins, whales, pirates, slave ships, treasure, and deadly sea battles, where poisoned arrows were often used. The beautiful and exotic Mrs. James Radstone would, in her terse manner, nod and verify the accuracy of the tales—after all, she had witnessed almost everything from her perch high above the deck of the *Freedom*.

After distinguished naval careers, the three Radstones entered Parliament, where they campaigned to abolish slavery. They did not live to see their efforts succeed. The next two generations of Radstones, however, continued the fight against slavery, and in 1807, England outlawed the Atlantic slave trade. For decades thereafter, the British navy maintained a squadron in the South Atlantic for the sole purpose of intercepting and seizing slavers. Many sailors in the navy called the South Atlantic duty "freedom patrol." Although there was no absolute corroboration of it, the Radstones liked to believe the term "freedom patrol" referred to that legendary ship, now a prominent part of the Radstone family history. In 1833, over a century after the exploits of Claire Riley and the Radstone boys, the British government abolished slavery throughout the Empire.

Claire Riley married Charles Garrison and they lived in Bantry for all their years. Claire bought Radstone manor and much of the surrounding land. She renamed the manor "Bantry House" and regularly opened her doors to anyone who was in need of a meal or a place to sleep. The school she started in the house overflowed year round with students. Claire and her English husband used their wealth and position to constantly and peacefully influence both sides in the quest for Irish independence from English rule. The Garrisons fought against the slavery imposed by men and the slavery caused by ignorance. Claire and Charles had three daughters. One married a successful businessman in London. The second married a Spanish nobleman, who took her to South America. The third followed her husband to the colonies in America.

The Radstone children loved visiting their Aunt Claire and their cousins at Bantry House. All fourteen of them would descend on the manor at least once a year. Most years they tried to visit when the two sapodilla trees growing in the greenhouse hung heavy with fruit. The children loved eating the exotic fruit. On each of the trees a brass plaque read, "Planted in honor of Lady Elizabeth Radstone and Mary Riley."

In the evenings, the children would sit in the parlor, mesmerized, as Auntie Claire would reverently take the necklace of shells and shark's teeth out of its glass box. She would tell the stories of the great and wise Gani, along with many others. All agreed that Auntie Claire told the stories with a most wonderful theatrical bent. The children of James and Ada particularly loved the story of their mother flying out of the water while balancing on the nose of a dolphin.

Claire returned to the Caribbean once. The crew of the ship chronicled an amazing sight; a thousand dolphins and hundreds of whales joined her as she sailed to Saint-Dominque and Jamaica.

In their later years, Claire and Charles spent much of their time walking the shoreline of Bantry Bay. A few dolphins could always be seen just off the shore as Claire strolled. The people of Bantry thought that she was doing much more than just talking to water. Charles was sure of it.

As for Declan Flynn—he sailed the *Freedom* in the Caribbean for a year, giving away his portion of the gold and silver to the poorer people of the islands. The *Freedom* put into Nassau for provisions as she prepared to head for the South Atlantic and hunt for slavers. The ship left Nassau, and in the late afternoon, anchored off an uninhabited island in the lower Bahamas. The island had a shallow bay with a bottomless blue hole at one end. The men of *Freedom* were nervous; it was said that sea monsters with glowing eyes lurked in the hole. Declan was acting strange and detatched, and the men wondered why they had stopped at such a dangerous place. That night, Declan disappeared along with the tattered and faded, blue, green, and yellow flag of the *Freedom*. The *Freedom's* skiff was found on the beach near the blue hole.

www.ingramcontent.com/pod-product-compliance
Lightning Source LLC
Chambersburg PA
CBHW030029180626

46810CB00001B/285